RUTHLESS TOUCH

BORN VILLAINS

BOOK TWO

ABBI COOK

Gideon Rule, the consummate gentleman who runs the Villa Aurelia, has everyone fooled. They think he's simply a businessman catering to the wealthiest of the Amalfi Coast.

But I know what hides behind that mask of civility.

The younger son of Helix Rule has mastered the art of pretending to be that perfect gentleman while behind the scenes he's as ruthless as any of the villains in his family.

He claims he took me from my ex-boyfriend for my own safety, but it's him I need protection from once we're alone. The man whose job it is to gather intel for his father knows my deepest thoughts and desires.

And he intends on using them for his own pleasure.

CHAPTER ONE

ideon

I TAKE A DRINK OF SCOTCH AND LET IT SIT IN MY mouth for a few moments, warming the inside of my cheek before I let the liquid slowly slide down my throat. I've been avoiding the inevitable with Aria, hoping she'd be settled by the time I got back to the penthouse, but if security is telling Sasha there's a problem, it seems my time ignoring the issue is over.

For some reason, I feel the need to clear up my assistant's misunderstanding regarding Aria, so I swallow another mouthful of scotch and say, "There's nothing crazy about what's going on upstairs."

Sasha looks back at me and shrugs. "Okay. It just seems distinctly odd for you to keep a woman prisoner in your penthouse. That's all I meant."

She can be so melodramatic sometimes. Rolling my eyes, I say, "She isn't a prisoner. Think of her as more like an investment."

I get no response to that, which is fine with me. I have little interest in explaining that I paid two hundred thousand euros for Aria. That's between me and the man she used to call her boyfriend, a lovely soul who sold her to save his own skin.

On her way out of my office, Sasha says, "Well, your investment is threatening her security guard. Not that she could actually do much to him, but they thought you should know."

She leaves before I can thank her, no doubt in a hurry to get to her time off. I take another gulp of scotch and a deep breath in before heading upstairs to deal with the problem.

I arrive at my penthouse door to see Raphael standing guard as he's supposed to. Solemn looking with a giant head that fits with his giant body, he stares straight ahead as I approach him.

"Good evening, Raphael. Everything okay in there?" I ask with a smile.

I don't necessarily think Aria is lying in wait to attack me when I walk inside my home, but the thought has occurred to me since she's been threatening a man who towers over her by more than a foot. My prisoner, as Sasha likes to call her, isn't violent.

At least not so far. Then again, it's only been one day since she's been here.

Raphael turns to look at me, breaking his somber appearance with a look of worry. "Your guest seems unhappy, sir. I told her she had to stay inside, and she threatened to jump off the balcony. So I had Luca lock those doors from the outside."

I smile, imagining the two security guards worried what their boss's guest leaping to her death would do to their jobs. "Thank you, Raphael. I appreciate your quick thinking. We wouldn't want her to jump, now would we."

He doesn't respond, returning to his stoic self and staring straight ahead. If Aria has given him that much trouble, he very well might want her to take a leap off my balcony.

As soon as I open the door, she rushes toward me, green eyes full of blazing fury and her long, dark hair flying behind her. I must be out of my mind thinking I should keep this woman.

"I want you to release me! You have no right to keep me here like some prisoner."

That's the second time tonight some woman has termed this my keeping her prisoner. I push past her as she stands at the door with her hands on her hips.

"Nobody is a prisoner here. You're my guest, so why don't you try acting like it?" I say as I shrug out of my suit jacket and drape it over the back of the black leather couch.

"Let me free. You do nothing with me, and I'm stuck here all day alone with that behemoth you have watching over me," Aria complains.

I close my eyes and hope to God my head doesn't start pounding. Maybe if I have another drink. As I make my way to the bar in the corner of the room, I look over at her to see a scowl marring that beautiful face of hers.

"Freedom is an illusion. There are just varying gradations of imprisonment for all of us, not only you," I say as I pour myself another drink.

"That sounds terribly interesting, but I want to be free, no matter what definition you go with, Gideon Rule."

I take a sip of scotch and let it slowly roll down my throat before turning to look at her. She really is beautiful, even as she stands there with her arms folded across her chest and pouting because I won't let her leave. Long, brown hair hangs down to just above her breasts. Her oval face with perfect cheekbones is made all the more gorgeous with deep green eyes that stun even when she flashes nothing but hatred at me.

"What's wrong? Is lounging around my penthouse difficult? Is it some kind of chore for you? My chef makes you food people pay dearly for." I look around my home and add, "And on top of that, I'm willing to bet you've never spent a day in a place as luxurious as this."

My questions are met with a scowl, and she marches over to stand in front of me. Just a few inches shorter than my six-foot four height, she levels her gaze on my face with such disgust that I feel like I should turn away.

"You paid all that money for me, but you barely talk to me, much less do anything else. Why don't you just let me go?"

I lift my glass to my lips and take another sip of twelve-year-old scotch. "Because I didn't pay for you."

Aria has no idea what I'm talking about, and at this moment, I have no interest in explaining myself. We stand there facing off, two people staring at one another until one of us breaks.

I watch her grow more frustrated by the moment, but she really is stunning. Something about green eyes never fails to intrigue me, and hers are the color of dark emeralds. The longer I stare at her, the more I see flecks of gold dance around her pupils. She looks exotic, like something foreign washed up on the shore that rivals anything beautiful I've seen on the Amalfi Coast.

Finally, she gives in, her entire body trembling when she realizes she can't convince me to let her go.

"What do you mean you didn't pay for me? Franco told me you did. I told him he was crazy and that I wasn't going to be sold to anyone, but he told me you bought me, which by the way isn't legal."

"Well, I didn't. I paid for something else entirely."

"Then why won't you set me free? What good do I do you? I've been here for more than a day already, and not once have you said more than ten words to me before now, and that's only because I'm forcing you to."

Her delusions amuse me, so I smile and shake my head. "You couldn't force me to do anything, Aria. As for why I won't let you go, that's my business. For now, you'll stay right here in this hotel and in this penthouse where you want for nothing. As for how much I speak to you, that depends. Right now, this conversation is over since I want to go to bed. I've had a long day, and nothing is more desirable to me than sleep at this moment."

When I turn to walk to my bedroom, she touches my forearm, sending a rush of excitement coursing through my body. I can't deny how desirable she is and the effect she has on me. I felt it that night at Angeloni's villa, and as I stand here with her now, I'm already hard.

"Nothing?" she asks, her eyes full of something I can't place at the moment. Seduction? Manipulation? Whatever it is, she knows how to use it because all I can think of as she looks at me is how much I'd like to be balls deep inside her right now.

Aria steps toward me, brushing her fingertips over the front of my black dress shirt. "I will do anything you want. Name it. Just don't make me sit in this penthouse alone for another day."

I let my gaze drift down her body, exciting me even more. Beautiful with curves most men would love, she's nothing short of breathtaking in the pale-yellow sundress she's wearing.

Unfortunately for her, I don't need that in my life. Want is an entirely different story, however.

Dragging my fingertip along her collarbone, I smile at the thought of what she's willing to give me. "I'm not the kind of man you should offer anything to. Trust me, I'll take it all."

"Whatever you want as long as you don't make me feel like a prisoner, Gideon."

"I'm not a man who plays games. If I do as you want, I'll expect something in return. Something big."

As I speak, I stare into her eyes to make sure she understands the bargain she's about to make. I'm not the Devil, but I'm closer than she's used to, for sure.

She hesitates for a moment before answering, "I'll do whatever you demand if you let me feel like I'm not trapped here. All I ask is one thing."

Intrigued that she thinks she should be bargaining for even more at this moment, I ask, "And that is?"

"Don't let any harm come to me. If you do that, then I'll do whatever you command me to. I'll be at your beck and call for anything and everything you want. Just keep me safe and let me feel like I'm not a prisoner."

She wants a protector and is willing to trade anything to get one, including her body? That's an offer I can't pass up. I'd be insane to even consider saying no.

I press my hand to hers and shake it to seal the deal. "Done. You're mine to do as I please whenever and wherever I please, and in return, I promise to keep you safe. Welcome to the Villa Aurelia."

Sliding my arm around her waist, I pull her to me so she can feel how hard she makes me. "Let me show you to your new bedroom, Aria."

Her eyes grow wide, but in them I see not fear but desire. Good. She bartered with her body, and now I plan on using it as payment as often as I want, and I expect her willing compliance.

"Know this," I warn her. "I expect you to obey me. Do that and we'll get along fine."

In a trembling voice, she asks, "And if I don't?"

"I have a reputation for being aloof. You don't want to see how cold I can be. Be a good girl, Aria, and we'll get along fine."

As I escort her to the bedroom, I sense fear begin to grow in her. She thought she escaped a bad man and found a good one in me. But she didn't.

She found a villain.

Or at least the member of a family of villains.

Aria looks around my bedroom and smiles at me. "Very nice. Very you."

"Undress," I order, surprising her, oddly enough.

Didn't I just say I expected her to obey me? Aria's not a stupid woman, so how she could be surprised at what's about to happen doesn't make sense. She wants something from me, and at this moment, this is what I want from her.

"Oh," she murmurs as she stares innocently at me.

I take her by the shoulders and spin her around so her back is to me. Pressing up against her, I whisper in her ear, "You made a deal, Aria. Now it's time to start living up to it."

She doesn't respond, and I'm not in the mood to seduce her. Our time out in the living room excited me, and I want to fuck, so I lift her dress and hastily tug her panties down her legs. She lets out a tiny cry, but I don't sense she's afraid.

In fact, I sense just the opposite by how drenched those white cotton panties are. Nice touch, although I doubt she's that innocent, considering who she was with until a day ago.

I unzip my pants and free my rock-hard cock before pushing her shoulders down toward the bed. After giving my cock a few strokes, I nudge her legs open with my knee and step forward.

"Can I be on my hands and knees?" she asks in a tiny voice. "I like it better like that."

With a shrug, I stop myself from plunging into her cunt. "Fine. Up on your hands and knees."

She surprises me by stripping off her dress first, leaving her in just a pink bra that seems far too sweet for what I'm about to do to her. My gaze fixes on her round ass stuck high in the air in front of me. Fuck, she's perfect.

Aria lowers her head to the bed and lets out a heavy sigh. "I'm ready."

I doubt it, but that's neither here nor there. Taking hold of her, I pull her back toward me and thrust my hips so my cock slides into her. She's tight and wet, and for a moment, I forget that I shouldn't feel anything other than pure pleasure.

From the second I saw her at Angeloni's party, I wanted Aria. The dark hair. The emerald green eyes. A mouth a man can only imagine wrapped around his cock. A body made for pleasure.

And that's all it was when I saw the opportunity to have her for my own. Or at least that's all I wanted it to be. Nothing but carnal desire.

Then memories began to invade my thoughts of her. Memories of a time and a woman I've tried so hard to forget. I thought if I just fucked her and got it over with, that somehow that's all Aria would be.

A body I could use and get lost in.

But now as I bury myself in her and listen to her

tiny moans of need, something's changed in me. She's not the same as that woman from so long ago, but she makes me feel things only she ever could. I suddenly want to revel in the feel of Aria's body instead of merely fucking her and getting off.

She backs up toward me, pressing her ass to my groin and taking every inch of me into her tight cunt. I don't want to feel this way. I can't. Not again.

So I grab her hair hard and pull her head back, forcing her up off the bed. She cries out in what has to be sheer agony at how tightly I'm holding her hair, nearly ripping it out by the roots.

Yet she never stops driving her ass back toward me, fucking me as I try to find a way to stop feeling anything for her.

Her hands push against the bed, making her back arch, and as much as I wish I could just pull out of her perfect body and walk away, I can't. I pump into her, the muscles in my thighs tightening with every rough thrust into her. She has no idea what she's doing to me. As much as I try, I can't make this a simple quick fuck anymore.

So I step back, releasing my hold on her hair. Aria falls to the bed and looks back at me in confusion.

"You're not done, are you?" she asks in a soft voice.

I shake my head and scoop her up around her waist to pull her to me as I sit down hard on the bed. This was just supposed to be sex, but now as I position her on my lap facing me, it's something else entirely.

Quickly, I unhook her bra and toss it onto the floor before I turn my focus to her tits. She isn't top heavy by any means, but her breasts are full and right for her body. I dip my head and take a deep pink nipple into my mouth, sucking hard. Aria moans and grinds her pussy against my cock, as needy to feel me inside her again as I am to be there.

I lift my head and pick her up by the waist to position her over my stiff cock. She bites her lip, desperate to have me fill her again, so I lower her down onto me and close my eyes as her cunt surrounds my cock.

My hand pulls her head to mine so I can kiss her, and when our mouths meet, it's like every part of my body is more alive than it's ever been. I don't kiss women when I fuck them. I haven't for so long I forgot how good it feels when I'm inside a woman and she's taking every inch of me as she craves the feel of my mouth on hers.

Her tongue snakes into my mouth, teasing my tongue and sending a thrill through my body straight to my cock. I hold her head, needing to feel her lips on mine as she rides me. What began as me fucking her has morphed into us fucking one another. We're raw and needy, each for our own reasons, and with every time she sits down on my cock and takes me inside her, I inch closer to coming.

Aria's sighs and moans fill my ears, and for a moment, it's all I can do to not pull away and watch her as she makes those sensual sounds. I want to see her ride my cock, but I don't want to let her mouth off mine. I'm greedy and want to feel it all. Fuck watching. I'll do that another time.

For now, I simply want to bask in every sensation her body offers.

I feel her cunt begin to tighten around me, and a second later, her teeth sink into my lower lip. It doesn't hurt so much as excite me even more, so I finally pull away and look down between us to see the final moments of her fucking me before she comes.

The scene is erotic, and with each time her body writhes and rolls against me, I can't think of anything else but how good it will be to fill her with everything I have inside me. She sits down hard on me one final time before falling still, her cunt squeezing over and over as her release tears through her.

Aria's arms tighten around me as she whimpers in my ear. It's the sound every man loves to hear. She's sweet and sexy, and for the first time in so long, I enjoy seeing a woman come on me.

My release follows hers, hastened by her body milking my cock. Aria sags against me as my body sends jets of cum into her.

By the time I'm finished, I can't think of anything else but her.

That can't be. I can't let myself feel this way again.

The last time nearly ruined my life. I won't let that happen again.

I lift Aria up off me and set her on her feet before standing up and walking into the bathroom. When I see my reflection in the mirror, I stop dead, recognizing that look.

No. Not again.

CHAPTER TWO

ria

THREE WEEKS. THAT'S HOW LONG I'VE BEEN HERE IN Gideon Rule's penthouse. He promised me he wouldn't make me feel like a prisoner, but not an hour after that deal between us was struck, he went back on his word and left me here in my gilded cage with my trusty guard stationed outside the door so I don't get away.

Not that Gideon does anything with me.

I felt how hard he was that night when he agreed to protect me. He wanted me as much as I wanted him. And then he fucked me, and it was incredible.

Yet since then, he's never touched me. Not again that night or any night since. I sleep beside him in his bed every night, but he doesn't even seem to know I'm there.

Or maybe it's that he doesn't care if I am.

Filling my lungs with a deep breath, I work to calm myself as my thoughts of him next to me every damn night makes an ache form between my legs. He's nothing short of beautiful, and that's not a term I normally use to describe men. Gideon Rule is, though. Like a priceless statue carved out of marble, he's breathtaking while at the same time colder than any man I've ever encountered.

Those expensive suits that fit every inch of his body perfectly do little to conceal how truly stunning he is, but that night as I watched him strip out of his clothes, even I was surprised at how powerful his body is. Muscles appear to strain beneath his skin, corded and taut like an animal set to attack. They're a complete contradiction to his face, which always seems so cool with its restrained expressions that rarely let on what he's thinking.

I've had nearly a month to study the man who insists on keeping me here with him, despite the fact that he treats me like something to be looked at and never touched, and I've come to the conclusion that Gideon Rule is a vicious as the rumors say he is. The problem is his disinterest in nearly everything about me has created a need to know every gorgeous inch of the man.

The sound of the penthouse's front door closing

rouses me from my daydreams about my captor, and I sit up in bed, clutching the covers to my chest. It's an instinctive motion, not one that's necessary since I've walked around this place completely naked, and I swear he hasn't given me a second glance.

"Aria?" he says in his deep voice with that lilt to it that always makes him sound slightly annoyed whenever he says my name.

I don't answer him, wanting to make him come back to the bedroom he left hours ago. When he appears in the doorway dressed in his dark grey suit and black dress shirt with that silver and red tie he's worn twice in the time I've been here, I level my gaze on him and wait for him to tell me what he wants. I suspect it's something important since he never returns here during the workday.

Gideon is nothing if not a dedicated employee of his family's business. Or maybe he's merely a workaholic. A cold, unfeeling workaholic who prefers to be downstairs dealing with things that assistant of his could do instead of spending long, luxurious hours in bed with me.

That thought makes me salty, so when he gives me the slightest hint of a smile, I don't give him one back. I'd smile if he didn't leave me alone in this goddamned gilded cage all fucking day. Or if he showed me a hint of kindness or interest once in a while.

"I called for you. Why didn't you answer?" he asks, his tone clearly aggravated now.

His dark brown eyes narrow to slits when he's upset, and right now, I have to wonder if he can even see me with how they look. I wish that made him unattractive, but somehow even when he's angry he's beautiful.

It must be all the time I spend alone up here. That's the only explanation for how I could possibly still want this man after the weeks I've been neglected here.

As irritated as he is, I mumble, "If you must know, I was busy."

"Doing what?" he asks as he steps into the bedroom. "You're still in bed at nearly noon. That doesn't sound busy to me."

His dismissiveness annoys me, so I roll my eyes as I say, "I was constructing a wonderful fantasy of being held prisoner in a beautiful penthouse and not being ignored for weeks on end. I planned on playing with myself afterward to ease the tension."

Gideon's eyes open slightly wider, a sign I've surprised him. Good. He should be ashamed of himself for how he's behaved toward me for the past few weeks.

"You asked," I say with a chuckle, enjoying how little control he has of this conversation after only a few moments.

"I did," he says, his smile growing a little. "Well, if you're finished enjoying yourself, I have a surprise for you."

That makes my ears perk up. "Really? Planning on actually paying attention to me today?"

He stops beside the bed and looks down at me. "Something like that. I need you to get up and get ready. You'll be accompanying me to an event here at the hotel tonight, and you need something to wear."

My mouth drops open in shock as I process his words. Accompanying him? "You're letting me leave the penthouse here? This must be some special event. Is it bring your prisoners to work night?" I say with a chuckle.

Gideon smirks at my attempt at a joke. "Something like that. Now get up and get ready. Sasha will be here in a few minutes to take you shopping."

Sasha. His gorgeous blond assistant who always seems to be far too close to him whenever they're together. I don't know what nationality she is — maybe Russian or Swedish — but she's as beautiful as she is. Every time she comes up to the penthouse, I can't help but wonder if she looks at me like I don't belong here and she does. I'm sure she and Gideon have been together. Maybe they're still together. That would explain why he never does anything with me even though I'm right next to him in this bed every night.

Disappointed to hear he's handing me off to my babysitter again, I sigh. "Sasha. You know, I don't think she likes me. Maybe you shouldn't make your girlfriend deal with the woman you keep captive up here. It seems like a rotten way to be to such a gorgeous woman."

His dark eyes focus on mine as he shakes his head. "Sasha isn't my girlfriend. Now get up and get ready. She'll be here in less than five minutes."

I throw off the sheet and stand up to face him, toe-to-toe with the man who seems to not care one bit that he has a naked woman in his bed he does nothing with. Staring up into his face, I have to fight the urge to smile at how appealing he is.

"She's going to have to wait then because I can't be ready in that time. I haven't even showered today."

He sighs heavily, like everything about me and having to deal with me is an enormous burden. "Fine. Get ready."

Nearly his height, I only have to tilt my chin up ever so slightly to show my insolence. "I like long showers. You'd know that if you ever took the time to get to know me, Gideon."

Once again, his eyes narrow, and I know he's angry with me. But his voice doesn't indicate it when he quietly says, "I have no problem telling Sasha to get into that shower with you and drag you out by your hair if you keep her waiting. Don't test me, Aria."

"Or what?" I ask as I stare up into his eyes in defiance.

We stand there like two warring factions for what seems like forever, neither of us willing to give any ground. He has no idea how long I can do this. Unlike him, I have nowhere to go. No work to get to. Nothing to make me want to give in.

Finally, he takes a deep breath in and lets it out slowly before saying, "Enjoy your time shopping. Feel free to get anything you want in addition to a dress for tonight."

And with that, he turns on his heel and leaves me alone and naked once more in his bedroom.

I'm victorious in our standoff, but it's a hollow win. At least I'll get to go out today, even if it is with his icy assistant.

AS WE EXIT THE ELEVATOR ON THE FIRST FLOOR, Sasha turns to look at me and smiles in a way that can only be described as predatory. Her grin doesn't look happy or cruel. Just dangerous, like this woman would eat me alive if she could.

"It's important you look like you belong on Gideon's arm tonight, so I'll be helping you pick out a dress at the boutique. I've had them assemble a selection for you out of the ones I thought would look good with your body and your coloring."

Even though I feel uncomfortable talking to her, I can't stop myself from asking, "What does that mean? My coloring?"

Again, she smiles as her right hand gently touches my back just below my bra. "It means your dark hair and green eyes, which by the way, are nothing short of enchanting. I'd kill for eyes like yours."

Hmmm. So the ice princess doesn't hate me. At least not my eyes.

"Oh. I thought you were insulting me because I don't have blond hair and blue eyes like you," I say as we walk across the black marble lobby floor toward the boutique near the terrace where hotel guests sit eating lunch.

"Not at all," Sasha coos as her gaze travels down my body. "I like the way you look. I told Gideon that."

"And what did he say when you said that?" I ask, eager to know what my captor thinks of me since he can't seem to be bothered to let me know himself.

His assistant answers with a shrug. "I don't think he said anything. Gideon isn't a man who spends time thinking about things like that."

"Things like what?"

"The color of a woman's eyes or her hair. If anything, he's more of a holistic type of person."

We walk into the boutique as I translate that into the truth. He doesn't have any interest in me or what I look like. That his behavior begs the question of why he's keeping me in his home doesn't seem to bother anyone else, even if it does me.

The painfully thin woman with jet black hair and tan skin scurries out from behind the counter when she sees us, her expression one of pure joy, as if she's been looking forward to this task all her life. I can't imagine Gideon told her to act this way, so I have to assume she's always like this with customers.

Clapping her hands together so her bangle bracelets make a tinkling noise, she gushes, "Sasha, it's wonderful to see you and your friend this afternoon. I have the dresses you chose waiting for you in the dressing area."

"Wonderful! Aria, this is Dominique. She'll be helping us today. Dominique, this is Gideon's date for tonight, Aria."

The way she says that, like the woman he'll be with tomorrow night will change and I'll be left as unwanted trash on the side of the road, makes my stomach clench. So much for his assistant being nice to me.

I eek out a hello for Dominique to be pleasant since she's done nothing bad to me and follow the two women to the dressing room. Far more than the cramped cubicles in most stores, the boutique's dressing area is spacious and bright with pale cream-colored walls, tan carpeting, and a crystal chandelier hanging from the center of the ceiling. Two navy-blue upholstered chairs provide a place for sitting, and a raised, carpeted platform in front of a bank of mirrors offers the chance to see what you look like from all sides.

As I look around at the room, Sasha and Dominique discuss which of the dresses will look best on me. I guess I don't have a choice in this matter, just like I have no choice in anything else here at the hotel. Glancing over at the dresses hanging on display, I see Sasha's taste is good. That I can be thankful for, at least.

Lost in thought about her comment about me being Gideon's date for the night, I don't notice that Dominique has vanished from the dressing area, leaving me alone with Sasha. The touch of her hand on my arm rips me out of my daydream of being consigned to the penthouse tomorrow night as he goes out with someone else.

"Why do you look so sad?" Sasha asks in a voice that doesn't contain a hint of irony. "Look at these gorgeous dresses. You can have all of them, if you choose, but we need to decide on one for the event tonight. Do you have a favorite?"

Her question rhetorical, she moves quickly from being concerned about my being sad to admiring the dresses. I can't figure this person out. One minute, she seems like she's made of something inhuman, and the next, she's expressing worry that I might not be happy.

Why anyone would think I should be the least bit happy is beyond me.

I study the dresses for a long moment, silently admitting each one of them is beautiful. She wants me to have a favorite, so I paste a smile on my face and point at the black one with the very low-cut neckline that I instantly worry might include me flashing guests my breasts if I move the wrong way.

"The black one is nice. I'm not sure I can carry it off, but I like it."

Sasha makes a face that tells me she thinks I've said something outrageous, her eyes opening wide like she's shocked about something. "Are you kidding? You have a gorgeous body. That's why I chose that dress. I love it too. Try it on!"

She hands it to me with so much enthusiasm that I can't stop myself from mumbling, "You sure do get excited about clothes. Who knew?"

"Clothes are a means to an end, dear Aria. They are there to make others desire you. Then once they do, they're meant to be a way to further excite someone as they remove them from your body."

As I open the curtain to the dressing room, I look back at her and smile. "And here I thought they were merely to cover up so we aren't all walking around with our bits and pieces hanging out all over the place."

That makes her throw her head back in peals of laughter. "You are so adorable. No wonder Gideon likes to have you around."

I wait for her to explain that ridiculous statement, but she simply shoos me into the cubicle to try on the black dress. Gideon likes to have me around? He must be telling her that because he certainly hasn't shown me any evidence of that in the weeks I've been living with him and sharing his bed. Most of the time he seems to have to work to tolerate me, and other times, I suspect he regrets taking me altogether.

As I slip into the barely there floor length black gown that definitely shows more cleavage than I think I can do, I say to her, "I think you must be mistaken. Gideon doesn't even like me, much less like having me around. He'd be quite happy if I disappeared today and was out of his hair."

"Stop being humble. You snagged the best man on the entire coast."

Now she sounds like she's disgusted with me. This woman's moods change like lightning.

I tuck my breasts behind the fabric and look down my body. I do like this dress. It actually holds me in nicely. I wasn't expecting that. Now to see how it looks in the full-length mirror out there with my babysitter.

The moment I pull the white curtain back to reveal myself, Sasha's mouth drops open. When I step out in the dressing area, she sighs and shakes her head.

"No good?" I ask as I step up on the raised platform in front of the mirrors.

She follows me up there so I have to step forward, and behind me she sighs again as her gaze trails up and down my body. "It's even better than I imagined. God, you look good."

Her hands cup my bare shoulders, instantly setting me on alert. No one has touched me the entire time

I've been here at Gideon's hotel after that one night, and the feel of her fingers and palms warming my skin makes me suddenly emotional.

Forcing a smile, I look at her in the mirror. "Okay, so this one is in the running. We could just stop now and settle on this one."

It's not that I don't want to try on more dresses. It's just that Sasha standing behind me so her body's pressing against mine while her hands now softly stroke down my arms is making me feel something I can't explain.

I watch in the mirror as she rests her chin on my shoulder and smiles. "I love it, but let's try the dark green one. I chose that because it's going to make your eyes pop. With your dark hair, I bet that will definitely be in contention."

As she speaks, her hands continue to caress my arms, sending waves of excitement through me. It must be because I've been starved for attention for the past few weeks because I've never been attracted to a woman. Whatever it is, I don't know how to handle it, so I awkwardly step down off the platform and hurry over to where the green dress is hanging on the rack.

"Okay. Green dress it is next. I'll be right out," I say, the words tumbling out of my mouth at a rapid pace so I sound like I'm nearly rambling.

Yanking the curtain closed, I take a deep breath into my lungs and let it out in a rush. I don't know why I'm getting so flustered. It's certainly better that

Sasha might like me rather than how I thought she felt about me until today. Gideon is close to her, so it might help if his righthand woman approves of me.

The green dress feels cool against my skin since it's satin, and when I finally get everything situated, I notice that the back is so low on this one that my ass is nearly showing. I wish I had used these past few weeks to workout. Gideon's chef loves to cook rich meals, so I think I've put on a few pounds.

When I step out into the dressing area again, I hear Sasha's audible gasp. "That black dress doesn't exist now that I've seen this on you. Turn around and let me see the back since that's where all the action is on this one."

I do as she commands and hear her gasp a second time. "Stunning. Okay, that's it. No more trying on dresses. This is the one. I'll have Dominique get it ready. Do you want me to have her send all the rest of them upstairs so you can try them on when you feel like it? I'm sure Gideon will have more events he expects you to attend with him."

Unsure what to say as her comment about my going to more events with Gideon fills my head, I press a smile onto my lips and nod. "Okay. Sure."

Sasha strides out of the room, leaving me alone to see how this be-all-end-all dress actually looks on me. Even without stepping up onto the platform, I have to admit she's right. It is stunning. In fact, in this dress, I feel more beautiful than I've ever felt in my life. It hugs me in all the right places and all the right ways while still hanging perfectly on my body. While not as low-cut as the black dress, it still shows off a good amount of cleavage. When I turn around, I see the back is quite flattering on me and I haven't lost all the tone in my ass after three weeks of sulking around Gideon's penthouse.

So green dress it is. Now to see if it has the same effect on him as it did on Sasha.

CHAPTER THREE

ideon

I GLANCE DOWN AT MY WATCH FOR THE SECOND TIME in minutes, wondering when Aria will be ready. Cordelia Anzeloni's ball is scheduled to begin in less than half an hour, and I prefer to be on site when the festivities begin.

On the table behind the couch sit the masks I had Sasha get for Aria and me. She spent nearly fifteen minutes raving about how the gold mask will go perfectly with the green dress Aria will be wearing, and when she began talking about how stunning she looked in it this afternoon, I had to stop her. She has far too much interest in my houseguest.

"Aria, we have to go now. Whatever you're doing, wrap it up in there and let's go," I call out toward the bedroom door.

As always, she can't just hear what I say and do as I want. She has to answer back, wasting yet more time. "I'm finishing my makeup right now."

"I wouldn't worry too much about that. It's a masquerade ball, so you'll be wearing the mask I have for you."

That gets me no response whatsoever, which may be a sign she's almost ready or might be a sign she's sulking. I wait a few moments before walking over to the bedroom door and throwing it open. Whatever she looks like, she needs to be ready to leave.

I stop dead as Aria walks toward me in that green dress Sasha couldn't stop raving about. She wasn't wrong. It's nothing less than stunning, and on her, it's utterly breathtaking.

"Why didn't any of you tell me it's a masquerade ball?" Aria asks in complete frustration as she storms past me into the living room. "I know I don't mean much in the big scheme of things here, but that seems like a detail I should have been told at some point. Why do you look like that?"

I pull my gaze up from her beautiful ass and shrug. "Like what?"

She hesitates for a moment, giving me more time to admire how beautiful she is. "Like you're surprised.

Or maybe something else. I'm not sure. You just look different. Maybe it's the tux. I'm sure you know this, but you look great in that."

"Thank you. We have to go, but there's one more thing you need to wear," I say as I walk across the room.

"Is the gold mask mine? It's beautiful," she says with a smile in her voice.

That may be the first time Aria has sounded truly happy since she got here. Who would have thought a mask would do that for her?

"Yes. Mine is the black one. I don't like to call attention to myself. Now come over here. I have something else for you."

"Other than the mask?"

Always with the questions and comments.

Aria stops next to me in front of the table, and I open the black jeweler's case containing the necklace I got for her to wear tonight. As I carefully lift it out of its velvet home, I hear Aria inhale sharply.

"You want me to wear that?"

I nod, holding up the diamond necklace for her to see. "The jeweler told me it would be perfect for what you're wearing."

Her eyes as wide as saucers, Aria stares at the necklace for a moment before saying, "I've never seen anything so beautiful. You must really want to impress people tonight dressing me up in this gown with that rock hanging around my neck. How many carats is that large diamond in the center?"

I gently press my hand to the small of her back, noticing how soft and warm her skin is against my palm as I move her toward the mirror on the wall nearby. "Fifteen. The total carat count is forty when all the smaller diamonds in the necklace are counted."

Stopping her in front of the mirror, I slide the necklace around her neck and watch as her eyes grow even bigger. I didn't think it was possible for her to look more beautiful than she did just a few moments ago, but now I'm speechless at how incredible she is standing here.

She softly runs her fingertips over the large diamond hanging between her perfect breasts and smiles. "This is like nothing I've ever worn in my life, Gideon."

I see in her green eyes admiration unlike anything she's shown me in the entire time she's lived here with me. Not that I've done much to deserve it. I know that, but I can't help but admit I like when she looks at me like this.

"You'll be the most beautiful woman at the ball tonight," I whisper next to her ear as I feel myself begin to get hard.

Aria feels my cock press against her ass and looks at me wide-eyed in the mirror. I'm sure she's wondered why I never touch her, even as she sleeps naked next to me every night. It's not that I don't want to. I just can't let myself get caught up in her.

"Thank you for this and everything tonight, Gideon."

Stepping away from her, I turn around and try to contain my desire as I grab the masks off the table. "Sasha says this gold mask will be perfect for your dress."

The mention of my assistant makes Aria's expression fall. "Oh? I'm sure it will. She was the one who decided this green dress was perfect," she says quietly as she takes the mask from my hand.

I fix my mask over the one side of my face it's made to cover and turn back to see Aria wearing her gold mask that only covers around her eyes. If I could, I'd rip that mask off, along with that green dress, and take her right here wearing only the diamond necklace.

"Time to go," I say as I take her hand in mine and begin to walk toward the elevator.

"What kind of event is this?" Aria asks, once again sounding happy like she did before I mentioned Sasha.

As the elevator doors close, I give her hand a gentle squeeze. "A very unique one. Just do as I say, and you'll be fine."

I expect to hear some complaint from her, but she says nothing. I'd tell her what she was in for once we reach the ballroom, but Cordelia's parties are better experienced firsthand to understand just what they involve.

ARIA'S SURPRISE AT SEEING NAKED WOMEN WITH their bodies painted as we enter the ballroom makes me smile. I could have told her, but why ruin the surprise? She's in for more tonight too.

"Exactly what kind of ball is this?" she whispers in my ear as we walk toward where we'll watch the festivities for the night.

"The best kind," I answer with a smile. "Don't worry. We're spectators here tonight, assuming you do as I say."

She tightens her hold on my hand, clearly afraid now. "You've said that twice. What does that mean?"

I stop and turn to face her, gently pushing her long hair off her shoulders. "It means do as I say, Aria. Whatever I tell you to do, do it."

Even behind her mask, the fear in her eyes comes through loud and clear before she quietly says, "You promised you wouldn't let anyone hurt me. Is that still in force?"

Nodding, I smile. "Yes. I swear I'll protect you, but all you have to do is obey me tonight."

Her hand trembles in mine, so I bring it up to my lips and kiss her knuckles. "Don't worry. I promised you and I live up to my word. Now time to watch."

Cordelia loves to create the feeling of a Roman

orgy for her parties, so they always begin with dozens of beautiful women naked with their bodies painted. I watch Aria's expression as they parade into the ballroom and take their positions around the room. Tonight, they're made to look like marble statues, but I'm damn sure I've never seen any statue with a body like these women have.

It's erotic and titillating, exactly what Cordelia loves.

Aria turns to look at me and whispers in a voice full of shock, "They have no clothes on."

With a smile, I nod my head and answer, "You're right. And this is only the beginning. The host didn't tell me specifically what these women will be doing, but I don't imagine they'll be standing like marble statues all night."

I see in her eyes this scene arouses her. Good. I like that.

"You keep me cooped up in that penthouse for nearly a month, and tonight for this you bring me out. Why?" Aria asks with utter suspicion in her tone.

"Because I wanted you here with me."

"Please tell me you aren't going to make me do something with one of these guests, Gideon."

She has no idea how off base she is with that request. I don't want her here because I want some other man to fuck her. I want her here because I want to see if she can handle what comes with my world.

The music changes to something far darker and the

lights around the ballroom dim, alerting me to what's coming next. As usual, Cordelia's parties only get more sensual as the night goes on.

"I'm not. Now come over here and stand in front of me."

Her expression filled with defiance, she tilts her chin up and levels her gaze on me. "What? Why?"

Leaning in next to her ear, I whisper, "I told you that you must obey me tonight. Do as I say. Stand in front of me and don't say a word."

Defiance morphs into fear that fills every inch of her beautiful face. "Gideon, why? And don't say because I told you to."

Sure if I don't get her in place in the next few seconds that the rules of the party will mean she ends up with someone else, I pull her in front of me and whisper in her ear, "Cordelia has a ritual she likes to do for her parties. Nude women with painted bodies come first, followed by the male guests walking around the room choosing any female who speaks to have sex with them on that dais in the middle of the room. Now stand completely still and silent until I tell you otherwise."

For once, Aria obeys me and stands in front of me, as still as those women nearby pretending to be marble statues. But since she's who she is, she can't stop herself from talking, which is the singular thing that's going to get her onto the stage in the middle of the room with a man fucking her for all to see.

38

"So you don't want to see me with some stranger?" she asks as a man stops not five feet away and takes a good long look at her.

I slide my hand around her throat and lean my body in against her back. "No. Now no more talking or that man right there is going to expect to have you all for his own tonight."

A man I assume may be around twenty-five stops in front of her, and it's clear he wants her. Rubbing his hand over his cock, he's hard and ready to take her to the center of the room and fuck her. His gaze rolls over her body as he smiles and licks his lips as possessiveness fills me at the sight of him. She isn't for the taking, but the rules are the rules, and if Aria speaks a single syllable, he can have her.

My hand stays around her neck, but now I step closer to her so my entire body presses against hers and slide my arm around her waist to make sure whoever this man is that he knows she's not available. I'm as hard as a rock, my cock nudging her ass as everything around us falls away until it's just Aria, this man who wants her, and me.

I hold my breath while I silently say what I've wanted to for weeks. She's mine. Only I can have her. Only I can give her what she needs.

Aria's breasts rise and fall as she begins to breathe heavier, and the man takes a step closer to her. His eyes open wide, and he licks his lips again.

Not a single word or you'll be his, Aria. For once, do as I say so I can keep my promise.

She angles her body so her head is nearly resting against my shoulder, a clear sign she doesn't want this man. It won't matter if she can't keep her mouth shut, though, so with every second that ticks by, I silently pray she'll obey me for once.

Finally, he gives up and walks on to the next woman nearby. Aria's body slumps in relief, and she turns to look at me as if to say thank you, her eyes filled with gratitude.

I smile and in her ear whisper, "You don't have to worry. I would never let anyone touch you. You did well, Aria."

When all the men have their partners, the orgy that always happens at Cordelia's parties begins in the center of the room. We watch as bodies writhe against one another and moans fill the ballroom. There's nothing like seeing strangers fucking, and Aria's reaction tells me she's never experienced anything like this.

Her eyes wide, she looks back at me. Assuming she can talk now since all the men are occupied, she says, "I bet you're used to this, but this isn't something I see every day."

"It's just one part of the world I live in. And here you thought I was all work and no play," I say with a chuckle.

She doesn't respond, choosing to turn around and

watch the sensual scene of people fucking in front of us instead. I let my hands fall from her body since the danger is over, giving her a tiny bit of freedom, but she searches for them and reaches back to take hold of my hand. Pulling my arm around her, she sets my palm against her stomach and lets out a sigh.

CHAPTER FOUR

ria

I'VE NEVER SEEN AN ORGY. BY THE WAY GIDEON seems utterly blasé about the whole scene playing out in front of us, he's clearly experienced this before. I can't help but wonder if he's ever been one of the men up there on that stage fucking some beautiful stranger.

My gut reaction is no, he hasn't. He's had me sleeping in his bed for weeks without touching me, and tonight is the first time he's ever shown me any hint of his attraction to me. I can't imagine him on display in front of all these people like that.

The feel of his hard cock pushing against my satin dress makes it difficult to stand here and pretend I'm shocked or appalled by what I'm seeing. All I can think about is how much I want to be back in his penthouse with him buried inside me.

As the orgy continues, the painted women meant to look like marble statues begin to walk around the room just as the men had a short while ago. Are they going to choose a woman now, or will they be taking a man?

"Do I have to stay silent for them?" I ask Gideon.

He shakes his head and smiles. "No. They're choosing men to grow the orgy on stage."

"So now you have to be quiet?"

Again he shakes his head. "No."

"But what if one wants you?" I ask, instantly unhappy with that idea.

Gideon gently pulls me back against him, and I feel his cock again. It excites me even as I worry he might go with someone else.

"You get to decide that. If one of them stop in front of you, it's your choice if she can have me or not."

By the look of utter happiness on his face, I assume he'd be perfectly fine if I handed him over to some gorgeous model painted up to look like a marble statue. Jealousy surges through me at the mere thought of it.

After three weeks of waiting, there's no way one of these statue girls can have Gideon. Go find another guy, ladies. This one's mine.

"Well, sorry, but you don't get one of them tonight. Maybe at the next orgy your date there will be okay with it."

That gets me a genuine smile that makes him even more gorgeous, if that's even possible. "Whatever you wish, Aria. It's your choice."

Angry he's so fine with the possibility of me handing him off to some beautiful woman, I grumble, "Maybe I should. I bet everyone on the coast would love to see the upright businessman who runs the Villa Aurelia buck naked and fucking someone for all to enjoy."

I spin around and stare straight ahead, so full of jealousy at the thought of him doing what I just said that I can barely see straight. When he slides his hand around my throat, my eyes flutter closed as feelings of need course through me.

In a low voice, he whispers in my ear, "I will do as you insist, but I don't want any of these women, Aria."

I don't ask it, but all I want to know is, does he even want me?

One of the marble statues stops in front of us and smiles up at him, completely ignoring me, the person who gets to say if he can go with her or not. So much for following the rules. Or maybe there are no rules when it comes to this part of the night.

With a shake of my head, I let the beautiful blond statue woman with big boobs and a tiny waist know she can't have Gideon. She gives him a tiny pout and goes on her way to the next couple standing near us. He's bald and looks like he wants to jump over his woman to get to the statue girl.

"Thank you, Aria. I prefer to watch the events at parties like this," Gideon says sweetly in my ear.

Again, I don't say anything, but I think to myself that I've endured far too many nights wanting him to simply hand him over to some stranger so he can fuck her. If he's having sex tonight, it's going to be with me.

I feel Gideon's hands leave my body, instantly missing his touch. Looking back to see why he let me go, I notice Sasha approaching. My mood changes in a flash, and it's like my arousal disappears the moment she takes her place next to him.

Dressed in a red dress that shows off great legs and leaves little to the imagination, she looks like she belongs here. Unlike me. Sasha has probably taken part in the orgies here at the hotel. She's probably participated with Gideon. On most days, she's as cold as a real marble statue, so I wouldn't be surprised if she was one of those painted girls here tonight.

That thought makes my mood sour, and I step away from them before jealousy overwhelms me. Why the hell is she always around? Even better, why does he like having her around so much?

"You look stunning, Aria," Sasha says, sounding genuine. "That dress steals the show here tonight."

Begrudgingly, I give her a smile and reply with a

compliment of my own for her dress. "You look great too. You fit in perfectly here."

Both she and Gideon turn their heads to stare at me. Good. I hope you both understood clearly I'm not happy she's here. Maybe now she can leave, and Gideon and I can go back to enjoying our time together.

As I seethe my unhappiness at our twosome becoming a threesome, Sasha begins to chatter on about some issue happening outside the ballroom. The entire time she's talking, her hand drifts along Gideon's tux jacket lapel and then his shoulder, like she's grooming him. It's intimate and unnerving, yet he doesn't flinch for a second as she touches him.

If anything, he looks pleased to have her there straightening his jacket and brushing a piece of dust off him. While they talk about how to handle whatever the issue is, it's as if they're the couple here tonight, not Gideon and me.

I watch them and can't help but wonder if that's why he hasn't done anything with me in the entire time I've been here at the hotel. Is it that he's in love with her? If so, then why aren't they together?

Or have I simply been too blind or stupid to see they are already?

Finally, he remembers I'm there and turns to speak to me as Sasha leaves. "Aria, I need to deal with something outside the party. I'll be right back. Don't do anything stupid, or I will send you back up to the penthouse. Understand?"

Sasha gets smiles and gratitude for running her hands all over him. I get threats if I'm not a good girl.

"Fine. Enjoy your little time with Sasha. Maybe next time you should bring her instead and just leave me upstairs. That seems to be where I belong."

I spin on my heel and turn my back to him before he can say a word, but I see in his eyes and his frown that he's unhappy at what I said. Good. That makes two of us who aren't having a good time.

Left alone, I consider trying to escape the hotel, but I have to assume he's told security to be on the lookout for me going anywhere but this room. I should find a way to get out, though. Now that my hopes are dashed for anything happening between us, what's the point of staying?

Lost in my misery, I don't see the handsome man stop in front of me. When he clears his throat, I look at him and smile, unsure if I can speak now. Then again, why shouldn't I, even if that means I have to have sex up on that stage? It's not like the man I want gives a damn.

This man is almost as tall as me with light brown hair and brown eyes that look out from behind a silver mask covering only the span around them. Although I can't be sure, I get the sense he isn't from the Amalfi Coast area. Something about him says he's American.

I don't say anything, but it doesn't matter because the man asks, "Would you like to dance?"

While my brain confirms his accent is American, I look around me and realize there are people dancing while the sex show is going on in the center of the room. I was so consumed first by the orgy and then by my jealousy over Gideon and Sasha that I never even saw all the couples on the dance floor.

After glancing in the direction of the door to see if Gideon has returned, I give the man another smile and take his hand. "That would be lovely. Thank you."

As we take our place away from the orgy over near the floor to ceiling windows that look out onto the terrace below, he takes me into his arms in a polite way and says, "My name is Marcus. What's your name?"

"Aria," I answer, enjoying the sound of his deep American voice.

"You're not from here," I add as I look up into his dark eyes and like what I see. They've got a sweetness about them I haven't found in most men.

My statement makes him grin, and I see he has a nice mouth too. Not as sexy as Gideon's, but he's not here right now.

As his hand presses ever so slightly more against my back, Marcus says, "I'm from the US. Have you ever been there?"

I shake my head. "No. I'd like to, though. It seems

incredible," I lie, preferring not to let on anything real about me.

That makes him roll his eyes and his smile broadens. "I don't know if it's all incredible, but where I'm from is. I would love to take you away from here and show you."

God, he's charming. It's so refreshing to have a man actually want me instead of treating me like I'm a piece of furniture in his penthouse.

"I wish you could, Marcus. I think it would be lovely."

He slowly turns me as he leans in and says in my ear, "I can promise you lovely would be the least of what it would be if you were with me."

I close my eyes as his words filter through my brain. I like being desired. I'm not ashamed of that. I would love if Gideon showed me even a tiny shred of what Marcus has done in the past minute or so.

Our bodies gently sway to the beat of the music, his strong hands holding me against him and making my body come alive. If only it was the man I wanted making me feel this way.

When I open my eyes, I see Gideon and Sasha walk through the ballroom doors. Instantly, he looks toward the spot where I was and then swivels his head to search for me. His dark eyes meet mine, and for a long second, it's like time stands still.

He rips off his masquerade mask and glares at me dancing with another man. What did he think I was going to do when he left me alone to go do something with his favorite person? If he wants me to be at his beck and call, maybe he should show me he gives a damn before I'm dancing with another man.

As his stare intensifies, I see something in his eyes that hasn't been there the entire time he's kept me in that penthouse of his.

Jealousy.

CHAPTER FIVE

ideon

I CAN'T STOP MY HANDS FROM CURLING INTO TIGHT fists at my side as I watch Aria dancing with whoever the fuck that guy in the silver mask is. His hand cradling her back makes my rage surge until all I want to do is kill him.

"Looks like your pet found a new owner for this dance," Sasha says with a chuckle.

"Who the fuck is he and why is he in my hotel?" I bite out through clenched teeth.

She hesitates, so I tear my furious gaze away from Aria and glare at Sasha. "I asked who the fuck is he? I want to know his name and why he's here. Now!"

Sasha smiles and runs her fingertips down my arm in that way she always does when she feels like she needs to calm me down before I do something I might regret. Except I won't be regretting anything I do to this motherfucker.

"He's an American. Very nice. I believe he's Cordelia's nephew. Or maybe grandnephew. I spoke to him earlier today out on the terrace. Very sweet. I bet Aria is loving the attention from him. He's got a real nice guy thing going. Not my type since I'd devour him whole, but after a month of being ignored by you, I bet she's eating up every word he's saying to her."

At this moment, I can't decide who's made me angrier, Aria or Sasha. Or that fuck who's got his hands on what's mine. The problem is he's the relative of one of my hotel's best patrons, which means I can't have my men toss him out on his ass.

"I want you to have security remove him before I do. Understand?"

My assistant nods and asks, "And Aria? Should I take care of her too?"

"No. I'll take care of her. You just get that fucking man away from her."

Knowing I have to handle this far more delicately than I've just instructed Sasha to do, I grab her arm as she turns to leave and add, "Don't have them make a scene. Tell security they need to check something for him because there's been some kind of threat. Make up something believable. Just get him the hell away from her now."

Sasha smiles and gives my hand a squeeze. "Of course. Consider it done. Maybe you should go dance with her. She seems to enjoy it."

Seething, I watch Aria and the American sway to the music and hate him without knowing another detail about him. It doesn't matter. He shouldn't be anywhere near Aria. As for her, she obviously can't behave herself and this was a mistake tonight. I should have attended with Sasha, like I usually do for these things. It allows me to fulfill my obligations without having to worry about dealing with some female.

A minute later, security politely escorts Cordelia's great nephew or whoever the fuck he is off the dance floor, leaving Aria alone like she should have been the entire fucking time I was gone. Five minutes I was absent from this room. Five fucking minutes and she ends up dancing with some guy.

I storm over to where she stands and wrap my hand around her arm. "Time to go. Come with me."

By the time we reach the elevator in the lobby, she's in tears, but I don't care. She's lucky I'm succeeding at controlling my temper right now. If I wasn't, she'd have something to cry about.

Nearly jamming my finger through the button for the penthouse, I watch the doors close before the elevator begins to ascend to the top floor. Beside me, Aria complains about something, but I'm lost in my own thoughts about how seeing her with that man made me feel.

"Are you hearing me? Why did you do that? You aren't going to hurt him, are you? He did nothing wrong. Either did I, by the way."

"Enough, Aria," I bite out, working harder than I ever have in my life to keep my cool.

"Just tell me you didn't hurt him, Gideon. He didn't hurt me. He was nice and sweet."

I snap my head to the left to glare at her. Damnit, I'm sick of hearing how fucking sweet this guy is. Good for him. He's like a goddamned dessert. Sweet can go fuck itself, though, for all I care.

"Didn't you hear me? I said enough."

When the elevator stops, she bolts out the doors toward the penthouse, catching Raphael off guard. He hurriedly rushes toward the door to open it, and as I march by after her, I give him a tepid smile, the most I can muster for him or anyone at this moment.

Christ, why am I feeling like this? I'm never jealous. I don't get that way with anything. If I want something, I have it. If I have to take it, then so be it. I can have anything I desire, so jealousy isn't an issue.

So what the fuck is wrong with me when it comes to Aria?

She stomps over to the couch and throws herself onto it before jumping up again to come toward me, her hands flailing in front of her. "I can't believe you, Gideon Rule! Why are you like this? What do you care if I dance with some nice American who was sweet and did nothing to hurt me? You weren't around. You were off like you always are."

My gaze skims over her body in that green gown that highlights every beautiful inch of her as I try to come up with an answer to her question. I don't know why I'm like this when it comes to her, and until tonight, I wouldn't have thought I'd give a single fuck about any woman I'm with innocently dancing with some guest of my hotel.

"You need to stay here. It's clear you can't behave, so no more ball."

Aria's green eyes open wide as they fill with tears. "Behave? You dress me like someone for sale, and then you leave me to go off with your favorite girl. Then you get angry when I simply agree to dance with one of your guests? Fuck you, Gideon!"

She turns away so I can't see her cry, but the sound of her sobs is enough to make me want to change my mind, so I turn to leave before I make a mistake. Aria needs to stay here. I have too much going on tonight to be able to watch her like I need to.

A few minutes later, I find Sasha waiting for me in the ballroom, but disappointment is written all over her face. "Where is your pretty plaything?"

"Where she belongs," I snap as I scan the room and the orgy still going on at center stage.

Beside me, Sasha pouts, "I wish you'd let her come out and play. I like her."

Feeling my rage begin to build again, I turn to look at her and angrily ask, "What do you think you're doing? Aria is mine to do as I choose. Not yours. Do not question me about how I handle her."

My assistant stares into my eyes in that ice cold way she can and then smiles as she slides her palms over my tux jacket lapels. "You don't handle her at all, Gideon. If you want to do that, fine, but don't get angry when other men and I want to be around her."

I shake my head as my anger subsides. "You wouldn't like her if you got to know her. She's high maintenance."

Sasha grins wickedly. "Give me a chance with her so I can see for myself."

"No and stop asking. It irritates me."

Disappointed, she shrugs. "Fine. Then let's focus on our work tonight. Is he here? I can't see him anywhere."

Looking around, I sigh. "I don't either. He'll be here, though."

"I know you think this hotel is your own personal fortress, Gideon, but is it a good idea to invite the one man who's sworn to kill every Rule he can find?"

While I keep my focus on the crowd, I answer her. "What better place to meet him? I'm protected by security here. Outside this hotel, who knows what might happen? This is the best way to handle this."

Sasha pushes her arm against my elbow, drawing my attention away from everyone else in the room.

When I turn to look at her, I see real concern in her eyes.

"What?"

"I just hope you're being careful. Please? I'd like to keep you as my boss."

"Not to worry. If they take me out, you can always go work for my brother," I say, even as I hate that idea.

Her eyes get wide. "Alex? He doesn't have any of your charm to soothe the rough edges. Mine or his. He's all dark and jagged. We'd probably kill each other by the end of our first week together."

"Then I guess I better stay alive," I say with a smile, touched by her concern for me.

Out of the corner of my eye, I see the man I've been looking for all night. Marcello Angeloni. He vowed to take down the Rule family after the Rossettis told him it was a Rule who killed his brother last month. Alaric swears it wasn't him who got rid of Lucius, although I wouldn't blame him if he had.

Leaning over, I whisper to Sasha, "This fucker is all slick and smooth. Is he more your type?"

She looks in the direction of my gaze and sees Marcello. Shaking her head, she says, "If it's a choice between him and your brother, then I'll take Alex. Darkness is one thing. This guy is all cockiness, and I don't think he has enough between his legs to back it up."

Not surprising. That's what you get with the prodigal son.

"What are you planning to do? I hope you've got your temper under control after that Aria situation. You can't let Marcello Angeloni see someone can get to you. He'll use that against you, Gideon."

She and I watch him walk toward where we stand. "Relax. This is just a chance for two men to talk. We'll have a conversation here in the safe confines of my hotel, and I'll see what he's got on his mind."

"What he has on his mind is to kill everyone with the last name Rule. Please don't underestimate this man. I know he's the baby of the Angeloni family and he's been gone from this coast for years, but he's not a boy. Remember that."

Just then, a man I know all too well joins Marcello as he makes his way through the crowd. "Some people just can't get it through their heads that they should stay away."

Sasha watches the men for a moment and asks, "Is that Franco Marchetti? I thought you said he left town and wouldn't be back."

"He's not supposed to be back. Looks like he made a new friend."

This changes my plans. I still need to talk to Marcello Angeloni to find out what he has planned, but Franco's showing up here tonight with him tells me I need to make a point he didn't understand when we last talked.

"Go get Aria. Make sure she's wearing her mask, but I want her down here with me. Now."

My assistant hesitates for only a moment before hurrying away to do as I ordered. Franco wants to show up at my hotel? Then he needs to remember what I got in exchange for him leaving town.

CHAPTER SIX

ria

MY BLOOD FEELS LIKE IT'S BOILING AS I PACE BACK and forth across the living room in Gideon's beautiful penthouse, or what I affectionately like to call my fucking prison. That bastard! He has that ice princess of his dress me up to look all pretty, and then when a single person has the nerve to appreciate what I look like in this green dress, he forces me to come back up here and he goes back to the party! He's probably there with Sasha, and the two of them are having a grand old time.

I pass that white and blue vase I saw him place on the table behind the couch the other day like it's some priceless thing and stare at it. He gives that more care than he does me. I should accidentally push it onto the floor as I walk by next time.

He's such an ass! Who takes a woman to stay with him and then does nothing with her, and then the one time he actually lets her out of her gilded cage, he stuffs her back in for doing nothing wrong?

Marcus wouldn't treat a woman like that. The memory of the sweet American with the gentle eyes stops me for a moment, and I feel like shit that I'm the reason he's probably wandering the streets of the Amalfi Coast with no place to stay because Gideon threw him out of the hotel.

Fed up, I storm to the front door and fling it open to find Raphael standing there doing his usual impression of a statue. God, that pisses me off even more! Does this guy actually like simply posing like an inanimate object day in and day out?

He doesn't glance over at me, even though I know he's fully aware I'm standing here. If I thought it would make me feel better, I'd punch him. Not that he'd feel it. The guy's like a mountain of flesh, bone, and muscle. My fist hitting him would feel like a flea landing on his skin.

I have to do something, though, so I ball my hands into fists and scream, "You know, you could at least acknowledge I'm standing right here! It's rude to not even turn to ask if I'm okay or if I need something. Not that anyone in this fucking place cares about that, but still, it would be nice."

That gets a reaction from him, and he slowly turns his big, stony head to look at me. "Do you need something, miss?" he asks in that robot-like voice.

"I need to get the hell out of this penthouse and out of his hotel. Any chance you can assist me in that?" I pointedly ask, knowing he wouldn't help me even if he could.

Raphael purses his lips, and for a moment, I wait for him to reply to my outburst. It never happens, though, and a few seconds later, he simply turns his head to face forward again.

More infuriated than I was before, I snap, "Nice chat. We'll have to do it again sometime."

He doesn't respond, so I slam the door and begin pacing again. I guess I could have tried to make a break for it and run to the elevator to escape this place, but he'd have me in his grasp before I could even press the damn DOWN button.

I hate him. I hate Gideon. And I hate Sasha. Not in that order, necessarily either. In fact, Gideon should be at the top of the list because he's the architect of all my misery. The other two are simply his minions helping him to make my life awful.

I head out to the terrace and look over the side at the hill below. I should throw myself over and save Gideon the trouble of unceremoniously having me escorted out of the building and tossed into the streets like my American dance partner. If he does that tonight, I'll be sure to look for Marcus. Maybe we can find a place to stay together for the night.

It's the least I can do for him since he was punished because of me.

Tilting my head back to look at the dark night sky above, I silently remind myself that's wrong. He wasn't punished because of me. He was punished because Gideon is a complete asshole who got jealous over nothing.

If he cares enough to be jealous of my innocently dancing with another man, then maybe he should show me that instead of forcing me back into his penthouse like some disobedient child.

I take a deep breath in an attempt to calm down and let myself enjoy the scent of lemons in the air. That's always been one of my favorite parts of living here on the coast. No matter how bad things ever got, the beauty of this region made me see I had something to be thankful for.

Behind me, I hear the door to the penthouse open, but I don't turn around to face him. If Gideon wants me to pay attention to him, he's going to have to at least apologize for being so terrible about my dancing with Marcus. If not, then I can stay out here and ignore him all night. It's not like we ever do anything together other than actually sleep when we're both here anyway.

"Aria, Gideon wants you to come back downstairs," Sasha says brusquely.

The sound of a voice I hadn't expected makes me turn around, and in just a few steps, Gideon's all too beautiful assistant is standing right in front of me. I scan her expression and see she isn't as angry as she sounded a moment ago. In fact, all I see in her face is nothing less than fascination.

She truly is odd. One minute it's like she hates me, and then the next minute she gives me a look like she wishes she could have me.

Is she gay? No, I don't believe that. My gut tells me she and Gideon have been together. For all I know they still could be. But I know the look in her eye right now. I've seen it before in men. She may be crazy about him, but she's got something going on for me too.

"Please tell Gideon I'm not interested in leaving my opulent prison."

Sasha doesn't respond for a long moment, simply staring into my eyes with an intensity that unnerves me. I fight against looking away, though. Something tells me with a person like her I need to stand my ground.

Out of the corner of my eye, I see something move. Looking down, I watch as her right hand holding her mask shakes like she's angry.

"Aria, make this easy on both of us and come with me. Gideon needs you downstairs."

Her use of the word need makes me roll my eyes. "Gideon needs me? What a joke. Gideon never needs me. If he did, he wouldn't keep me prisoner up here, never paying a moment's attention to me when he comes home every night."

She takes a step closer to me and lets out a heavy sigh. "I understand. He can be a difficult person to appreciate if you aren't like him. Gideon just has his way of doing things. He means you no harm. So let's go back down to the ball."

I study her nearly perfect face and feel jealousy surge inside me. "Well, how nice it must be for you then since you're just like him. Two peas in an ice cold, feelingless pod. Why don't you go back downstairs and you be his date for the night? It won't be the first time, I'm sure, and likely not the last either."

My insult doesn't seem to affect her at all. She continues to stare into my eyes like I'm the most intriguing thing in the world right now.

Reaching her hand out, she caresses my cheek, sending chills through me. "It's true he and I are very much alike, but that doesn't mean he doesn't care about you. You need to be patient with him. He has a lot to handle with this hotel and his family."

God, I'm so sick of hearing this woman defend Gideon Rule! Can he do nothing wrong in her eyes?

I push her hand away and step around her to walk back into the penthouse. "Poor Gideon. He's so busy. Why should anyone expect him to be kind or show me any attention? Maybe in those hours when I'm here with him after long days downstairs he could do something like talk to me or show me he likes having me around. But no. He's done none of that. He simply walks in, looks at me like he's pleased I'm still here waiting for him in the exact spot where he left me twelve hours before, and goes to bed. Sorry, but I have no time for being patient with your favorite guy. You go be patient with him, Sasha. I'm sure he'd like that more anyway."

In a flash, she's behind me. Before I can turn to face her, she spins me around so we're toe-to-toe with one another. I see something other than interest in me now in her eyes, and whatever she's thinking scares me.

"You're a beautiful woman, Aria. Maybe that's why you can't see a good thing when it's standing right in front of you."

"Are you talking about you or Gideon?" I ask, truly unsure what she means at this moment.

That makes her smile, and her eyes soften again. "Well, to be honest, I could mean either of us, but right now I'm referring to Gideon. He can give you anything you could ever want or need. You just need to give him time. He'll come around. Just be patient."

Sensing she might actually tell me the truth, I take a step closer to her so our bodies are nearly touching and our lips are only inches apart. "Tell me, Sasha. What kind of man can lie in a bed with a beautiful woman night after night and not touch her? What exactly am I patiently waiting for? He's hard nearly

69

every moment he's around me. Tonight downstairs, he was as hard as a rock behind me. I felt his cock pressing against my ass. So why doesn't he do anything?"

For a long moment, she doesn't say anything as her eyes scan my face, giving me a reprieve from her intense stares. I wait for an answer, truly needing to know what I'm waiting for from a man who clearly wants me but won't do anything about it.

Finally, she answers, "If you're asking me if he's said why he doesn't do anything with you, all I can tell you is he hasn't. Gideon and I don't talk about you."

She stops and gives me a big grin. "Well, except for when I tell him he should bring you out to play more and he tells me to stop. You see, I agree with you. I think he should have done something by now. I think he might believe you still care about your ex, so he doesn't feel like he should bother getting attached. But that's just my opinion."

Her answer stuns me. Shaking my head, I step back away from her, needing space to understand what she just said.

"Why would he think that? Franco happily handed me over to Gideon, although once again I feel the need to mention to anyone who'll listen that selling a woman isn't okay or legal. I wouldn't have anything to do with Franco ever again."

Sasha takes my hand in hers and smiles. "Well, when you have the chance to show him that, I suggest you do and see if that thaws things out between you two. Now, come on and let's get back down to the party. He wants you down there with him."

I give in, unable to fight her anymore after hearing her crazy idea about Franco. Why would I feel anything for a man who happily gave me away for money? That's insane.

"Fine. Let's go."

She keeps her hand on mine and leads me through the penthouse, grabbing my gold mask off the table on our way toward the door. I shouldn't trust her at all since she's loyal to only Gideon, but I can't help but feel there's something good about her.

As we step into the elevator and the doors close in front of us, she drops my hand to press the button for the first floor. We begin to descend back toward the party, and I ask, "Do you ever get annoyed by having to run these errands for him?"

She doesn't hesitate to answer, shaking her head as she says, "Never. That's my job. Whatever Gideon needs me to do, I do. Whatever he requires, I make sure it happens. It's all there is to being an assistant."

No wonder he adores her and barely tolerates me. She's there at his beck and call, waiting on him hand and foot. If he expects me to be that, I'm afraid we'll never be together.

I'm not a Sasha. I never will be.

. . .

WHEN WE RETURN TO THE BALLROOM, GIDEON gives me a smile as he adjusts my mask around my eyes. "Thank you for coming back, Aria."

I try to return the smile, but all I can think is I'll never be what he wants. Why he doesn't just let me go so he can be with the woman he truly cares about I don't understand, but I can't keep letting myself get hurt waiting for him to show me he cares.

He falls silent, so I look around for his assistant since I'm sure she'll say something, but she's nowhere to be found. "Where did Sasha go?"

Gideon turns to face me and answers, "She's doing what she's supposed to do. I don't need her here with us right now."

I can't help but feel happy about her being gone. I may not think she's completely made of ice anymore after our little conversation upstairs, but when she's around, he's never going to see me.

"We're going to be talking to someone in a few moments, Aria. Stay by my side and don't say a word," he instructs me.

"Is this more orgy rules? I had no idea random fucking of strangers in public had so many regulations," I say with a chuckle.

Just then, I see two familiar faces and my entire body tenses. Marcello Angeloni and Franco walk toward us carving their way through the crowd like they own this place. The youngest Angeloni brother wears a tux with a red mask that only covers near his eyes and contrasts with his jet-black hair. Franco looks like he always has—like a man perpetually looking for a fight, even though he's in a tux. His mask resembles a white skull and covers all of his face except his mouth.

I clutch Gideon's arm, immediately terrified at what's going to happen next. Is he going to hand me back to Franco because he thinks I still care about him? He can't do that!

"Please, Gideon. You promised to keep me safe. I can't believe you let that man in here. I hate even seeing his face," I say as I press my body against his side, silently praying to God he doesn't plan to simply abandon me with my ex.

He doesn't answer, except for a single nod, and then slides his arm around my waist to pull me close to him. Marcello and Franco stop directly in front of us, and even though I can't imagine Gideon could want people like them here in his hotel, he greets them like a gentleman.

"How are you tonight, Marcello? It's good to see you here. Have you been enjoying the party?"

Marcello smiles a slick grin that reminds me of how a snake would show his happiness and answers, "I have to say you and your guests know how to have a good time."

"That we do," Gideon says with an air of confidence that makes the two men in front of him seem unsure of themselves.

I avoid even glancing in Franco's direction, but he can't pretend to be a gentleman and snaps, "Being a slut looks good on you, Aria. Nice rock."

Every muscle in my body tightens in fear that he's going to reach out and slap me across the face, but Gideon quickly says to Marcello, "Remind your man he's a guest in my hotel. I would hate to have my men have to throw him out because someone like him doesn't belong here like Aria does."

Franco practically seethes, but his boss doesn't hesitate to send him away. "I apologize for him. I'm afraid he lets his emotions get the best of him. He's not like us, Mr. Rule. I'll let you get back to your night. I simply wanted to say hello and let you know I'm looking forward to sitting down and talking sometime soon."

"As do I, Marcello."

When he walks away leaving us alone again, Gideon turns to look at me and I swear I see concern in his eyes. Is that for me after what Franco said or is it for whatever situation there is between him and Marcello Angeloni?

Quietly, in a somber voice, Gideon says, "It's time to go back upstairs, Aria."

My blood practically boils at the idea that he had that assistant of his bring me down here just to make me face Franco. Is he truly that cruel?

Tears well in my eyes as I struggle to keep them at

bay. "Did you want me back down here because you knew Franco was here and he'd say something to me?"

Whatever that expression in his eyes from a minute ago that I wondered about returns in full force, and Gideon shakes his head. "No. I wanted you down here because you belonged at my side."

"And yet now that he and Marcello Angeloni are gone, I'm forced to go back to my prison?"

He slides his mask over his head so I can see his entire face, and I recognize the look of irritation I've seen so many times in the past few weeks. "I didn't mean just you. Now let's go."

Before I can say a word, he takes me by the hand and leads me out of the ballroom and across the lobby toward the elevator, all the while remaining silent. I want to ask why he's angry now—is it what I did or the meeting with Marcello—but I don't. He probably wouldn't answer me anyway.

We stand quietly waiting for the elevator, and then when we step in, I notice he doesn't release his hold on my hand and instead reaches across his body with his other hand to press P on the panel of buttons. He'll talk now, I'm sure, not that I really know if I want to hear what he has to say considering he's still frowning as he stares straightforward toward the gold elevator doors in front of us.

But even though we're alone, he says nothing. It must be me he's angry at, although I don't understand why anything I said would upset him. Then again, can I really say I understand anything about this man?"

The doors open and we walk out into the hallway where Raphael stands guard outside the penthouse like always. With a smile, I nod at him, but he doesn't respond.

"Does that guy ever move from that spot? I'm beginning to think he's a statue," I say with a chuckle as Gideon and I walk into the penthouse.

Yet again, my words are met with silence. It's becoming deafening, and I have to say something. I can't live like this.

"What did I do to make you so angry? Please, Gideon. Tell me."

Finally, he speaks, but it's only a single word. Turning to look at me, he shakes his head and says, "Nothing."

That's it. Nothing. And still, he acts like he's furious with me.

I open my mouth to ask what the hell the problem is then, but he simply walks away toward the bedroom without saying another thing. Following him, I try to distill what I'm feeling into a simple statement because I sense he's not going to listen to much more than that.

But he makes a move toward the bathroom, robbing me of my chance to start any conversation, so I blurt out, "Why are you like this? You act as if I didn't something wrong, but then you tell me I didn't nothing. So why are you acting like this toward me?"

Gideon stops and levels his gaze on me, and now I'm certain something's wrong. I just don't know what. I wait for him to tell me, to give me some clue as to what's happening between us right now, but he denies me that when he slowly turns away and walks into the bathroom, closing the door behind him.

And again, I'm alone.

CHAPTER SEVEN

ria

FOR THE SECOND DAY IN THE ROW, I OPEN MY EYES to see Gideon standing by the bed staring down at me. After last night's silent treatment, I'm still angry, so I don't give him the opportunity to say anything and instead throw the sheet off me before swinging my legs over the side of the bed and pushing past him.

If he wants to live in silence, then so be it. I can do silence too. It doesn't come as naturally to me as it does to him, but I can do it.

Just before I reach the bathroom, I hear him say, "Aria, you'll be spending time outside the penthouse today."

I close my eyes and stop walking as I decide

whether I want to engage with him. He makes it next to impossible not to since he says so little and every statement that comes out of his mouth practically begs for me to respond.

As much as I should remain silent and give him the same treatment he gave me last night, I can't. Spinning on my heel, I face him and see his eyes widen for just a moment. I don't know why. I sleep nude right beside him every night. He can't possibly be shocked by seeing me standing naked in front of him now.

"Why? Where are you consigning me to today? Do I get to watch the gardener as he waters flowers on the terrace while your other guests enjoy a nice breakfast? Are you training me for a job at your hotel, Gideon? That would at least make some sense, as opposed to what we're doing here each night."

He merely stares at me, his dark eyes laser-focused on my face. "Wear the blue dress with the little yellow flowers along the hem. One of my security guards will be here to get you at ten."

"You're picking out the clothes I have to wear now? What's that about?"

But, of course, he has no answer for me and simply turns to walk out of the room. Fed up with whatever game he's playing, I rush over to block his path and reach him just before he gets to the door. The look of shock on his face is real, although I don't know why he should be surprised.

A person can only take so much before they can't control themselves anymore.

"Stop and explain to me what the hell is going on. You get jealous when I dance with another man last night, so you send me to my gilded cage, only to have that woman come get me so I can be right beside you when Marcello and Franco show up. You pretend like we're some happy couple for them, although I have no idea why, and when my ex calls me a slut, all you do is threaten to throw him out of your precious hotel. Not that I guess I should expect anything more since you took me and have clearly decided you don't want me. But then you give me the silent treatment, despite the fact that I did nothing wrong. Why are you like this?"

The words stream out of my mouth like I've rehearsed every syllable night after night for nearly a month. Never before have I sounded as strong and confused at the same time.

He listens to every word, never once moving to force me out of his way. His dark eyes stay fixed on mine, like the clue to how he should answer can be found in them. When I finish, I wait for him to say even a few words, unwilling to deal with silence anymore.

If he wants out of this room, he needs to say something. I might not be as big as him, but I can put up a fight like a cat trapped in a bag.

When he finally does speak, I take a step back in shock.

"I'm like this because this is who I am. I told you last night that you did nothing to anger me, and that was the truth. I have a lot of things on my mind, Aria, and it would be nice if for once, just once, you didn't have to be one of the problems I have to deal with. You don't want to stay here all day, so I made arrangements so you don't have to. Please get dressed and be ready for when security comes to get you at ten."

I don't think Gideon has said that many words at once to me in the three weeks I've been here. Maybe I touched a nerve. But he still has one question to answer for me before I move out of his way.

"Why the blue dress with the yellow flowers? Why that particular dress today?"

For the first time this morning, he smiles, and it's like someone turned a light on inside him. Even his dark eyes brighten. Best of all, he looks like my question made him happy.

"Because I think it will look beautiful on you. That's why."

"Will you be wherever your security guy is taking me? Where am I going anyway?" I ask, pushing my luck but eager to keep him talking.

"It's a surprise," he answers, his smile still as big as it was a moment ago.

"Will you be there for this surprise?"

I don't know why I keep hoping at some point he's

going to finally look at me and realize he wants me. If it hasn't happened by now, it's not going to happen.

But when he's sweet and he smiles like he's happy to be with me, I can't help but wish it would.

Gideon leans down to position his mouth next to my ear and whispers, "I'm always there when you're in my hotel."

His warm breath brushes against the shell of my ear, exciting me. Pressing my thighs together, I feel an ache begin to form. If only he would touch me, we could have fun. I'm already naked, and it wouldn't take much for him to be.

My hopes for any kind of morning rendezvous are dashed when he gently moves me out of his way and walks out into the living room. Disappointed, I don't ask him anything else and slowly mope back to the bathroom. On my way, I glance over at the clock on the wall and see it's nearly ten already. I guess there won't be time to me to masturbate in the shower.

I swear to God this entire place is just one tease after another, with Gideon being the biggest tease at all. As I wash my hair, I close my eyes and let the water run down over my head as I wonder if he does it intentionally or is he really just like this and none of how he behaves is deliberate.

Whichever it is, this whole cat and mouse game he's playing with me is driving me nuts. It's also making me so sexually frustrated that he shouldn't be surprised if I start coming on to Raphael, my favorite guard and statue.

After taking one last look in the mirror at myself in the dress Gideon ordered me to wear, I walk out into the living room reconsidering these shoes with their three-inch heels. Glancing down my body, I study them for a moment and wonder if lower shoes might work better.

"This would be so much easier if I knew where I was going."

I assume it's nowhere that will involve a lot of hiking or running since he pointedly commanded me to wear this dress, but with Gideon, who knows? The man might tell me to go shopping up and down the coast for some unique item he insists I have for only reasons he understands.

A knock tears me out of my deliberations about my footwear, and I hurry over to answer the front door. I'm not sure why Raphael is knocking anyway. He only does that when Gideon is home. I suspect he's been told to never knock when it's only me here so he can possibly catch me doing something.

As if I'm up to something nefarious here all day.

I fling open the door and see not Raphael waiting for me but a new security guy. As big as my usual guard, this one has light brown hair and blue eyes that instantly remind me of Marcus. God, I hope he didn't end up wandering the streets because of Gideon's jealousy.

"Hi. Who are you?" I ask as my gaze travels down his very muscular body and back up to his attractive face.

"Phillip. I'm here to take you to the eighth floor," he says in a soft voice that seems odd coming from someone his size.

"Phillip? That sounds distinctly un-Italian. Are you from here, Phillip?" I ask as I grab my purse to leave.

I check to make sure I have my phone while my new bodyguard explains he's an American who works for Helix Rule and has been assigned to the hotel for the remainder of the month. I listen, smiling as he talks and wondering if he's done something bad to be sent here by Helix or if this is a move upward for him. I decide not to ask since I have a feeling he won't tell me anyway.

Everyone here is all about keeping secrets. It's like this hotel does something to them as soon as they step foot in the front door.

"Well, lead the way, Phillip."

Closing the door behind me, I step out into the hall to go to the elevator and see Raphael. As always, he's silent and as still as a stone. I bet he's happy he didn't get stuck touring me around the eighth floor today.

"You get a break, so ease up, Raphael. Maybe

smile. Or would that make your face crack?" I say with a giggle.

He doesn't respond. I watch to see if he even blinks before the elevator doors close. Nothing. Maybe he is a statue.

Thankfully, my new guard is more talkative, so I turn to look at him and ask, "What's on the eighth floor that I need to be there today?"

"An art gallery," he answers. "I'm not sure why you need to be there today, but that's where I was told to take you."

"Were you told anything else?"

Phillip shakes his head and frowns like he's disappointed he can't help me with an answer. "Nothing. Just pick up the woman at the penthouse and take her down to the eighth floor."

"Do you know something about art?" I ask as the elevator begins to come to a stop. "Is that why you got this assignment today?"

My question gets me a broad smile. "Not a thing. Sorry."

As the doors open and I step out onto the eighth floor, I wonder why this particular guard was chosen by Gideon to escort me around the hotel's art gallery. Why wouldn't Gideon just do it himself since I'm sure he's quite proud of the pieces in his hotel's collection?

Then again, why does Gideon do or not do anything? The man is a complete mystery to me.

Unlike the main floor with its black marble floor

and enormous marble columns and the penthouse floor that always seems dark, the eighth floor has pale marble floors and white walls. Lighting is situated overhead so it focuses on the pieces of art hanging on the walls and showcased on pedestals throughout the floor.

I look at Phillip and smile. "This is nice. Have you ever been here before?"

He shakes his head and looks around. "No. Too bad I don't know a thing about art. This might be really great if I did."

Unsure how this is supposed to work, I ask, "Were you ordered to walk around with me? Or am I on my own?"

Phillip points at the glass doors we just walked through when we got off the elevator. "I'm supposed to wait here."

Of course he is. It's the only way to leave this floor, so naturally, Gideon has told him to position himself there so I can't get away. Even when he does something nice, it turns out that I'm still treated like a prisoner.

"Okay. I'll be back in a little while," I say as disgust fills me. Not at Phillip, who's only doing his job. No, at the only person in this entire building who deserves my anger and resentment.

Gideon Rule.

I wander around the gallery admiring the artwork on the walls, none of which I know anything about.

Some are landscapes, while others are still lifes. That's about all I know of art. Well, I know about the Mona Lisa, but that's not going to be hanging on the wall somewhere here.

It's all very nice, and one or two of the black and gold pottery pieces make me think I'd like to know more about them, so I read the caption on the gold plate below each one and find out they're Etruscan. I vaguely remember learning about them in school. They disappeared from Italy before the people considered to be Romans came on the scene. History was never my strongest class, so I'm actually surprised I recall that at all.

As I continue my walk through Gideon's gallery, I wonder why I needed to wear this dress to see all the pieces of art here today. Not that I would want to walk around naked to admire them, but I could have dressed in my yoga pants and a T-shirt and felt the same way about all I'm seeing. It's not like there's anyone else here with me to see what I'm wearing either.

I'm beginning to feel like I'm in one of those foreign films where nothing makes sense and even subtitles don't help. Like the ones where you're certain an important part of the movie was edited out, leaving you to wonder what's going on.

Just as I'm sure this day can't get any more confusing, my phone begins to ring. No one has called me in the three weeks I've been here because I couldn't get any reception that whole time. I found out when my phone fell silent for two days right after I arrived and wanted to call my mother to tell her I was safe.

Reaching into my purse, I pull it out and look at the number on the screen. I don't recognize it, but I'm curious enough to answer. "Hello?"

"Are you enjoying your time in the art gallery, Aria?" Gideon asks in a low voice that I swear hits me somewhere deep inside I didn't know existed until this very moment.

"Yes."

I want to ask how my phone seems to work now when it hasn't for weeks, but before I can get a chance to, he replies, "I'm happy you're enjoying it. We made sure to put that upholstered bench in front of the Modigliani. What do you think of it?"

Turning around the room to figure out which piece he means, I see the bench in front of a painting of woman lying nude on a red sofa. Unshaven under her arms and between her legs, she has a long torso and rounded hips. I also can't help but notice she's extremely well-endowed.

"I think there weren't breast implants whenever this was painted, so this model had a very nice body naturally."

When I finish giving my commentary, I realize he knew exactly where I was when he called me. "How did you know I was standing near this painting?"

"I told you. I know where you are at all times in my hotel, Aria. Do you like the painting?" Gideon asks, his voice practically beaming a smile.

With another glance at the nude woman, I shrug. "Not really, to be honest."

"Why?"

I hear the disappointment in his voice, but I see no reason to lie. I don't have a problem with nudes. I just don't like this one much.

"She's not appealing, I guess. Isn't art all about personal taste anyway? I'm guessing whoever this painter is, he wouldn't care one bit that I don't like his nude woman on a red sofa."

That gets me a deep chuckle before he says, "That's true. What I like you might not."

"Why didn't you tell me about this gallery before today?" I ask as I sit down on the white tufted bench. "It would have been nice to see it on all those days I was just stuck in the penthouse. I might not love art, but this is better than sitting around all day doing nothing."

"What pieces do you like?" he asks, disregarding my question entirely.

I turn my head to look over at one of the Etruscan pottery pieces and say, "I like the black Etruscan water jug. I like the way people are painted around it."

"Interesting. So you prefer much older artwork. Modigliani's portrait is from the early twentieth century," Gideon explains.

"I guess. I'm not really knowledgeable about art. I'm thinking there are far better people to ask about art than me."

"Except I want to know your opinion, Aria, so you're the only person to ask."

I should encourage him to keep asking me what I like since this is the most we've spoken in all the time we've known one another. The problem is I don't have many other opinions about the artwork in this gallery.

You know who I bet knows all about art? Sasha. I'm sure she could give him chapter and verse about what's great about the big breasted lady lying back on that uncomfortable looking sofa with her armpit and crotch hair hanging out and how the pottery I like isn't anything close to being great and only some uneducated fool would enjoy it.

"Why are you pouting?" he asks, instantly ripping me from my sulking.

I look around for any sign of cameras but don't see any. "How do you know I'm pouting?"

Gideon chuckles at what must sound like a ridiculous question to him. "I told you. I know where you are at all times in my hotel."

"Well, I don't see any cameras, and unless you have Phillip there relaying all my expressions, I can't figure out how you know," I say, frustrated he seems to know everything about me and I know nothing about him, as usual.

"Just assume I always know, Aria. So you enjoy

Etruscan artwork. I think that surprises me. I like that."

He sounds so smooth and so pleased that I don't bother to mention that I don't love it as much as he seems to think. It's nice, but I think I prefer the blue and white vase in the penthouse more, even if it's not priceless art.

"For once, you're quiet. Why is that, Aria?"

"I don't know. I guess I'm like a fish out of water here. Maybe you should ask someone who knows about art to talk about these things. I'm sure your assistant could do the job far better than I can."

My jealousy comes through loud and clear, and I don't care. Unlike him, I have no problem admitting when I'm jealous. It's perfectly normal to feel that way. Maybe if he understood that, poor Marcus wouldn't have been unceremoniously tossed out of the hotel last night.

"I'm not interested in Sasha's point of view right now. I'm interested in yours," he says sternly.

"Tell me what you did to that man I was dancing with last night. I want to know."

"Only if you do something for me."

Frustrated he won't give me a simple answer, I sigh. "Fine. Tell me what piece of art you want me to look at and I'll tell you what I think of it."

"No, that's not what I want. Lie back on the bench as we continue to talk."

Confused, I look up to see if there's some painting

hung on the ceiling but see none. Lie back on the bench? Why?

I could ask, but what's the point? We've done this my questioning and him not answering dance so many times in the past few weeks that I know what the outcome will be. I'll waste my breath and he'll tell me nothing.

When I'm fully reclined, I take a deep breath in and let it out in a rush. "Okay. What am I looking at?"

"Did you do anything in the shower this morning, Aria?" he asks in a whispery voice that hits me deep inside again.

Does he mean what I think he means?

CHAPTER EIGHT

ideon

"DO ANYTHING? WHAT DO YOU MEAN?" SHE ASKS with a tremor in her voice.

I don't answer for a long moment but then ask, "Did you touch yourself? You seemed very excited when we were talking this morning."

There's no point in her lying. She was practically begging for me to fuck her, even if she didn't say a word about it this morning in the bedroom.

"No, and not because I didn't want to. You gave me so little time to get ready before Phillip arrived that I couldn't squeeze it in."

"Then I think you should now."

She swivels her head to look for where the camera must be as her mouth drops open in surprise. "You want me to play with myself here? In your art gallery? Why?"

"Because it would make me happy."

"Ah, now I get it. Gideon likes to watch. Okay. That doesn't mean I want to just slide my finger inside my panties and get off right here, though."

"Why not?"

Everything with this woman ends up in a struggle. For once, can't she just surrender and do as I want without asking questions?

"What about your security guy Phillip? He's right at the door. What if he sees?"

"He's been told to watch the door and not bother you. He won't see anything."

"So you watch while I play with myself? Will you be doing something wherever you are?" she asks, sounding suddenly more excited than even this morning back in the penthouse.

"No, I won't be doing anything here in my office," I answer.

"I think you should," she says with a smile that makes her even more beautiful, still looking for the camera somewhere in that room.

"Take your panties off," I quietly command.

"So you're just going to watch and not do anything? That doesn't sound like fun."

Standing from behind my desk, I button my suit

coat before I make my way toward the door. "Do as your told, Aria. Take them off."

As she slides them down her legs, she says, "I had no idea you were this kinky, Gideon. Who knew you had a peeping Tom thing going?"

"Now close your eyes and run your finger through your pussy. Tell me if you're wet."

I listen, wishing I could see her do what I ordered her to do. Her breathing grows ever so slightly heavier, telling me she's enjoying this.

"I just hope Phillip doesn't walk in on me."

"He won't. Tell me what you're doing."

"Even though you can see? You are kinky. Okay. I'm sliding my finger through my folds and over my excited clit, arching down to dip my fingertip inside me. I'm soaking wet, even though in the back of my mind I can't help but worry I'm going to be seen by someone other than you."

"You're fine. Keep going," I say as I walk toward the elevator, waving off Sasha as she hurries toward me.

I don't care what she has to tell me at this moment. All I care about is listening to Aria as she plays with herself and tells me about it.

"What do you want me to say?" she asks in a tone so innocent my cock stiffens to as hard as a rock as I enter the elevator.

"I want you to tell me everything. How it feels. How close you are. Everything."

I press the button as she begins to describe how it feels lying there in my art gallery touching herself with her bodyguard nearby. She sounds so perfect that I can't wait to see in person how beautiful she looks there with her finger deep in her cunt.

By the time the elevator reaches the eighth floor, my cock hurts it's so hard. My plan was to simply surprise her while she does what I want, but that might have to change if I want to get any work done today.

"Gideon, is this why you wanted me to wear this blue dress today?" she asks breathlessly.

I step out of the elevator and point at Phillip to move. Covering the phone, I say to him, "Stand in front of this elevator and don't let anyone onto this floor. Understand?"

He gives me a somber nod of his head, and I pass him on my way to Aria. I see her lying on that white bench with her dress hiked up around her waist and can't think of anything else but burying myself inside her.

I answer her question with a quick yes before stopping behind her. Eyes closed, she doesn't see me standing there watching, my cock aching to get in on the action.

"Oh, God…This isn't going to take long. Three weeks of nothing with another human being is a long time," she says sweetly as her body tightens.

"Good. I want to watch you come," I say into the phone right behind her.

Her eyes fly open, and she looks up at me, instantly pushing her dress down over her hips. "Gideon!"

"In the flesh. Now get back to what you were doing."

She sits up and pouts at me. "No. You tricked me. And I want to know where that damn camera was."

I can't help but smile at how cute she is when she's flustered. Pointing up toward the ceiling at the tiny camera right below the crown molding, I say, "Right there. It gave me a perfect vantage point. Of course, that was the point."

Still sulking, she stands up and faces me. "I thought the point was for me to get off without you having to be involved at all. That seems to be your whole focus with me."

With two strides, I'm directly in front of her as she continues to scowl. "I was involved. It was me directing this whole thing. I got you here. I had you lie down on the bench. I told you to play with yourself. See? I was part of it all."

Her green eyes flash her unhappiness at me as she says, "You're like some unbelievably frustrating online boyfriend who only likes to watch but never participates and never comes to town to have the real thing."

"The real thing?" I ask before snaking my arm

around her waist to pull her to me. "Is that really what you want? Right here in front of that camera?"

Aria's eyes grow wide before she glances up at the ceiling in the location of the camera. "Who would see? You're here."

I hesitate to tell her the truth, but she asked. "Sasha might see if she's walked into my office. I left my laptop open."

"Oh, really? Is she into watching people have sex?"

Leaning down, I whisper into Aria's ear, "She's into anything. Just a fair warning. She likes you, so she'd probably enjoy watching us fuck right here."

I feel Aria's hand slide down the front of my pants, and a second later, her fingers wrap around my hard cock. Staring into my eyes, she says with a smile, "Then I say we give her a show."

It occurs to me I haven't kissed Aria since that one night we were together, so I dip my head to press my lips to hers. She's soft and tastes like peaches, although I don't know why since there isn't a single peach in this hotel. I want to devour her mouth like I want to devour every other part of her.

She returns my kiss with a neediness I can't help but love, and a second later, I sit down on the bench, my cock dying to be inside that wet cunt. I see her panties lying on the floor and smile as I unzip my pants.

Aria returns her hand to where it was a minute

ago, stroking my cock up and down and making me feel like the top of my head is going to blow off. I slide my hands up under her dress and sink my fingertips into her hips as I guide her onto me.

"We're really going to have sex right here?" she asks as inch by inch my cock fills her.

I nod as my eyelids flutter closed. She feels even better than I remembered from weeks ago. Tight and wet, she's perfect.

But she's still dressed, and that needs to change.

Yanking her dress up, I tug it over her head, surprising her. "Gideon!"

After I toss it onto the floor on top of her panties, I turn back to face her on my lap in only her white lace bra. As nice as it is, that needs to go too. So I quickly unhook it and toss it onto her dress.

"Now that's how you should look when I'm fucking you."

Her thighs skim my sides and hips as she begins to ride me, but even now she can't stop with the questions. "Why didn't you do something all those times I was upstairs naked in the bed next to you?"

Unable to answer her, I silence her mouth by kissing her as my hands force her down hard on me. She lets out a tiny squeal when I finally fill her completely, making my cock grow even harder. Her tongue slides over mine before she moans softly, and I lift her off me.

"Even in sex, you're in total control, huh?" she asks against my lips.

I look up into her green eyes hazed over by desire and nod. She smiles and kisses me. "Let go of my hips. I want to be in charge."

Nobody ever says that to me. Not women I fuck. Not people who work for me. Nobody. I'm always the one in control.

When I don't release my hold on her, she begins prying my fingers from her hips. "Gideon, let go. Trust me. You'll be happy you did."

I reluctantly agree and put my hands up to show her I did as she asked. With a smile, she sits back down on my cock and sighs.

"Enjoy yourself for once. You might like it."

Without answering, I let my hands come to rest on her waist and watch her as she begins to ride my cock in earnest. She's sensual and open, unlike I've ever seen with her before. Regret for waiting this long fills my brain, but that's pushed out when she rolls her hips to take all of me again.

"Tell me how much you love the feel of me riding your cock," she whispers breathlessly.

I open my eyes and look down as her body takes all of me. Every fiber of my being wants to grab hold of her hips so she'll go faster. I know that's because I don't have control right now, but it's taking every ounce of willpower in me.

She's waiting for an answer, so I try to focus on her face and say, "More than you know."

It's not what she wants to hear, and she stills on my lap and pouts. "Is it that you don't want me? It seems like you do. You're hard. So why does it seem like you aren't enjoying this? You set this whole thing up today, not me. You dressed me like you wanted, brought me to this place, and then undressed me just as you wanted. What is it, Gideon? What's wrong?"

Staring up into her beautiful face, I know as much as I don't like to admit it, I'm wrong. I have been for so long that I don't know how to be right again. It's not Aria. I wanted her that night at Angeloni's party and I've wanted her every day and night since. I made that deal with her asshole ex-boyfriend because I couldn't stand to let him have her any longer.

None of that changes the fact that as much as I can want her, I can't have her the way she wants.

I close my eyes and take a deep breath into my lungs. Letting it out slowly, I lift her off me and set her on her feet. "Get dressed."

When I look up at her again, her expression is pure hurt. Seeing her like this makes my chest ache, but I can't change what's happened.

Quickly, I straighten myself and stand up from the white bench I intentionally positioned here so I could watch her this morning. Why didn't I just stick to that plan? I know what I'm like. I knew if I came up here and actually fucked her that it wouldn't go well.

"Phillip will take you back upstairs," I say as I begin walking toward the door.

Behind me, I hear her begin to cry. I'm sorry. I wish I wasn't the man I am. You have no idea how much I wish I could be something different than what I am.

AFTER AN ELEVATOR RIDE THAT GAVE ME ALL THE time I needed to hate myself, I walk across the lobby and hope I don't have to deal with Sasha right now. I just want to be alone. No Aria and her disappointment that I'm not the kind of man she wants. No Sasha demanding I do something for this goddamned hotel. No anyone insisting I be exactly what they want at just this moment.

Just me alone with my regrets.

The moment I open my office door, I see that won't be happening. Sasha stands behind my desk watching my laptop, as I guessed she would.

"Well, that went swimmingly, don't you think?" she says with a devilish smile.

"Unless you have something that needs to be attended to in the next thirty seconds, you can go, Sasha. I have things to do," I say as I make my way to my chair.

All I have to do is keep busy and I won't think about Aria and how sad she looked as I left the gallery.

Like every other time I couldn't forget, all it will take is work to make me feel better.

But Sasha doesn't move as I sit down behind my desk. Still watching my laptop screen and the feed from the camera in the gallery, she sighs, and I can't stop myself from looking. Aria sits on that white tufted bench dressed in that blue dress with the yellow flowers and staring at the Modigliani she doesn't like.

I slam my laptop shut and glare up at Sasha. "Didn't you hear me? Go!"

"Gideon, it's no crime to be who you are. Why don't you just tell her? She'll understand. She's crazy about you, you know. I'm sure if you explained yourself that she'd be thrilled to see it isn't her, because that's what she's thinking right now."

My head begins to pound with every word that comes out of my assistant's mouth. She acts like it's so easy. Just explain yourself. Tell her you can't let go of the past and she'll be fine with it.

"Oh yeah? Tell me, Sasha, how would you feel if a man you wanted told you what's stopping him is something long gone?"

A slow smile lifts the corners of her mouth, and she answers, "I would feel better knowing that it wasn't me. So you can't forget your past? Maybe Aria can make you forget."

"Just go. This isn't helping."

I hang my head and silently wish I wasn't like this.

It's been long enough. I shouldn't feel anything for my past anymore. Aria is right here. Even though I've kept her in my penthouse for weeks, never touching her and barely speaking to her, she still was willing in the gallery. I should take the chance like anyone else would.

"Listen to me, Gideon. She doesn't have a clue that you aren't like every other man she's ever met. She thinks you don't care about her. She thinks you don't find her attractive. The other night I told her she just needed to be patient with you when she asked me why you don't touch her even though she sleeps next to you each night. It's okay to not be able to let go of the past completely. Tell her what's going on. All she wants to know is you want her. You do, don't you?"

I spin around in my chair and face her as my headache grows exponentially worse. "Stop acting like all I have to do is tell her I'm fucked up and everything will be fine. There's a fucking reason I'm alone. Don't you get it? I can't just explain the shit that happens when someone gets close to me and think she'll fall into my arms afterward. Why would she? Aria wants a man to love her. The best I can do is adore her from afar because I'm fucked up."

Sasha's smile fades until she looks as sad as Aria did when I left her a few minutes ago. "Then you should let her go. It's not fair to her that you know what's going on with you and you refuse to tell her about it. I think you're wrong, though. I think she'd be fine if you told her. I mean, Jesus Christ, Gideon.

Look at the guy she was with before you. If she can be fine with that troll, she'd be over the moon to be with a man like you."

"A man like me. I can't tell you how much I wish I was more like that troll than myself," I say quietly, hating how true those words are.

My assistant touches my shoulder in a rare act of kindness for her and quietly says, "It's not a crime to not be able to forget how much you loved someone once. Tell her what's going on with you. She'll understand, Gideon. It's not like you can't give her what she wants. You can make her the happiest woman in the world. She just needs to see that the happiness you offer is slightly different than what other men can give her."

If only it was that easy.

CHAPTER NINE

ideon

By the time I got back to the penthouse last night, Aria was sound asleep on her side of the bed. Then when I woke up this morning, she was out on the terrace staring out at the water. I thought about talking to her, but Sasha has it all wrong. It isn't just a matter of explaining about what I can't seem to forget. I'm fucked up. I always have been. It's not going to be enough to explain that and expect her to be fine with it.

So now I'm back at my office in one of the few places I can relax lately. How messed up is that? A man who can only be comfortable at the one spot in the world he never wanted to be in the first place.

Christ, I really am fucked up.

My phone rings, thankfully interrupting my self-loathing session, and I pick it up to hear my father already talking. "So he'll go later today. Let him know so he can make arrangements."

"Hello?"

"Ah, Gideon. Good. I was just finishing up with Isaac. How are things there on the beautiful Amalfi Coast?" my father asks, his way of easing into whatever he has to tell me.

I lie and try to conceal how miserable I am. "As beautiful as ever."

"You sound strange today. Not your usual businesslike self. Something wrong?"

I don't sound like a machine like usual, so there must be something wrong with me. Nice to know even someone thousands of miles away can pick up on my defectiveness this morning.

"I'm fine. Isn't it the middle of the night on the island? Or have you and Isaac taken the business on the road?" I ask, eager to get the attention off me and onto any other topic.

"Yes, it's still night here, but I have plans to make, so I'm up. Your mother wants me to tell you she's sending you a gift. I'm assuming it's a birthday present. You know her. You're a grown man, but to her, you're always her baby."

"Great. I'll look for it. So why are you calling this morning?"

I can't even attempt to sound happy that he's making some plans because I know they'll be affecting me in some way that's about to throw my daily life into chaos. He knows how much I fucking hate it when he does this.

"Alaric is going to be coming to see you there. He's got some work to handle for me."

Instantly, my meeting with Marcello Angeloni and the threat he's made to our family flashes in my brain. "I wouldn't suggest that, Dad. Not now."

"Why not? I need something done, and Alaric is the man to do it. You sound like your mother. She thinks I should give him some time off so he and Sienna can enjoy being together."

"That's not it. There's something else. The new head of the Angeloni family, Marcello, has made it more than clear to anyone who'll listen that he thinks someone from our family killed his brother. He's vowed to kill every single Rule. I've been trying to get him to see it wasn't any one of us who shot Lucius, but so far, I don't think I've made much headway."

"Fine. I'll come instead. Make sure that suite I like is ready for me."

Why is he not listening? He's a Rule, so Marcello Angeloni wants him dead too.

"I don't think you should. Give it a couple weeks.

That's not a lot of time. Whatever you need Alaric to do can be accomplished later."

Still, he won't listen.

"I'm coming. Expect me tomorrow."

And this day keeps getting better.

"Are you killing people now?" I ask, confused why he needs to come to my hotel at all.

"What? No. Why?" he says in a stunned voice, as if jumping to that conclusion is insane of me.

"Because that's what Alaric does for the family."

My father lets out a hearty chuckle, like I said something amusing. "He does other things too now. It's one of those tasks I'm coming to your little corner of the world for. Not that I can't kill people. I just don't have to right now. So expect me tomorrow, and have some good scotch in the suite. You know how I hate flying, and I'll need some twelve-year-old scotch to make me feel better."

"Got it. Suite and scotch. Anything else?"

He doesn't answer for a long moment before finally saying, "You don't sound happy to hear I'm going to be paying you a visit. Is there something going on that I should know about at the hotel?"

Other than I have a woman living with me I have no interest in talking about, no. Everything in this place runs like clockwork because usually I run like clockwork.

"No. Just had a hard time sleeping last night. It's

made today difficult to get started," I answer, every word a lie.

"Well, get some sleep tonight because I'm going to expect you to at least have dinner with me while I'm there. Maybe I should grab your brother and bring him along. We could have a nice meal, just the three Rule boys."

Nice to know he's taking Marcello's threat seriously.

My father doesn't ask how his idea sounds because he knows I hate the idea even without asking my opinion. I don't get along with my brother. He's the king of chaos, and every time he steps foot into my world, it's like it's turned upside down. The last thing I need now is to deal with Helix and Alex Rule together at the same time.

"Okay, well, I need to go attend to your suite so it's ready for tomorrow. Have a safe flight."

Without missing a beat, my father asks, "You do delegate menial tasks like that there, don't you, Gideon? I mean, if you have to order that assistant of yours to do it, then you should."

His subtle attempt to make me see that I don't need to handle everything here at the hotel doesn't go unnoticed by me. "I know, Dad. I just like to pay special attention to certain guests. You know, the ones who are important?"

I intentionally stroke his ego to get the focus off the fact that I enjoy paying attention to details. I always have. It might be a part of what's wrong with me, but it's not one of the bad parts, at least.

"Okay. I'll see you tomorrow. Maybe your chef will make that dish I liked so much the last time I was there."

"I can make sure he does, Dad. Just say the word."

"Great! I'll see you tomorrow."

And with that, he ends the call and I sit back in my office chair dreading the next twenty-four to forty-eight hours. Even worse will be if he brings my older brother. Christ, I don't need to deal with him right now.

In the middle of my misery my office door opens, and in strolls Sasha with her usual leather planner in her arms. With a smile, she points toward the chair in front of my desk and sits down.

"I'm guessing by the look on your face that something bad has happened?"

"My father is coming tomorrow. He's got some errand he needs to run. He might bring my brother."

As if a dark cloud covers her face, Sasha's expression drops. "God, why? Doesn't he have enough to do where he is?"

"Which one? My father or Alex?" I ask, genuinely curious since the question could apply to either of them.

That makes her wince, and I sense she thinks she's

offended me. She hasn't. My father can be as difficult to deal with as my brother, depending on the situation.

"Your brother, of course. Helix Rule isn't bad. He's a little destructive. I mean, if he's coming to the hotel here, then he must be coming for work. Unless your mother is coming with him. Is she?" she asks, her eyes filling with hope by the time she's finished.

Sasha, like most people, likes my mother. She softens my father's jagged edges, and if she's with him, then he's not here for work.

"Not that I know of. Just Helix and possibly Alex."

"Oh."

We sit in silence for a few moments before Sasha asks, "Does your father know about Aria?"

I shake my head as the thought of telling him that fills me with dread. "No. And I don't want him to, especially if my brother comes with him. She'll need to stay in the penthouse the entire time."

"As if that will be any different than the rest of the past three weeks?"

I sense Sasha wants to talk about what happened yesterday, but the last thing I want to do is have that discussion. Unfortunately, before I can dismiss her, Sasha gets her question out.

"Did you talk to her when you went upstairs last night? What happened?"

The hopefulness returns to her eyes, but I have to

disappoint her. Avoiding her gaze, I look at my computer and answer, "No."

"So you're going to let her go?"

Rage fills me at the thought of losing Aria, and I shake my head in disgust that she could even suggest that. "No. Why do you think it has to be one or the other?"

"Because that's the least you can do for her, Gideon. You don't have an incurable disease or anything that will harm her. You simply can't let go of the past. Not yet, at least. She deserves to know that if you want to keep her."

A single thought fills my head and escapes from my mouth before I can stop it. "And if she can't live with that?"

"That's for her to decide, isn't it?"

Sasha's answer doesn't make me feel better. "Since when did you begin to side with a woman in my life over me?"

She stands from her chair and smiles down at me. "You know I'd die for you, Gideon. I'm as loyal to you as anyone can be to another person, but if you don't tell her the truth about you, then you're just being cruel."

"I thought you liked it when I was cruel. You once told me that's what makes me such a good businessman, that I'm ruthless. What's changed?"

Sasha shrugs and shakes her head. "Aria isn't business. She's a woman you want who wants you.

The only thing stopping the two of you from being together is that you're still haunted by something that happened, even though it wasn't your fault. I think she'll be happy to find out you do care and the way you show it doesn't mean you don't, but it should be her decision to stay, and it should be a fully informed decision."

If only everything with Aria was as simple as business. Then I wouldn't be so miserable.

"Not that I don't love having this same conversation as yesterday, but has the P.I. arrived yet? He said he'd be here mid-morning."

"Cesare Bellucci is coming?" Sasha asks with surprise. "Maybe you should tell your assistant that, Gideon. It might be nice for her to know your schedule."

I smile at her sarcasm since I know it means she's miffed at me. "I'm sorry. I thought you assumed he'd be coming since I mentioned calling him while we were at the party. I need him to do some investigating for me regarding that Marcello situation."

"See how easy that was to be nice to someone? You even apologized for making my job harder. I guess I better get out there and intercept him when he arrives since last time he nearly accosted one of the desk clerks. That man is a pig. You know that, right?" she asks, twisting her face into a look of pure disgust.

"I don't care what he is if he finds out what I need

to know. Just make sure the desk clerks don't get too close to him."

As she turns to walk out of my office, she says, "I notice you aren't worried about my having to deal with him."

"You'll eat him for a snack if he gets out of line with you. Even he knows that. So I don't have to worry."

Sasha throws me a dirty look over her shoulder. "You're lucky I can handle myself, Gideon Rule. Maybe you need to remember that not all women are like me."

She slams the door behind her, and I can't figure out if she's angry about the P.I. having to come here or how things are with Aria. I don't know when it happened, but my usually ice cold and emotionless assistant has somehow become the champion of the woman I'm keeping in my penthouse.

Cesare interrupts my thoughts about the situation between Aria and Sasha when he walks into my office without knocking as usual. A hulking creature close to my six foot four inches, he has the largest neck I've ever seen on a human being and eyes so dark they're practically black. He's nothing less than formidable, and the first time I saw him I couldn't believe he could be a private investigator. Even now as I watch him walk toward the chair in front of my desk, I can't imagine how he skulks around unnoticed. It's like seeing a mountain move in front of you.

I stand to shake his huge hand before the two of us sit down to discuss why I needed to see him so soon today. "How are you, Cesare?"

"How I am is fucking tired. Do you know I was out until three this morning on a job? I swear to God I don't know why I still work the goddamned cheating spouses shit. Well, except for the fact that the pay is fucking sweet with these high rollers on the coast. The man you see in front of you today got next to no sleep because some bitch decided she likes the boy who trims her hedges more than she likes her husband's bank account. Stupid bastard. You should see her too. A fucking knockout. How he got her I have no idea, but even more, how the hell did he think he'd keep her with his wrinkly sixty-year-old balls when he hired that boy with muscles on his goddamned muscles to be his gardener? Love is not worth it, Gideon. Mark my words. Not worth it."

My private investigator never fails to make me smile when he tells me stories about his other jobs. He does far too many spying on cheating wives cases, in my opinion. Not that anyone asked, but he should stick to the kind of jobs I give him. I pay him enough.

"I'll keep that in mind. Love is not the subject of today's meeting, though, so I think you'll be happy about that."

His jet-black eyes light up. "The nastier the better when it comes to your jobs. You know what my favorite one was? That time you had me check out that guy who you thought might be stealing from you. I got to exercise my own muscles on that one. Any chance this new job is like that?"

I shake my head and smile at how vicious he got with that guy. Turns out, he wasn't stealing from me, but if he had been, going up against Cesare on that dimly lit road that night would have made him think twice.

"Not this job, but you never know what the future will bring. As for this one, I want to know everything there is to know about Marcello Angeloni and his men. Everything. Understand? I want to know where they go and what they do when they get there. If they're fucking someone, I want to know what color her hair naturally is and if the carpet matches the drapes. If they're stealing from someone, I want to know who and if they know. Got it?"

A smile pushes up his giant cheeks into the fat folds around his eyes. "Got it. Everything from A to Z. How soon do you need this information? Marcello Angeloni might not have a huge crew yet, but the family has tentacles in nearly everything on the Amalfi Coast."

I lean back in my chair and sigh. "As soon as possible. Whoever you work with that you trust, get them on this with you. Money is no object. Whatever it takes, I'll pay. But don't bring anyone on who can't keep their mouth shut because if they talk and it fucks me, I'm going to make sure they don't see the sun again."

Cesare nods his understanding. "Got it. Fast and complete. The word on the street is Marcello has a hard on to prove he's not someone to be taken lightly."

With a chuckle, I diagnose the problem immediately. "Youngest son syndrome. He thinks he has to whip out his dick all the time to show he's got what it takes. The fuck actually made it known that he intends on killing every Rule he can find. Who the fuck does he think he's dealing with? He's lucky my father hasn't come over to cut his dick off and shove it down his throat."

"Ah, that's why you want everything on him. How's Helix feeling about a threat to the family?"

"He hasn't said much about it, but you know him. One minute he's all calm, and then the next minute he's cutting off someone's fucking hands and feeding them to their dog."

That visual makes Cesare laugh, and the sound is booming, like some kind of deranged Santa. "Good old Helix Rule. You have to appreciate a man who once used a woodchipper to get rid of someone. I'll never forget that night when you introduced me to him, and he ended up telling me that after a few drinks. Motherfucker knows how to make a point. I'll give him that."

I don't say anything to Cesare, but I know the reason my father told him that story was because he wanted to make sure my P.I. got the point that fucking with me meant fucking with a man who would stuff a fat fuck into a chipper and let the machine chew up every last inch of him. My father can be difficult, but he looks out for his family.

"Get back to me the moment you know something. I need dirt on Marcello. Dirt I can use. The nastier the better."

"So no cheating wife bullshit? We're talking hardcore here?" the private investigator asks with a wicked grin.

"Yeah. Hardcore and fast. As always, you get me what I want and I'll take care of you, Cesare."

That's all he needs. He stands from the chair with a groan and extends his enormous hand to shake mine before he leaves.

"I'll let you know as soon as I find anything."

"Good. I'll be waiting."

As he makes his way to the door, he turns back toward me and smiles. "You know, you have the most beautiful desk clerks of any hotel on the coast. Did you know that?"

"Yes, and make sure you keep your hands off them."

My warning makes him throw his head back as he lets out a big belly laugh. "Bad Cesare. I'll make sure to be a good boy whenever I come to see you. Promise."

He closes my office door, and I can't help but feel

exhausted after dealing with him. Talking to most people takes it out of me, but Cesare Bellucci makes me need a fucking nap after our conversations.

I could go upstairs and do just that. Then again, that would mean I'd need to see Aria. That can't happen. Not yet, anyway.

CHAPTER TEN

ria

TEN HOURS. FOR TEN LONG HOURS, I'VE WAITED for him to return to this penthouse. After eight, I began wondering if he ever intended on coming home again.

He's avoiding me. I don't understand what happened yesterday, and when he got back here last night, he wouldn't speak a word to me.

This silent treatment nonsense is ending today. When he walks through that door, I'm going to get him to talk to me or the two of us are going to spend a very bad night together.

It's his choice.

The sound of the front door opening alerts me he's

back, and I hear him having a pleasant conversation with Raphael. Good to know he can do that with someone. Just not me.

But that's going to change right now.

Our eyes meet as the door closes behind him, and I swear I see something in his expression that makes me think he's dreaded this moment for hours. What is so terrible about having to talk to me?

"Gideon, we need to speak about what happened. Actually, we need to speak about whatever we're doing here, but we can start with what happened in the gallery."

He sighs, and I think I see a hint of a nod, so my spirits soar. We're actually going to have a discussion!

But then he quickly turns to make his way toward the bedroom, dashing my hopes. That's not going to dissuade me this time, though. I'm not so easily put off tonight. He has no idea how many times I've practiced what I want to say today as I sat here alone as usual in his penthouse.

I follow him, fully intending on starting this conversation whether he likes it or not. He's undressing out of his work clothes, so I wait until he's only wearing his shirt and pants to begin.

"Gideon, you can't keep ignoring me. I've let it go on long enough, but I'm done. If you don't talk to me, then I'll talk to you and I'll keep doing it until you finally can't take it anymore and you have to say something."

My early attempt at an ultimatum seems to fall on deaf ears as he doesn't even look at me when I finish to acknowledge what I just said. This man must be a master at hearing only what he wants to hear. No doubt Sasha is partly to blame for this too. She's probably been filling his head with ideas about how he doesn't have to speak to me because I don't deserve it.

I'm only the woman he keeps prisoner in this penthouse. Why would I deserve the decency of a conversation?

After giving him a few moments to respond, I launch into what I've practiced all day.

"Fine. I'll go first. I don't know what happened yesterday, but for the record, I'd like to say I was having a very nice time. Now maybe you're used to controlling things during sex. I can appreciate that. It's not like I'd know that going into yesterday's time together. I mean, we were together that first time, but who knows? But assuming this is a control thing, I just want to say that if that's the way you are, all you need to do is let me know. I don't need to be the one holding the reins. I'm fine with going along for the ride."

The words tumble out of my mouth as if they've been waiting for hours to hit the air, which I guess they have. Thankful to at least have said that much without him bolting, I smile at him and patiently wait for something to come back at me.

Anything.

Just one word.

Maybe a smile or a nod of his head to let me know he's alive in there and not just a mannequin someone dressed in an expensive Italian suit.

But he gives me nothing.

How is it possible this man can hear all of what I said and not respond?

Well, he's going to. I'm just getting started.

I watch as Gideon methodically unbuttons his blue dress shirt, each button slowly undone before he moves his hands down to the next one. It's almost hypnotizing to see, but since my brain is moving at a million miles an hour, I have a hard time focusing on that for longer than a few seconds.

He usually undresses in the bathroom, so I can't help but wonder why he's doing it right here in the bedroom. Then a thought dawns on me. He's planning for us to have sex now. This man actually thinks he can cut me off in the middle of the act in the gallery yesterday and then just expect me to be at his beck and call, wet and willing for him now that he's finally decided it's time for us to be together again.

Hell. No.

When he shrugs out of his shirt, my brain takes a tiny siesta from all my planned speech to admire his body. He really is beautiful. Toned and muscular, his torso shows evidence of him spending some time in the gym. When he does that I have no idea, but let's be honest. How much do I really know about what he does with his day since I'm stuck up here on the top floor the whole time?

My gaze travels down from his face to his strong shoulders and arms, over his toned pecs, and finally coming to rest on his washboard abs. Yes, he's definitely someone who spends some time working out.

I want to say something to continue the conversation I started a few minutes ago, but the sight of him makes doing anything but watching him difficult. I hate that, to be honest. Not that I think it would be better if he was some potbellied ogre with a body that repulsed me, but I have the feeling that he's using his to manipulate me at this moment.

"So you have nothing to say to all I just said?"

Gideon lifts his head as his hands drift down to unbutton his pants and lower his zipper. With a hint of a smile, he finally answers me. "No. I just want to take a shower, relax, and have a nice dinner. I'm assuming you're hungry? Feel free to order whatever you want and get me the salmon. I'm in the mood for fish tonight. I think I saw some kind of fruity dessert when I walked through the kitchen earlier today. Order me that too."

And just to punctuate his statement, which I swear sounds like utter madness right now after all I just said to him, he slides his pants off his right leg and then off his left one before setting his clothes on the chair near the bed. For any normal couple, this might pass for a proper conversation.

For us, it's like we're living two different realities, and his revolves around food, oddly enough.

"Gideon, didn't you hear a word I said?" I ask in stunned irritation.

He takes a deep breath in, expanding his broad chest, and nods. "I did."

"And all you have to say is you want the salmon and some fruit dessert the chef made today? Do you plan on just walking by me and getting into the shower without saying a word about all I said to you?"

With each moment that passes, my voice gets higher and higher until by the time I finally reach the end of my question and the word you comes out as barely a squeak. I swear to God this man is trying to drive me crazy!

He doesn't answer either of my questions and begins walking toward the bathroom in his black boxer briefs that always make his legs look good. But I don't want to think about how great his legs are now! I want a damn answer or at least some recognition of what I said. Either I was completely off base, and he needs to explain how it wasn't a control problem yesterday, or I was right, and we can agree that if he wants to be the one in control, then that's fine.

But this not saying anything is not working for me. In fact, it's making me want to lash out, and I swear to

God if he walks into that bathroom and closes the door without answering me, I'm going to lose it.

I watch in stunned disbelief as he does exactly that, and I swear he's wearing a smile as he does it. That's it! Gideon has finally pushed me too far.

My heart slams into my chest as I turn to follow him, each step sealing a fate he created. All he needed to do was talk to me. Now he won't have a choice but to listen because he'll be a captive audience.

Captive and naked.

My hand touches the doorknob and twists, giving me a sense of relief that it isn't locked. Foolish mistake, Mr. Rule. Not that I wouldn't have said my piece, but this will make it much easier since I don't have to yell through a damn door.

He's already in the shower, and when I look through the glass door, I see his entire body there on display. God, Gideon really is stunning.

No! Do not think like that. This man has kept you prisoner here in this gilded cage for nearly a month, and then when he finally decides to show you some affection, he cuts it off in the middle of what was shaping up to be some great sex. Whatever he looks like naked as the water rolls down over the peaks and valleys of his muscular abs before trailing over his long, thick cock has nothing to do with why you're in this bathroom right now, Aria. Keep focused.

I take a deep breath of warm air into my lungs and hold it there before letting it out slowly. All I have to do is keep calm. He's a master at that, but I'm not, so I have to truly keep my head in this if I want to get my point across.

"As I was saying, if it's a control thing, all you need to do is tell me. I'm fine with that, Gideon."

His face comes close to the glass shower door as he looks out in shock at me standing there. "Aria? What are you doing?"

"I'm having that conversation I told you I wanted to have. I assume you thought it had ended simply because you didn't want to talk, but oh no. I have some things to say, and you're going to listen to me. If it means I have to stand in this hot bathroom as steam fills every inch of space around me and I can't even see you as I say what I came to say, then so be it."

"You're crazy. You know that?"

His attempt at insulting me misses its mark completely. With a chuckle that I admit sounds a bit more manic than I'd like, I say, "Well, you'd be crazy too if someone kept you cooped up inside for weeks, only to let you out to have fun and cut it short, which by the way, was very frustrating. I liked the way you were when you came to the gallery, Gideon. You were sexy and fun. Why did that guy disappear?"

I think I hear him sigh heavily over the sound of the shower before he answers, "He didn't. He just didn't feel right being there at that moment."

"Why? I want to know, so please tell me."

He falls silent, and as I listen to the sound of the

water, I can't help but notice he's actually doing a lot of talking for him. Now I just have to keep it going.

"I know you want me, Gideon. You were so hard your cock could have cut glass. So don't try to tell me you didn't. At least deal in facts so we can get past this."

"Go out into the bedroom. I don't want to have this conversation right now."

And there he goes trying to ignore the problem again.

"Well, I do, so I'm not going anywhere. In fact, if you don't keep talking, I'm going to come into that shower so you can't avoid me. Your choice. You talk to me, or we take a nice shower together like normal people."

Gideon presses his nose to the glass shower door in front of me. "You think this is normal? What about any part of us is normal?"

"Fine. We aren't normal. No, it's not normal to take a woman and keep her in your house for weeks on end. No, it's not normal to finally initiate sex only to stop in the middle when there was no good reason to stop. And no, it's not normal to have conversations like this, but you left me no choice."

"You always have a choice, Aria."

He's right. We do always have a choice, and after looking at the outline of his naked body through the glass for the past few minutes, I've decided to make mine.

I quickly strip off my shirt and yoga pants, tossing them onto the white tile floor before opening the shower door. Gideon turns to look at me in utter surprise, but I don't know why he's so shocked. I did say I would do this.

"So much for obeying the rules you yourself set down," he says as he slides his hands through his dark hair to get it off his face.

"I changed my mind. Anyway, you weren't really talking, so I'm not technically breaking any rules," I say with a smile as the hot mist from the shower begins to hit me.

Still stunned, he shakes his head. "Do you routinely get into the shower with men who don't ask you to?"

Always so serious this one. You'd swear he never had someone invite themselves into the shower with him. Or maybe he hasn't. He does seem to enjoy having control.

I take a single step toward him and stop, enjoying the view from where I'm standing but wishing we weren't still talking. "No, but to be honest, most men I've met wouldn't have any problem with me getting into the shower with them. Do you?"

As much as I don't want to think it, I know that leading question might result in him telling me he does have some issue with me just jumping in the shower with him. I'm not actually sure what I'll say to that if that's his reply.

At least he'll still be talking, though. A girl has to count her wins wherever she can find them.

Instead, he asks me another question of his own. "Are you always this insistent?"

There's a trace of a smile on his lips as he says that, so I'm hoping this is some kind of sexual banter of his and not the prelude to him telling me to get the hell out of his shower and stop bothering him. Not that I will. I'm past the point of no return now. This shower isn't going to end until we both come.

"Only when I really want something."

I take another step toward him and stop, only a few feet away from him now. He's stopped washing up and simply stares at me like he doesn't understand what I'm doing. Maybe I'm going too slowly for him. I would be for most men, but this particular man is unlike anyone else I've ever met in my life. Any other man would already have me in his arms with his cock deep inside me.

Water pours down over his face, so he scrubs his eyes with his hands before stepping toward me. "What if I don't want you?"

I glance down between us and see his cock standing straight up at attention against his belly. Looking back up at him, I can't help but grin at how silly his question sounds.

"You should tell your body because it seems to have gotten a completely different memo."

"You don't want me, Aria. Trust me on that," he says, his words tinged with sadness.

That's my cue to take another step forward, and when I do, my breasts softly touch his body, exciting me. He doesn't move when I reach out to slide my arms around his neck, so I tilt my head back and smile at him.

"I do want you, Gideon. I wanted you that night at that party. I wanted you later that night when you weren't around and I had to listen to Franco berate me for talking to you. I wanted you the day he said I was to go with you, and I've wanted you every day since. I haven't been the one fighting this."

He looks into my eyes and winces like what I just said caused him pain. "No, I've been the one who was fighting it."

"Please stop. I'm here. I want you, and you want me. Stop making whatever it is we can be impossible. Whatever the problem was the other day, I don't care. All I care about is us in this shower and what we could be doing if we weren't talking."

That makes him smile, and he really is more incredible than any man I've ever seen in my life at this moment. "Weren't you the one who said you wanted to talk?"

He's cute and sexy, and it's too much for me to bear, so I press a kiss to his lips as water streams down between us. His lips are soft and willing, and it takes no time at all before our tongues are mingling together, each of us exploring the other's mouth.

Gideon stuffs his hand into my hair and tugs my head back so I'm forced to stare up at him and that beautiful mouth I want more of. "I tried to keep you at arm's length. It was for your own good, Aria."

"What if I don't want you to look out for my own good? What if I want you, no matter what?"

"I'm not what you should want."

His words sound so full of sadness I don't understand, but I'm here with him in the shower and he's as hard as a rock pressing against my pussy, so I don't care. He is what I want. I can't change that, and I don't want to.

I kiss him hard, wanting to feel everything he has press against my lips. He doesn't hold back this time, and the sensation of his tongue teasing mine while his hands slide down my back to cup my ass thrills me.

A second later, he lifts me in the air and fills me with one slow thrust. I close my eyes as his groans fills the shower around us. He's as raw and needy as I am, and the two of us quickly fall into a rhythm with his cock thrusting deep inside me and my hips tilting to take every delicious inch of him.

My hands cling to his neck with his soaking wet hair tickling my skin. Even drenched, it's soft, and I can't stop myself from running my fingers through it. His mouth plunders mine like the very essence of all he needs can be found in my kiss, and I revel in how sensual this man is.

When he pulls away to kiss my neck, I moan his name. "Gideon, don't stop...please, don't stop."

His teeth gently sink into my shoulder as he begins to thrust faster into my body, sending my need to come into overdrive. It's been too long since I got to enjoy that feeling of release, and after being so close to him for all these weeks without a single kiss until the other day, I'm desperate to finally orgasm.

His cock jackhammers into me, sending waves of need coursing through me. I tilt my head up to feel the water from the showerhead hit my face. The warmth contrasts with the feel of the marble tile pressing against my back when he pushes me to the wall. His hands let go of my ass so all that's keeping me on him are my hands clutching his neck and my legs wrapped around his waist.

Gideon leans forward, positioning his hands against the wall on either side of my head, before dipping his mouth to mine in another mind-blowing kiss. I open my eyes to see him staring at me like a ravenous animal set to devour me. He's more intense than I've ever seen him in all the time we've been around one another, but I'm not afraid.

"Give me what I need. Please," I beg, unashamed of wanting to come.

"Tell me what you need, Aria. I want to hear you say it."

His husky voice sounds like he's on the edge of losing it just like I am. The thought of finally seeing him let go excites me more than I thought possible.

"I want to come. Please, let me come, Gideon."

He slides his hand around my throat and squeezes ever so gently, sending waves of desire washing over me. I don't know if his thing is control, and I don't care right now. Whatever it takes for him to get off he can do. I just want to orgasm.

In my ear, he says in a low shaky voice, "Come for me, baby. Come all over my cock and let me feel that cunt milk me dry."

His words thrill me, and a few seconds later, I feel my release tear through my body like a freight train. It's almost violent, and my hips thrust hard against him to take every inch of his cock into me. My fingernails tear at the back of his neck, making him growl not in pain but pleasure.

As I come, I feel his body still and then he fills me with all he has, warming my insides. His cock twitches inside me, sending ropes of cum deep inside. It's erotic and sensual and everything I've needed all these weeks.

I sag against his shoulders as my release slowly ebbs away, leaving only my thighs quivering from the aftershocks. My lips brush against his neck, and I taste a faint hint of saltiness on his skin.

"That was incredible," I whisper and then let out a heavy sigh of pure contentment.

Gideon is silent for so long that I finally lift my head to see what he looks like, and for the first time since he brought me to his home, he looks pleased. It's not a laughing or joking around kind of joy but a quiet happiness that makes him even more appealing. His dark eyes seem softer when I look into them now.

Finally, he responds to me with a tender kiss that makes my heart soar. Maybe we aren't so bad together, after all.

FOR THE FIRST TIME SINCE I BEGAN STAYING HERE with him, Gideon and I have something that resembles a normal dinner. Not that he does a lot of talking, but he seems different now after our time in the shower.

He takes a drink of his scotch and sets the glass down in front of him with a sigh. He doesn't look unhappy, but that sigh tells me there's something on his mind.

"Did you enjoy your salmon?" I ask, suddenly needing to fill the silence with talking.

Gideon surprises me by nodding and giving me a smile. I wait for him to say something, but he stops himself. Always so in control.

"What? You were going to say something. What was it?"

He looks around at the terrace and sighs again. "Why didn't you try to get away? Three weeks and you never tried even once. Why?"

I can't stop the chuckle that escapes from my throat. "Get away? How? Raphael isn't exactly a man you can get away from. He would have grabbed me before I even got to the elevator. I guess I could have tried to make my way down the side of the building over there, but I'm not exactly the type of woman who's up for that."

As I explain why I didn't try to leave for the past month, Gideon nods like what I'm saying makes perfect sense. When I finish, he seems to want to say something, but once again, he remains quiet.

"Do you want to ask me something else?"

I wish I wasn't so curious about this man. Things would be so much easier for me if I wasn't. I wouldn't want so much to hear what's on his mind, and I wouldn't be so frustrated all the time.

He doesn't answer me for a long moment, but finally, he says, "For three weeks, you've slept next to me in my bed. Why didn't you ever try to do something to me in all that time? There are at least a dozen things in my bedroom you could have bashed my head in with and been free once I was dead."

That he actually wonders why I didn't try to harm him makes me wonder what kind of women he's been with in his life. I may not enjoy having to stay in this penthouse every day, but it never occurred to me to physically attack him.

"Gideon, I didn't want to hurt you. I admit this isn't a traditional situation here between us, and I would like to be free to leave this penthouse when I want to, but it never crossed my mind to use any of those things in your bedroom to kill you. Is that why you've been so reluctant to be with me? You thought I wanted to murder you in your sleep?"

He smiles like my explanation makes him happy. "No, that's not the reason."

I get the surest sense he doesn't intend on telling me why he's kept me at arm's length all this time, but strangely enough, I don't mind tonight. "Did you enjoy the dessert?" I ask, happy to change the topic.

Gideon nods again and stands from the table. "I have something else in mind I think we'll both enjoy. Let's go inside," he says in a low voice, holding out his hand for me.

I like this Gideon. He reminds me of that man who joined me in the art gallery.

"Something else? A second dessert?" I ask with a smile as I take his hand.

He leads me into the penthouse before bringing my hand up to his lips to kiss my fingertips. With a sparkle in his dark eyes, he answers, "Something like that."

Oh, I definitely like this Gideon.

CHAPTER ELEVEN

ideon

As I sit at my desk trying to get some work done, my mind continually drifts back to last night with Aria. Jesus, that woman is relentless. Not that I'm unhappy about the shower sex and then a second round of sex after we had dinner that left me exhausted in the best way. I just can't see how I'm going to keep her at arm's length if we're constantly fucking.

Most men would kill to have this problem, so I don't pretend to think I'm being tortured or anything. I just can't forget the past, which makes any present or future with Aria difficult, if not impossible.

"You look like a new man today," Sasha says in a lilting voice that borders on sing song, very odd for her. She's never this happy.

I look up from the papers I wasn't really reading and reply, "And you sound like a children's song. What's made you so chipper today?"

She gives me what I judge to be a genuine smile and answers, "I like seeing you happy. Don't ruin this. I like feeling as if you aren't the most miserable man on the entire coast. It reflects positively on me."

After plopping down in front of my desk, she asks about what I know she's been dying to hear. "So have things gotten better with your beautiful prisoner? I'm assuming yes since you look like the weight of the world has been lifted off your shoulders."

Sitting back against my leather office chair, I scan her expression and decide she really is interested in hearing about this topic. Too bad I'm not interested in saying anything about it.

"Do most bosses tell their assistants about their sex lives? I think the answer is no."

Sasha twists her face into a grimace and leans forward to tap the edge of my desk. "First of all, we aren't most bosses and assistants. Second of all, we've slept together, so I think that blows the usual protocol between bosses and their assistants out of the water. But most of all, you and I are closer than most family members, so why shouldn't I ask about something I know has been bothering you?"

She does make good points. We really don't have your usual boss and employee dynamic, especially after sleeping together. Even more, I'm closer to Sasha than I am with any of my family, except maybe Alaric.

Still, I don't want to tell her about my time with Aria last night. Something about that feels like it could take the magic away.

However, I know my assistant and she won't stop asking, so I have to give her something to pacify her. Maybe a few details will make her happy.

"Let's just say I think we may have reached a new understanding."

Her face lights up as her eyes grow wide. "Ooooh, tell me."

"No."

All the happiness in her expression drains away as she juts out her lower lip in a pout. "Why not? I'm living vicariously through you, Gideon, since you won't let me have any fun with her."

"About that. You need to stop talking about wanting to sleep with Aria. I think she's already jealous of you, and that doesn't help matters."

Sasha rolls her eyes as she sits back in her chair. "I don't say that to her. Only you. By the way, you should let me get to know her better. I like her. She's beautiful, and she's just my type."

So much for her stopping.

"No. And stop asking. I told you at the party the other night. It irritates me."

"I thought it only irritated you because you weren't with her. Now that you are, what's the problem? You and I have been with other women you were sleeping with. Is Aria different?"

Yes, she's different, but I don't want to get into that discussion with Sasha. It will only encourage her to chase after Aria more.

"Let's just say I don't want to share her and leave it at that. Why are you in my office this early in the morning? Do we have something big going on today?"

She levels her gaze on me and slowly smiles. "You know what today is. The visit from Daddy and possibly from big brother."

And with those words, my day is officially ruined.

"Right. I had forgotten somehow."

"I'm guessing whatever you and your beautiful prisoner did together last night caused that."

Hating the way she keeps using that term, I say, "Can you please stop calling her that?"

With a shrug, she seems to agree. "Fine. What would you have me refer to her as since I'm sure Helix and Alex are going to be curious?"

"You are to say nothing about Aria. Understand me? She'll be up in the penthouse away from everyone, so there will be no need to mention her."

Again, Sasha twists her face into a look of disgust. "A night of mind-blowing sex and you make her stay in again? That doesn't seem right."

As she stands to leave, I can't help asking, "What

makes you think that's what happened between us last night?"

Smiling, my assistant answers, "Well, you look downright happy today, happier than I think I've seen you in ages. Also, I've slept with you, Gideon. Trust me. When you're on, it's mind-blowing. Come to think of it, even when you're not, it's pretty great."

"I think you have a one-track mind, you know that?" I say with a chuckle.

She turns to leave but calls back to me, "I just call things as I see them. Gideon had great sex last night. I'm going to tell the rest of the staff so don't be surprised when they all gawk at you as you walk past them in the lobby today. I'll let you know when your family arrives."

I'm not sure who's happiest that Aria and I finally slept together, me, Aria, or Sasha. I wish I could keep this day feeling just as it does now. No problems. Just great memories of my time with her last night.

But my father will put an end to my good feelings, and if my brother comes too, I predict nothing but misery for me. Maybe they'll only stay for a few hours.

RIGHT BEFORE LUNCH, I HEAR SOMETHING OUTSIDE my office door, and a second later, Sasha comes rushing in followed by my father and Alex. She looks flustered, which can't be good.

"Gideon, sorry I couldn't get here sooner. I was

busy with Lila helping one of the guests. Your father and brother have arrived," she says, practically stumbling over her words.

As I stand from behind my desk and button my suit coat, I smile. "I see. Thank you, Sasha."

My father makes a beeline to where I am and wraps his arms around me in a big hug. "Good to see you, Gideon. The hotel looks stunning, as always. I like what you're doing with the hanging baskets of flowers out on the terrace. Nice touch."

Helix Rule never fails to say something nice to me right before he asks for something next to impossible. It's his version of the compliment sandwich, except he doesn't bother with the second compliment once he announces what he wants that invariably means my day has gone to hell.

"Hi, Dad. It's good to see you too."

I scan his face and can't fathom how he still looks so goddamned young. It must be the island because my mother doesn't look anywhere close to her age either.

Turning to look at my brother as he touches a piece of that black Etruscan pottery Aria so likes that I recently relocated to the cabinet in my office, I force a smile and say flatly, "Alex. Nice to see you."

He grins like I've said something funny before abandoning the art he didn't care about anyway. "Nice to see you too, little brother. Nice gig you have here. I'd love it if we could switch. You go manage the club while I hang out here in paradise with that gorgeous assistant. Where did you find her? Because I want one just like her."

Suddenly feeling protective of Sasha, I say, "She's one of a kind. You'll have to find your own assistant."

The mere thought of changing positions with Alex and leaving this hotel for his club makes my stomach twist into a tight knot. I have no interest in living my life in darkness like he does. I actually like seeing the sun more than once or twice a year.

"I'm surprised you came. Don't you usually sleep at this time?" I ask dismissively.

My brother isn't offended by my remark, though, and as he sits down in one of the chairs in front of my desk, he says, "Usually, but when Dad said he was coming to see you and asked me if I wanted to join in, I couldn't say no."

"He jumped at the chance," my father says, clarifying my brother's remark, as if it needed it.

With a grin I suspect means nothing good, my brother says, "Yeah, of course I did. I love to see how the other half lives. Now that I think of it, I don't think we could trade jobs. You couldn't handle the gritty life I have to lead."

This might be a record for Alex. He's been here for almost two minutes before he insulted me. Give that man a gold star.

"I'm sure." Turning my attention from him, I look

at my father as he sits down next to Alex. "So why are you here, Dad?"

"Well, I initially was coming to clean up a business deal that had gone sideways, but since you told me about the threat from the Angelonis, I thought I should look into that issue."

Great. Another county heard from. I don't need my father butting into this delicate matter. Nobody needs to get killed over this. Not yet, anyway.

"I'm handling this, Dad. You don't have to worry. If it becomes a bigger problem that I don't think I can solve, I'll let you know. Until then, trust me. I got this."

My father listens, nodding his head, and I can see in his expression he's willing to let me deal with the Marcello Angeloni issue. He may be a man who doesn't shy away from violence, but Helix Rule knows how to delegate.

And then my brother has to give his two cents.

"Fuck that. We need to start busting some heads and right now," Alex says in his usual over the top way. "Let them see what the name Rule means, motherfuckers."

That's all it takes for my father to go from zero to one hundred. Turning to look at my older brother, my father smiles and points at him like he just said the magic words.

"You're right, Alex. These motherfuckers don't know who they're dealing with. The name Rule means something around the world, and that asshole Angeloni needs to be reminded of that."

While the two of them look like they're about to start frothing at the mouth, I calmly try to interject some sanity into a meeting that's quickly going off the rails. "Can I remind you two of something equally as important? I have to live here. That means just killing anyone who dares to utter a threat against me or anyone in our family isn't a good idea. It's particularly bad if you want to keep getting intel on the families here and what they're up to. Who's going to do that if you get me killed?"

Alex throws his head back and laughs. "Me, of course. I'd run this hotel too. How hard could it be? I'll tell you one thing. Nobody would be cocking off about our family if I was here. That's for sure."

As much as I want to tell my brother to fuck off about his ludicrous ideas concerning replacing me, I try to keep my cool and focus on my father. "Let me handle this, Dad. Marcello Angeloni hasn't tried anything yet. I think he's angry about his brother's death and wants to put the blame on someone, but he's not actively sending anyone to do the job. I think he's just trying assert his power on this coast. As the youngest Angeloni, he probably feels like he has to in order to gain respect."

"Youngest sons are always the worst. Talk about insecure," Alex mumbles and then elbows our father.

Fuck, this meeting isn't ten minutes old and my

brother has already pissed me off enough to make me want to beat the hell out of him. Why does my father bring him along? His solution to everything is to pull out his gun and shoot everyone. The son of a bitch doesn't possess an ounce of finesse in his entire body.

My father seems unsure who to listen to, which is never a good position for me to be in. That means he's leaning toward doing what Alex wants since he never fails to side with him over me.

"Gideon, I trust you. You know that. I know you're skilled in handling things here on the Amalfi Coast."

I quickly agree with him, hoping to keep that thought going. "I am. Things aren't like they are in other parts of the world. We're relatively new here, so that means learning the lay of the land and building trust. I've done just that, and people up and down this coast see me as someone who should be respected. They respect our family because of that. Lashing out at Marcello Angeloni because he's blowing off steam could cause an erosion of that respect, and that's the last thing we want. You put me here to be the eyes and ears of the Rule family on the Amalfi Coast. I've been that to a T. Let me navigate through this Angeloni issue in my way. It's always worked before. There's no reason to think it won't now."

I see in my father's eyes a look that says he agrees with me, but once more, Alex chimes in and inserts doubt into his mind. "That's all well and good, but you don't let a threat go by unchallenged. This Marcello asshole needs to be set straight. Show him a little muscle and he'll find someone else's family to try to intimidate. We need to strike and now!"

Fuck me. My brother may very well be trying to get me killed. Maybe that's his plan. Make things unbearable here for me until someone offs me, and then he can step into my place and live the life he's always wanted to here. Not that he has a single clue as to what it takes to run this hotel. In his mind, all I do is get dressed in a suit and sit behind this desk every day.

What an asshole. How we can be related is beyond me.

Just as my father opens his mouth to say something, probably in support of Alex's insane suggestion, Sasha knocks on my office door and walks in. With a smile I can tell is fake, she says, "I'm so sorry to interrupt you. Gideon, there's an issue I need your help with."

"I'll be right back, Dad. We'll pick up where I left off in just a minute."

Happy to be relieved of that discussion, I walk out to the lobby to find Sasha standing behind one of the marble columns like she's hiding from someone. Confused, I look around to find the issue she needs my help with but see nothing out of the ordinary. My lobby looks just as it always does. Guests milling about. People checking in and checking out. The pianist dressed in a black tux and tails playing some melody meant to entertain people as they enter the building.

"What is it?" I say as I join her behind the column.

"Nothing. I knew you were likely unhappy in there with your father and brother since you're always surly when they come to visit, so I thought you might need a distraction. Was I right?"

I pinch the bridge of my nose and let out a heavy sigh, disgusted after only a few minutes around my brother. "Of course you were. If it was just my father, it would be okay, but fucking Alex...I swear he does things just to push my buttons."

Sasha smiles as she straightens my tie. "Family. You can't live with them. You can't live without them."

Looking down at she moves her hand up to tighten my Windsor knot, I joke, "I thought the saying goes you can't live with them, and you can't shoot them."

Although at this moment all I can think of is doing just that to my goddamned brother.

"Well, I didn't think you had that option, so I went for the family-friendly version."

She takes a step back and studies how I look for a moment before smiling again. "There. Perfect."

"What would I do without you?"

"You'd get along fine, but you'd have to endure more of these types of meetings without any reprieve. So it's really bad? Alex being his usual asshole self?"

Tension courses through my shoulders and neck on

its way to creating a splitting headache I know I'll have to deal with in the next hour. Tilting my head left and right, I try to stop it before it even begins by cracking my neck, but I'm so tight, nothing happens.

"He's his usual bombastic jackass self, which I think might get me killed if my father does what he wants. The son of a bitch thinks we should strike at Marcello Angeloni. I mean, I get it. He's weak now because he hasn't gotten his footing as head of the family yet, but for Christ's sake, why does everything with Alex and my father have to include violence? It's like they never think of the possibility that we can outwit people and achieve the end goal."

Worry fills her eyes as she shakes her head. "He's always such a brute. Why doesn't he understand the idea of subtlety? You want the same outcome as he does. And why does your father listen to that? He knows how well you've handled things here all this time, doesn't he?"

I take a deep breath in as I try to find the right way to describe why my father is like he is. After blowing the air out of my lungs, I say, "I think it's the oldest son thing, which is odd since to hear him talk, that's the one thing his father did that bothered him more than anything else. My grandfather always deferred to my Uncle Maddox since he was the oldest, and according to my father, that was a mistake because it ignored what he had to say since he wasn't the oldest.

Nothing like making the same mistakes your father made."

Sasha sets her hands on my shoulders. "You have to make him see your way is the right way. Let Alex pull that Cro-Magnon man shit at his own place. You have the right idea. Helix just has to see that."

"From your lips to God's ears. Was that all you wanted? To give me a break from the torment in there?" I ask, happy if that's all it was. The break helped more than she knows.

"No. There are no issues I need your help with, but Cesare is here and wants to talk to you. I have him waiting in the conference room."

"Good! Now that's the type of news I want to hear today. If I can just get through this meeting, here's to the rest of my workday going smoothly, assuming Cesare has something good to report. Keep him happy until I'm done. It shouldn't be long."

My assistant lowers her head and stares at me. "What that man would like to make him happy isn't happening with me, Gideon. And not with any of the people who work here either. He's a pig. He'll be lucky if I don't scoop out some slop on the conference table in front of him."

The way she talks about the one person who can help my day turn from the shitshow it's become back to good makes me laugh. "Just tell him I'll be there in a couple minutes. Turn on the TV for him. Keep him amused and I'll get to him as soon as I can."

The news of Cesare coming to see me so soon gives me hope that he has some dirt on Marcello I can use so I can assure my father things will be fine and not have to deal with my brother going all old school mafia on things here. When I return to my office, only my father is waiting for me, though.

This day keeps getting better and better. If he tells me Alex has left, I might let out a yelp of joy.

As I take my seat behind my desk, I ask, "Where did he go?"

"He was hungry, so I told him to go grab something to eat. We can discuss this Angeloni situation just the two of us because you're right. You do have to live here, and I do need you gathering intel on the goings on around here."

Finally, some sanity coming from someone in my family.

CHAPTER TWELVE

ria

As much as I still don't love the fact that I have to stay in this penthouse all day, I can't help but admit that sitting out on this terrace with the sun beaming down onto my face isn't the worst thing in the world after last night. I expect I'll have a much better tan after all the time I spend out here today.

Closing my eyes, I enjoy the warmth of the sun on my cheeks and take a deep breath in, letting it out slowly as the memory of my time with Gideon fills my mind. He's quite sexy, when he isn't doing that silent thing he so loves to do. I think we made a breakthrough in the shower. And later that night in the bedroom. Now I hope we can begin to be like normal couples.

Well, normal other than the fact that he's still not okay with me leaving this penthouse.

I take a sip of orange juice and sit back on the chaise lounge to work on my color. I had begun to get a little ashy sitting around inside for the past few weeks. I probably shouldn't have threatened to jump off the side of the building that first day here.

The sound of the door opening surprises me since it's the middle of the morning and Gideon never returns this early. I quickly swing my legs off the chair and hurry inside to see what's up, but I see a stranger instead of who I expect to see. He walks around like he belongs here, but Gideon didn't mention there would be anyone coming in today.

"Hello? Are you in the right place?" I ask as I walk toward the man.

Nearly as big as Gideon, he has a thicker build and a darker vibe to him. But I don't think he's a security guy. I don't want to feel frightened, but when he looks up at me after flipping through one of the books on the coffee table, I get chills up and down my spine.

"Hello. And who might you be?" the man asks with a wicked smile that does nothing to make me feel more at ease.

"I'm Aria. Who are you? Does Gideon know you're up here?" I ask nervously as the man's gaze rakes over my body.

Instinctively, I fold my arms across my chest. If I had known there would be strangers coming into the penthouse today, I wouldn't have worn my new bikini I got at the boutique.

"Aria. Beautiful name for a beautiful lady. No need to cover up on my behalf. I'm more than happy to take in the view."

This man scares me. I shake my head as I try to cover up even more of me. I don't want him looking at the view if that means he's just going to stare rudely.

"Who are you? Gideon isn't here, but you can find him down in his office, I bet. If not, find Sasha and she'll let you know where he is."

That's twice I've asked him for his name, and twice he's ignored me as he gawks at my body. Suddenly, I miss Gideon's way of being silent so much. At least I never feel like he's ogling me as if I'm a piece of meat and he's some kind of predator, which is exactly what this person feels like.

The man walks up to me and sticks out his hand. "I'm Alex, Gideon's older brother. He never mentioned having a new woman in his life. You'd think he'd say something if he had a beautiful woman in his penthouse."

Gideon's brother? Now that I hear that, I can see the family resemblance around the eyes. Both men have that dark, smoldering stare that unnerves me. It's just that with Gideon, I never feel like I'm in danger.

With this man, I'm sure I am.

"I didn't realize he had a brother. It's nice to meet you, Alex," I say as I tug my hand away from his hold.

"Same to you, Aria. My brother certainly has a type. When I first saw you, I thought you were Gia come back from the dead. Long dark hair, great body, innocent face. Gideon definitely likes that look," he says, his devilish grin growing bigger as he describes some woman his brother used to be with, I'm guessing.

I want to know more about this Gia woman, but I don't dare ask Alex. In fact, I don't want to continue this conversation at all he makes me so uncomfortable.

"Well, it was nice meeting you. As I said, Gideon is in his office, most likely, or somewhere in the hotel. Sasha, his assistant, can help you out."

Alex shrugs and rolls his eyes. "I know exactly where my little brother is. The same place he always is. All work and no play make Gideon a very boring boy. I'm just wondering how he got a woman like you to lounge around his penthouse like some Greek goddess. How did he snag you, Aria?"

I have a feeling telling Alex that his brother paid off my boyfriend and is keeping me here as his captive, even though I don't really mind much now, isn't exactly what Gideon wants me to let him know. Alex doesn't seem to be the type of older brother someone like Gideon would get along with.

So I lie.

"We met at a party. He's very sweet and kind to let

me stay here for a while. I can't tell you how much I appreciate his hospitality."

My answer appears to bore Alex since his gaze begins to travel down my body once more. "I'm sure. Hospitality is so very Gideon with his Italian suits and expensive leather shoes. I'd become convinced my baby brother didn't know how to have a good time. You make me question that belief, though."

He ends his statement by licking his lips, like he's imagining how I'd taste on his tongue. Why is this man here? And why hasn't Gideon come up to make him leave? He has no business being here.

I take a few steps back toward the terrace and force a smile to be polite. "Well, it was very nice meeting you. I'm sure you can find Gideon downstairs. I bet he's eager to see you."

But Alex follows me step for step until he's so close that our bodies are nearly touching. "I'm not particularly eager to see him, to be honest. I prefer the view here better. Since you're with my brother, I think I should get to know the woman living with him. Did he ever tell you about Gia? Because I can't get over how much you remind me of her. They had a love for the ages, or at least that's what she said to me one time. Ridiculous, if you ask me, but she was crazy about him, and the sun rose and set on her for Gideon. I don't think he's been with anyone since, which is so typical of my brother. Carry a torch for a dead woman for years. Even more ridiculous."

I listen to all he has to say about this woman Gideon loved named Gia and can't help but wonder if I'm some kind of replacement for her. If we look that similar, it would make sense. That could also explain why he waited so long to be with me and never even wanted to touch me for weeks on end, even though I was sleeping just inches away from him each night.

Instead of answering his question about whether Gideon ever told me about this woman from his past, I take two more steps until I'm outside on the terrace in the sun. Still with my arms wrapped around my body, I can't wait for my time with Alex to be over.

"Where are you going? We just met. I think we should hang out and get to know one another. You are my brother's girlfriend, aren't you?" he asks as he follows me outside.

The thought of getting to know Alex Rule terrifies me. He hasn't looked at me in a decent way since he laid eyes on me a few minutes ago, and the way he insists on crowding my space like some kind of hunter eyeing up his prey makes me feel helpless.

Girlfriend. I'd never thought of myself in that term before this moment. Gideon and I don't do regular things boyfriends and girlfriends do, so the idea of my being his girlfriend feels odd. Until the other day, I only considered myself his prisoner, but now that we've slept together a few times, maybe I would be his girlfriend.

"Yes," I say, my voice shaking as the chaise lounge

hits the back of my legs when I take yet another step away from Alex. "I am. I'm sure we can get to know each other later when he's around. Maybe we could all have dinner downstairs. The chef makes fantastic food. Have you ever had a meal in the restaurant or out on the terrace?"

Not that I'd know what either are like since I've only eaten the chef's creations right here, but this man doesn't need to know that. God, why hasn't Gideon or even Raphael come in by now? Someone must be looking for Alex.

He shakes his head at my suggestion we could meet later before he reaches his hand out to run his knuckle along my jaw. I don't want to look away and give him the thrill of frightening me since I'm pretty sure he's the type of man who enjoys that kind of thing, but the way he's staring at me like he plans to devour me at any second makes my skin crawl.

"You really are quite beautiful. How on earth did someone like my brother get you?"

"Gideon is a wonderful man. I don't know why you're talking about your own brother like that," I say defensively, hating how he refers to Gideon like he's not good enough for me because of how I look. "He's successful, runs this hotel expertly, and is respected up and down the coast. I'm sure if you ask around you'll hear the same thing from people who know him outside the hotel."

Alex purses his lips and moans as he steps closer to

me, pressing his body to mine. "Mmmm…beautiful and loyal. I like that. Where do I find someone like you for myself? I don't run a hotel, but I run a club and you'd be perfect there on my arm. I promise to show you the time of your life. What do you say? Chuck all this hotel stuffiness for a world that will make your body feel like it's never felt before in your life."

I open my mouth to tell him no, but before I can, he pulls my head forward and plants a hard kiss on my lips. I struggle to push him away, but I'm no match for him. His other hand roams over my body, grabbing at my breasts and my ass even as I try to wriggle out of his hold.

"Please! Don't do this! I'm with your brother!" I cry out.

He shrugs like that fact means nothing to him. "So?"

Thankfully, Gideon walks into the penthouse and sees his brother looming over me. "Alex! Back away from her right now. She doesn't need you terrorizing her in her own home."

I've never heard Gideon sound so brusque and angry. Not even with me, and I've tried his patience more than once in the past few weeks. He didn't even sound that way when Franco called me a slut.

His brother steps back from me, and I breathe a sigh of relief. When Gideon walks out onto the terrace, I hurry over to his side and grab onto his arm, still afraid but at least protected now.

He gives me a gentle smile and kisses me softly on the lips. "Aria, go inside and put on some clothes."

I hold back the tears as the thought that he thinks because I was in my bathing suit that I was inviting his brother's ugly behavior rushes through my head. I can't see by Gideon's expression if that's what he believes, though. He just looks hard and unreachable right now.

Without another word, he nudges me toward the doors, and I run inside to put a dress on over my bikini. I hear Gideon and his brother get loud but can't understand what they're saying to one another. When I look out from the bedroom door, I see Alex march through the penthouse and then hear the front door slam behind him.

Unsure if I should walk out, I take a few steps into the living room. Gideon is still out on the terrace, but he looks flustered and enraged as he runs his hands through his dark hair. I've only known him for a month, but when he does that, I know he's upset.

Cautiously, I walk out to join him and say in a soft voice, "I didn't do anything to make him do that. I swear. I was just sitting out getting some sun and he walked in. I told him to go find you in your office, but he said he wanted to get to know me. I didn't want to, Gideon."

"Come with me," he says gruffly, taking my hand as he walks toward the front door.

"Where are we going? Don't you have to go back to work?" I ask as fear courses through me that he doesn't believe what I said.

He doesn't give Raphael his usual pleasant chit chat and silently pulls me into the elevator. Not a word is said the entire time we ride down to the lobby, although he never lets go of my hand, so I want to believe his anger isn't for me but for his brother.

Sasha is waiting when the elevator doors open. Gideon hands me off to her and says, "Take Aria to get something to eat. Do it out on the terrace so she can enjoy the sun."

Before I can utter a word, he walks away and disappears into his office, leaving me with my babysitter again. When I turn to look at her, I can't even disguise how miserable I am about all that's happened.

"So first I get accosted by that awful brother of his, and now I get to hang out with an ice sculpture. Super."

"Maybe I'll melt in the sun as we have a bite to eat. I'm assuming you're hungry since Gideon told me to feed you."

Sasha begins to guide me across the lobby as I say, "Nobody asked what I wanted. I was just enjoying getting some sun, and the next thing I know I have to be given over to the babysitter again."

That makes her smile, strangely enough. "We'll have a nice time with some good food and sun, and you can tell me about what Alex did. I'm sure it's nothing I haven't heard before. He's a piece of work that one."

"I'm worried Gideon thinks I was coming on to him or something because now he won't even talk to me. I swear I was just relaxing in my bikini. I never once invited his brother in, and I certainly didn't give him any idea that I wanted to hang out with him."

With a look of disgust, Sasha says, "He's a thug. He's a dick to his brother, so I'm not surprised he got handsy with you."

We find a table just outside the doors and sit down as her attempt to make me feel better starts to work. "I just don't want Gideon to think I wanted him to act like that. I'm worried what happened is going to ruin everything between us, and just when things were starting to be good."

"No worries. It'll be fine. Gideon can't stand his brother, and I know he likes you, so chances are pretty good he knows exactly what happened had nothing to do with you wanting Alex to act that way. What that man needs is a woman to smack his face hard. Maybe then he'd get the idea he shouldn't go around touching people who aren't his to touch."

After the server takes our order for some biscuits, we sit together silently soaking up the sun until I can't wait any longer to ask her about what Alex said. "Sasha, who's Gia?"

She opens her eyes and turns her head to look over at me. "Who told you about Gia?"

"Alex. He said Gideon was in love with a woman named Gia and that I'm the spitting image of her. Is that true?"

Sasha studies me for a long moment and then tilts her head right and left. "You do resemble her now that you mention it. She had long brown hair and green eyes like you, except I think yours are actually a much nicer green. Hers were more of an olive green."

"You knew her? Were they really in love?" I ask, unsure I want to hear the answer.

"I didn't know her. I knew her through Gideon, just like I know you through Gideon. As for if they were in love, you'd have to ask him."

God, this woman can be infuriating! Always protecting him. Why not just say it? They were in love.

"I'm asking you. Were they in love?" I press, not willing to let go of this.

She looks up toward the sky for a few moments and then back down toward me. "Assuming I believe Gideon is capable of love, or whether any of us are, then I'd say yes, they loved each other."

All that to say he loved a woman who looked just like me.

"What happened to her?"

"She died. That was a long time ago. Don't go dredging up the past. It never turns out well."

I want to say that I don't know how I feel about being some replacement for another woman who Gideon loved and who died, but I remain silent as all Alex said about Gia and me being so similar fills my head. Am I just someone Gideon wants around because I remind him of her?

Has he been so distant because he's still in love with her? I made the move on him in the shower. Perhaps he doesn't care for me at all. Perhaps he just wants me around because I look like the woman he lost.

The woman he still loves.

CHAPTER THIRTEEN

ideon

My rage barely contained, I march into the conference room to find Cesare relaxed and watching soccer on the TV. At least one of us is having a good time today.

"Comfortable?" I snap.

The enormous man slowly swivels around in his leather chair and looks at me oddly. "Something on your mind today, Gideon?"

Pinching the bridge of my nose, I try to stem the headache that's settling into my skull. "No. Sorry."

"I saw your father in the lobby earlier. Family visits can be a bitch, can't they?"

As I sit down next to him, I mumble, "You have no idea. What a morning. No stress, but I'm relying on you to salvage this day before it goes straight into the toilet."

Cesare laughs and shakes his head. "Nothing like putting pressure on a guy."

For a few moments, I watch whatever match is on the TV and hope to escape my life here. I never wanted this for myself. When my father decided this was to be my fate in our family, all I could think was my fucking life was over.

I'd had such big plans. Once Alex had graduated and was gone from school, I was free to be who I wanted to be. Yes, I was still a Rule and the son of Helix Rule, which meant people always whispered whenever either my brother or I was around. They heard the rumors about what my father did for a living to afford to send us to the best private school in the States, and I always knew part of them would never accept us because of that.

Alex never gave a damn. He reveled in the idea that he could use our father's violence to intimidate classmates. He made sure to let them know whenever they fucked around with him that whatever they heard about our family was only the tip of the iceberg, and if Helix Rule was bad, Alex Rule was so much worse.

I never wanted people to see me like that vicious animal who'd willingly hurt others with my hands. Physical violence was never my thing.

Not that I was any kinder than my brother or father. I just had my own way of dealing with people who crossed me. While Alex would just beat the hell out of someone who pissed him off, I preferred to choose to fuck with them in other subtle ways that hurt far more than my fists ever could.

It didn't take long for my fellow classmates to figure out that messing with me was even worse than messing with my brother. Bruises and cuts healed quickly. The torment I visited on someone wasn't something a person could brace for or be stitched up from.

Fucking with someone mentally takes time, but for someone like me, it was the only way. I could inflict physical pain on those who fucked with me, but I found the joy of torturing people quietly far more exquisite.

"You okay, Gideon? You seem different today."

Cesare's question pulls me from my thoughts of prep school and all those plans I'd had before my father announced I was to be the manager of this hotel instead of finishing college. Those dreams seem like they're a million miles away now.

"Just the usual business I have to deal with," I say with a smile I have to force. Eager to forget all those thoughts of the past, I change the subject. "So what did you bring me today?"

The enormous man leans back in his seat, and I swear I hear the chair groan under his weight. Folding his arms behind his head, my P.I. seems uniquely pleased with himself today.

"I know you said you didn't want any cheating wife or girlfriend shit, but let's say it's the appetizer before I get to the main entrée," Cesare says, practically gloating.

Surprised, I nod at this bit of news. "Well, I'm in the mood for a good cheating story. What did you find out?"

My P.I. leans forward and smacks his hand off the table. With a hearty laugh, he says, "Marcello's girlfriend has a daddy thing going on. I followed her after she left the Angeloni villa, and she led me right to her side piece, who is definitely old enough to be her father."

"Tell me you got pictures of her fucking dear old daddy," I say with a smile.

He sends a manila envelope sailing down the table to where I sit. "It's all there. Be sure to check out the ones toward the end. Baby girl has a thing for getting fucked hard. But hey, what's a little blood, right?"

As I slide the photos out of the envelope, I murmur, "A little blood? Sounds kinky. Daddy must be really rough."

"Oh, he is. I was impressed since he's got to be in his late fifties. The guy must be taking care of himself. No low T there. Not like that wrinkly old bastard I was telling you about the other day."

I flip through the pictures and see a blond woman

getting fucking abused by some guy with gray hair. He does look like he's in good shape for a middle-aged man. I don't generally enjoy eyeballing stills of other people fucking, but for today's purposes, I'll suffer through it.

"And Marcello thinks she's his?" I ask as I stuff the photos back into the envelope and set it aside.

"Truly and forever," Cesare answers with a shit-eating grin. "I saw them out at dinner last night. They were all lovey dovey. Typical woman. Fawn all over a man at eight o'clock, and by ten, be on your hands and knees getting plowed by another guy."

Such a romantic.

"Okay, this can definitely be useful, but I'm eager to know what else you found out about him."

Cesare pulls another envelope from his coat pocket. This one is much smaller and white.

"I think you're going to like this. Seems our boy isn't the only Angeloni left. Here, take a look."

"What do you mean? I thought all the other brothers were dead," I say as I open the envelope to see what he's talking about.

My eyes scan the papers inside, and I instantly understand. Looking up at Cesare, I can't hide how happy this news makes me.

"Fuck me. You can find out secrets nobody else can. So Marcello Angeloni has a brother?"

Cesare taps his fat fingers on the envelope sitting in front of me. "Not just a brother. An illegitimate brother who I bet will be more than eager to get what is rightfully his because he's an Angeloni son. Keep reading, though. You haven't even gotten to the best part."

I drop my gaze to the papers and keep reading, dying to find out what he thinks is the best part. And then I come to it, and it's like Christmas and my fucking birthday all at once.

Looking up at Cesare, I shake my head in disbelief. "No fucking way."

With a huge grin, the P.I. nods. "Way. Marcello Angeloni isn't actually an Angeloni by blood at all. Motherfucker is adopted. Turns out his mother and father were some fucking teenagers who gave him up at birth and went on their merry goddamned way. The Angelonis adopted him, but he doesn't have the birthright that bastard son of his father's has. And the cherry on top of the cake? This illegitimate son doesn't know a fucking thing about it. He just thinks he had a wealthy benefactor who left him a bunch of money when old man Angeloni died."

"I think it's time the bastard found out who he really is. Any chance Marcello doesn't know about him?"

Nothing would be better than being able to spring that news on the asshole when we have our meeting.

With a huge smile, Cesare nods. "Believe it or not, I can't find any evidence that he knows a goddamned thing about it. So how'd I do, boss? Am I forgiven for getting fresh with that pretty redhead you have out there in your lobby?"

I stand and pat him on the shoulder. "You're forgiven. Just don't do it again or I'll let Sasha deal with you."

His eyes get wide, and I swear I see fear settle into them. "Got it. Behave or the gorgeous woman who I think might be the type to kill me in my sleep will come after me."

"You did good, Cesare. Be sure to stay and have some lunch. On me."

That makes him happy, and as he stands to walk out to take me up on my offer, he asks, "Anything else you need from me on this? I know I gave you all the info you need to fuck up Marcello, but if I can be a part of it, just say the word."

A little surprised to hear he wants to help me take down my newest enemy, I wait for him to explain what his problem is with Marcello. When he doesn't, I say, "I didn't realize you had an ax to grind with the new head of the Angeloni family."

He shrugs and answers, "I don't, but something about this fuck announcing to the world that he plans on killing any Rule he can pisses me off. I'm just saying, if you need help, just let me know."

"I will. Thanks for all of this, Cesare."

"My pleasure, boss. Now I'm going to enjoy a nice lunch out on your terrace and live like the other half does for a little while."

"Try the lemon pasta with shrimp. It's a specialty of my chef's," I say as I make my way toward the door.

I appreciate his offer of help to get that fuck Marcello, but I think this is something that needs to be kept within the Rule family. I won't forget the offer, though.

CHAPTER FOURTEEN

ideon

MY MEETING WITH CESARE HAS SAVED THIS DAY, thankfully. But my father and brother are still hanging around threatening to ruin it at any moment.

I see Alex and have to hold back the urge to beat the hell out of him for that shit he pulled with Aria. Not that I should be surprised. My brother has hit on every female I've ever dated, all the way back to when we were in prep school, and most he tried to steal away. It never even mattered that he had a girlfriend through most of high school. He just couldn't stand to see me have one.

"What's up, baby brother?" he asks with a laugh as

I walk out onto the terrace on the main floor looking for Sasha and Aria.

I look down at him sitting across from my father and don't even attempt to hide my sneer. "Dad, how long are you planning on staying?"

My father thinks about my question for a few moments and then says, "I'm happy to say the meeting I had scheduled for later this afternoon is now unnecessary, so your brother and I will be leaving in a few hours. Why? Do you have something you'd like to do while we're here? Do you know in all the time I've owned this hotel that I've never toured this coast? Want to act as tour guide and show me the sights? You look like you could use some time off from this place."

As much as I'd like to do that with him, the thought of spending even a minute more around my brother has me practically seeing red. I hadn't intended on mentioning anything to my father since what happened earlier is between me and Alex, but now as he sits here with a shit-eating grin on his face showing no remorse for his behavior, I feel like I need to say something.

"You know what, Dad? I'd love to, but to be brutally honest, I can't stand being around my brother anymore. This son of a bitch went up to my penthouse and put his fucking hands on my girlfriend. He's lucky I didn't throw his ass right off the side of my goddamned terrace. So no, I'll have to take a rain check on showing you around the Amalfi Coast."

My father listens to everything I have to say and then turns to look at my brother. "Is this true?"

Why my father allows the idea that I'm not telling the truth to creep into this conversation baffles me while pissing me off royally. Before Alex has a chance to say whatever shitty thing he intends to, I butt in and answer my father's question for him.

"When the fuck have you ever known me to lie? That's not me, Dad. That's this one. If I tell you he did what I say he did, then it's the truth. You should operate from that basic fact, not asking him if what I just said is true."

Rarely, if ever, have I ever defended myself like that to my father. The stunned look on his face tells me he didn't expect me to talk to him like that.

"Okay, fine. I'm sorry." Turning to look at Alex again, my father rewords his initial question. "You've obviously angered your brother. Why would you do what he claims you did?"

It still sounds like he wants to believe his older son is innocent, but with Helix Rule, you take your wins whenever you can and in whatever form they come.

For his part, Alex knows as well as I do that he's my father's favorite, so he merely shrugs off all my anger and my father's questions about what he did. "As usual, Gideon is making a big deal out of nothing. I went up to his apartment to find him and found a girl instead. I was just extending a welcome Rule hand since it was my first time meeting her. Have you seen Gideon's new girl, Dad?"

And just like that, my father's attention leaves where it should be—on my shithead of a brother—and returns to me and the idea that I'm with someone he hasn't met yet. Fuck, I hate Alex.

"I didn't realize you had a new woman in your life, Gideon. Why haven't you introduced her to me?" my father asks, like I'm a fifteen-year-old boy.

"Because I'm a grown man and I can't remember the last time I discussed a woman in my life with anyone in my family."

Out of the corner of my eye, I see Sasha and Aria walking toward where I'm standing. Jesus, how is it possible my assistant thinks this is a good idea?

"Here she is right now," Alex says. "I have to give you credit, little brother. She's a nice piece of ass. Too bad she's just a copy of that woman you can't seem to get over."

And that's enough to send me over the edge.

Too angry to think straight, I grab my brother by the collar and yank him up out of his chair. A second later, unable to control my rage, I shove him hard, sending him tumbling into the lobby as I follow after him. Alex is bigger than I am, but he spends too much of his time drinking and snorting shit up his nose, so he's no match for me in the furious state I'm in at this moment.

I hear people murmur around me, which should make me stop, but I can't. If my father isn't happy about my behaving like this, then maybe he shouldn't have brought my dick brother to town. Next time, let's hope he knows better.

"I've had enough of your bullshit, big brother," I say through gritted teeth as I grab him by the collar again to bring him to his feet.

"Gideon!" my father barks behind me in that tone that says he doesn't approve of what I'm about to do.

Too fucking bad. This has been far too long in coming. Seeing him with his hands all over Aria this morning just made it inevitable it would happen today.

A single thought of hurting him fills my mind, and a second later, I smash my fist into my brother's face. He falls to the floor, bleeding all over my fucking marble lobby, but I don't care if I have to spend millions to have this entire floor redone. Hitting him felt far too fucking good for me to regret anything.

"If you ever come near Aria again, I won't stop at breaking your goddamned nose. Now get the fuck out of my hotel!"

A hand touches my left arm, and I spin around to see Sasha and Aria standing there looking at me like they can't believe what just happened. "Gideon, I'm going to take Aria upstairs. Do you need anything?"

Taking a deep breath, I run my hand through my hair as my heart races. "Good. I'll be up in a little while."

The two of them hurry off toward the elevator as the crowd of people that had gathered around me and Alex begins to disperse, leaving just my father standing next to me. If he thinks I'm going to apologize, he's out of his fucking mind. He's lucky I didn't do more to my brother.

Next time he pisses me off, I swear I will.

"So much for brotherly love," he says in a low voice. "I had no idea you resented your brother so much, Gideon."

Is he really going to make this about me and my problems? Not today.

I turn to face him and shake my head. "You would if you weren't constantly acting like the sun fucking rises and sets on him and I'm some leftover you get to rely on who never lets you down. Tell Mom I'll be looking forward to seeing her birthday present. Have a nice flight back."

My father's eyes open wide as I say what I've wanted to say for years, but he doesn't respond. As I walk past my brother still sitting on the floor holding his bloody nose, I grimace. "Get up off the fucking floor, Alex. You look pathetic down there, and you're getting blood all over my marble."

I head toward the elevator but turn around to make sure he isn't coming after me because I know my brother. He fights dirty, and I don't see him letting this little incident go by without him wanting to retaliate.

It might not happen right now, but he'll get me back somehow.

What I'm certain of is he won't learn a goddamned thing from what just happened. He'll continue to be the asshole he's always been.

And Alaric thinks his issues with his brother were bad? I wonder if he ever sucker punched any of his siblings in public before. I'll have to ask him when he calls after hearing about this, as I'm sure he will since nothing in the Rule family stays secret for long.

By the time I reach the penthouse, my heart has returned to its normal beat, and I'm calm enough to deal with my assistant and the woman's honor I just defended. The two of them are waiting for me in the living room, and when I walk through the door, Sasha runs up to me, throwing her arms around my shoulders.

"Oh, my God! You finally did it! I couldn't believe my eyes. You hit him hard enough to make him fall to the floor."

I gently push her off me and nod, unable to keep the smile from my face. "Finally, right? I just hope it doesn't ruin the floor."

"To hell with the floor, Gideon! He had it coming in spades for years. It was the best thing I've seen in ages."

"Well, now I need you to go see if I need to spend a fortune to have a new floor installed. Have it professionally looked at, okay?" I say while I ease her toward the door.

I want to be alone with Aria right now, and any talk of my brother or bloody marble floors can wait for later.

Sasha, thankfully, understands without being told that she needs to leave, and hurries out. "I'm on it! That was the best thing, Gideon! It was like a Christmas bonus in September. So cool!"

When the door closes behind her and I'm alone with Aria, I'm surprised to see her looking unhappy. "Are you upset I caused a scene with my brother?"

She narrows her eyes at me and shakes her head. "I don't care what you do to your brother. In fact, I was happy you hit him. He's an ass, and he had it coming."

Slowly, I walk toward her as she stands over near the couch, her arms folded across her chest. "Then why don't you look happy."

"Gideon, did you do that to your brother for me?"

I stop and consider that question. It was definitely in part for her, but I'd be lying if I said it had nothing to do with wanting to beat the hell out of Alex for years. There's been too much bad blood between my brother and me to deny that.

"Yes. And no. But mostly yes."

"Then why when you walked into this penthouse did you immediately look at Sasha and not me? And why did she feel comfortable running into your arms the second she saw you."

I reach out for Aria's hand, but she yanks it away. "No. I want an answer first. Why was I an afterthought for you? You take me from Franco and keep me here like I'm yours. You defend me against your brother. But when it comes to actually dealing with me, Sasha is more important. So why am I an afterthought?"

"You're not an afterthought, Aria. To be honest, you're all I've thought about all day since I walked in and saw my brother with you."

Her eyes flash pure emotion. "Oh, that's because you were jealous. I'm not stupid. I picked up on the brotherly rivalry between you two. That doesn't mean I'm not someone you forget about whenever Sasha comes around."

"Sasha is my assistant. I'm used to relying on her. That's the only reason she reacted like she did. She knows how much I've had to deal with when it comes to my brother."

None of what I say makes Aria happy, though. Sulking, she walks out to the terrace and stares out at the water. I thought she'd be thrilled that I punished Alex for what he did. Instead, I'm the bad guy.

Needing to make her see I care, I make my way out to the terrace and slide my arms around her waist. I dip my head to her ear and whisper, "Please don't be mad at me. You're not an afterthought. In fact, since the other night, you've been one of my only thoughts."

She slowly turns around so she's facing me, and in her eyes I see true sadness. "Gideon, who's Gia?"

Only my brother would bring up my past to use it like a fucking cudgel on me. Fucking Alex.

"Nobody," I answer flatly, sure my expression isn't as calm as I'd like it to be at this moment.

"According to your brother, I'm the spitting image of her. Is that why you took me and keep me here? Do you like having the duplicate of the woman you loved around? He said you two had a love for the ages. Is that true?"

I step back away from her, dropping my arms from around her waist. "I can't imagine Alex said that without a mouth full of bile since he thinks of love as nothing more than a word you use to get people to do what you want."

"That doesn't answer my question, Gideon. In fact, it doesn't answer any of the questions I asked."

"Yes, you look like her. As for the rest of what my brother said, ignore him. It's not worth your time."

"Do I look exactly like her?" Aria asks, her voice shaking as the words come out of her mouth.

I don't have to think about the answer to that. She absolutely does. It's what drew me to her at that party weeks ago.

But that doesn't mean a goddamned thing. The problem is thanks to my shithead brother, now that's all she's going to think I want her for—as a replacement for a ghost.

"Men generally have a type. My brother likes any woman who will have him, but he prefers blondes with big breasts. He has mommy issues. I prefer women with dark hair and green eyes. It's nothing, Aria."

"Except I look exactly like the woman you loved. Tell me the truth, Gideon. Am I merely a substitute for this Gia person?"

I shake my head and frown. This day has gone from bad to worse. "No. Don't listen to my brother. He's wrong about nearly everything."

"You know what? I don't think he is. I think even worse than being an afterthought is being a replacement for someone. You can go to hell, Gideon. Take your huge gestures and your penthouse and everything else and go to hell!"

CHAPTER FIFTEEN

ria

I HURRY AWAY BEFORE I START CRYING BECAUSE I don't want him to see the thought of not mattering to him bothers me so much. It shouldn't. It's not like Gideon Rule ever promised me a happily ever after. He merely promised to protect me, and so far, he's lived up to that.

Everything else between us has been miles short of romantic. So we have sex. So it's great. That doesn't mean I matter, and I need to get that through my thick head.

I guess I just thought by the way he reacted when he saw his brother bothering me that he may have cared a little. Stupid Aria. He's a bad man who may be kind sometimes. I shouldn't confuse his willingness not to be a total villain with love.

He pads up behind me hiding in the bedroom and in a low voice says, "Aria, you aren't a substitute for someone else. Don't think that."

"But I do, and nothing you've said so far has convinced me I'm not."

"Turn around and look at me. I'll tell you anything you want to know about her. Then you'll see you have nothing to do with anything that happened with anyone in my past."

I do as he commands like I always do and see he looks sincere. Now I guess I'll find out when I ask him about her. If he avoids any of my questions, I'll know.

Not that it matters. I really need to remember that. Whatever we're doing here with him keeping me in this penthouse and us sleeping together isn't a relationship and it certainly isn't anything resembling love.

"Was what your brother said true?"

Gideon winces at the mention of Alex. "So little of what he says is true, Aria. Trust me on that. Don't believe him."

"Then make me believe you. Were you in love with this Gia woman?"

He doesn't hesitate to answer, surprising me. "Yes. I was crazy about her."

"Was it a love for the ages like he said?"

That gets me an eye roll and a smile. "My brother would have only said that to make fun of how we felt about each other. I don't know if it was a love for the ages, but we loved each other, and I would have done anything for her."

I was afraid how I'd feel hearing Gideon truly cared about someone, but listening to him now, I can't help but be relieved. At least he's capable to love. That's more than I thought about him until this morning.

"What happened between you? Sasha said she died."

He nods and lets out a heavy sigh. "She did. Her husband found out she was in love with me, so he killed her before I could get her away from him."

The sadness that fills his eyes as he says that makes my chest hurt. Gideon loved someone else's wife and blames himself for her death.

"Is that why you paid Franco so I would come with you?"

This time my answer is a simple nod of his head. No words. Just another sigh and a nod.

"Why? You and I didn't even know one another. We'd only spoken once at that party. It was because I looked like her, wasn't it?"

"No," he answers, shaking his head wildly. "That wasn't it at all."

God, I feel like I'm getting nowhere with this!

"Then what was it?" I ask, my voice verging on screaming. "Why would you care at all what happened to me? You barely knew me!"

All of a sudden, it's as something snaps in Gideon, and he becomes a different person right in front of my eyes. He storms over to me and takes my face in his hands before he kisses me hard, taking my breath away.

"I don't know why I cared for you after only meeting you, but I did. I tried to pretend like it didn't matter. I told my cousin it meant nothing, and I only defended you with Franco because it was the right thing to do, but I do the wrong thing more often than not, so that was a lie. I fought him and I hit my brother because the very idea of someone hurting you makes my chest feel like someone's fucking carving a dull knife into the center of it."

When he finishes speaking, he takes a deep breath and lets it out slowly. "So that's your answer. I did it because something about you touched me like no one has ever done before."

"Even that Gia woman you were in love with?" I ask, needing to know.

I wait, holding my breath as he takes another deep breath in and holds it in his lungs. Finally, he lets it out like the weight of the world comes along with it.

"Yes."

"But you were in love with her," I say, still not understanding.

Gideon doesn't say anything for a long moment, his stare remaining on my face the entire time. He looks like he doesn't know how to say what's on his mind.

Then a hint of a smile lifts the corners of his mouth. "I've been in love with you since that night we met."

I shake my head in disbelief. "How can that be? You slept next to me for weeks and never touched me. You barely spoke to me for the past month. That isn't love."

"Why? Why can't it be love? Why couldn't I feel that way? Just because it isn't the way most people act? Well, I'm not most people."

My mind whirls as I try to process what he's saying. Does he truly mean it? Does he actually love me?

"Then why did you make that deal with me the second night I was here if you were going to protect me anyway?"

"Because that's what I was supposed to do. I knew you'd never believe me if I told you how much I cared about you, so I played along. People around here think I'm like the rest of my family, so I act the part of a bad man. With you, though, I don't want to be that. With you, I want to be who I truly am."

The way he says that, like he isn't sure how I'll

react but he wants to chance it anyway, touches my heart, so I reach out and cradle his face in my hands. The stubble from his new beard growth scratches my palms when he smiles at me.

"So you love me?" I ask, still unsure I believe him.

"I love you," he answers quietly. "I know it doesn't make sense with the way I've acted, but I've loved you more every day you've been here with me. I can't imagine my life without you."

Pressing my lips to his, I kiss them softly and sigh. "I want to believe you. I do. It's just that nothing you're saying makes any sense when I think about how you've acted for the past weeks."

His dark eyes search my face like he needs to find something inside me to cling to in case I try to slip away. Pushing my hair off my shoulders, he smiles and says, "Then forget about all of that. Tonight, we start something new together."

As much as I love what he's saying, the truth of the matter is I'm still his prisoner here. If he loves me, that can't continue.

"Gideon, you keep me here and won't even let me go down to eat my meals without someone babysitting me. That's not love."

He winces at my description of what's been the truth of my life for the past month. "That's been protecting you, but you're right. Love should mean you can trust someone. If you want to leave the penthouse while I'm at work, you can from now on."

My heart soars at what he's saying. I won't be his prisoner anymore. I'll actually be Gideon's girlfriend, free to come and go as I like, at least during the day.

"And no Sasha watching over me?"

"Fine. No Sasha watching over you, but you can't leave the hotel without a bodyguard. I can't relent on that. You asked me for protection, so you'll get it."

I can live with that. I did ask him to protect me because I don't think Franco is done with me yet, so if I leave the hotel, I'll go with a bodyguard.

"Okay. That works for me."

We fall silent as I think about all he's told me tonight. He never asked if I love him, though. Is it that he doesn't care, or it doesn't matter to him?

Taking his hand in mine, I bring it to my lips to kiss his fingertips. "Are you wondering why I haven't said I love you?"

To my surprise, he shakes his head. "No. I haven't done anything to make you fall in love with me yet. I know that. I just have to hope in time you'll come to love me."

"It's only that I don't know how to feel, Gideon. You pay my ex-boyfriend to take me, you keep me locked up in this penthouse, and before today, I didn't even know what we were to each other."

"I understand. You're not a prisoner here as of tonight. Whenever I'm at work, you can go anywhere in the hotel you want, and you can go anywhere up and down the coast, as long as you're escorted by a bodyguard."

His attempt to sound like a normal boyfriend makes me smile. "I don't mean to ruin this beautiful moment, but you know most men don't say things like that to their girlfriends. Most women can go wherever they want whenever they want."

Gideon's eyes get a sparkle in them that looks downright devilish as he says, "I'm not like most men, Aria. I may not be the man most people think I am, but that doesn't mean I don't see the truth of what the world is. There are more than a few men who would happily take you from me for no other reason than to punish me because my last name is Rule. You're mine to protect, so that means your freedom comes with some restrictions."

Since I don't think I have a choice if I want to be with him, I nod my agreement. I do want to stay with Gideon here in his beautiful penthouse. Now that I know he cares about me, I can live with a few limits.

He takes my hand in his and leads me to the bed, gently lying me on my back. "Now that our negotiations are finished, can we finally get to something we both deserve after the day we've had?"

Giggling, I watch as he begins to undress in front of me. "I didn't realize those were negotiations. I would have asked for more if I knew."

He stops loosening his tie and looks down at me. "Didn't you get everything you wanted?"

I sense that's a rhetorical question, but he has a point. I can freely move about the hotel whenever I feel like it. I can even leave, assuming I have a bodyguard.

And best of all, I now know Gideon's in love with me. I got a lot out of our negotiations, it seems.

CHAPTER SIXTEEN

ideon

AS SHE LIES ON THE BED WATCHING ME, I UNBUTTON my black dress shirt slowly, button by button until there are none left. She doesn't join in undressing me, oddly enough. I can't figure this woman out. The other night, she walked into my shower to seduce me, and tonight, she seems perfectly content to simply watch me strip.

"Are you okay?" I ask, hoping she'll say something to make any of this make sense.

With a smile, she nods. "Yes. I'm enjoying the show."

I lean down over her and press a kiss to her lips before I whisper against them, "Join in then."

Aria looks up at me with those green eyes that seem full of mischief as her hand cups between my legs. I'm hard and ready, so the feel of her fingers pressing against me only serve to excite me more.

"You mean like that?"

Not exactly, but I'll fix that in a second. Standing up to my full height, I unzip my pants and slide my stiff cock out. She watches me give it a few strokes, smiling up at me.

Now it's her turn.

"Sit up," I order, and she does as I command.

Her beautiful eyes don't seem so mischievous anymore. Instead, all I see is uncertainty in their green depths.

Stuffing my hand in her hair at the back of her head, I gently pull her mouth to my cock. She hesitates just before her lips touch the head and looks up at me innocently.

"I haven't done this a lot. I might not be good at it. Just let me know if you don't like how I'm doing it."

Whatever kind of men she's been with in the past must have been real losers because I can't imagine watching Aria suck my cock ever being anything but pure ecstasy. As long as she doesn't fuck around with her teeth, I'm going to love this.

"Don't worry. I have no doubt you'll be good."

Her dark lashes lower so her eyes disappear

behind them, and a second later, that perfect mouth of hers touches my skin, sending strings of the most delicious sensations racing to my balls. Jesus, she feels good on me. I thought her cunt was the most incredible feeling, but now I'm not so sure.

She's tentative as she lowers herself down onto my cock, and I sense she really isn't confident in her ability. That's about to change.

I tug her head back so my cock pops out of her mouth. She stares up at me in confusion, and I think I see hurt in her eyes, so I quickly say, "I'll guide you. Don't worry. You'll love it."

Aria nods, but I can tell she's not sure. That's okay. I like having the chance to train someone in the way I like it.

"Lick your lips. The wetter they are, the better."

"I know," she says, and the hurt is evident in her voice. "I may not be good at this, but I know that."

Bending down, I kiss her sensuous lips I can't wait to have suck me off. "I can't believe with a mouth like yours that you won't be incredible at this. Ready?"

"I think I'm nervous, Gideon."

"Don't be."

I pull her head toward me and watch as her eyes slowly close once more. I'd prefer it if she was looking up at me while I fuck her mouth, but that can happen another time when she's more confident.

Her lips open at the first touch of my cock to them,

and I groan at the feel of her lowering herself down on me. That mouth feels fucking incredible.

After a few moments to get used to the size of me, I whisper, "Wrap your hand around the base. Not too tight."

She does as I order, adding another layer of perfect sensation to our time together. Her fingers are warm against my skin, and for a moment, I let myself revel in her touch.

"Look up at me, Aria."

Her eyes open wide, and I swear to God it's the most erotic fucking sight I've ever laid eyes on. "Good. Now try to keep your eyes on me up here. You don't have to do anything but make sure your teeth don't scrape me. Feel free to flick your tongue around my cock as I fuck that beautiful mouth."

She doesn't respond, and I push my hips forward, sliding my cock deep inside her mouth. I hold off on thrusting too hard at first so as not to scare her. I suspect she's gone down on men before by the way she knows how to run her tongue along the underside of my cock, but the way she looked like a frightened deer a few seconds ago tells me the last thing I need to do is jackhammer into her face the first few times.

We fall into a rhythm of me thrusting slowly and her teasing me with her tongue that sends waves of desire coursing through me. My hands in her hair keep things going at a tempo I like and doesn't scare her, and as I watch her suck me off, it's the best blowjob I've had in a long time. Maybe not technically but emotionally.

Aria's eyelids flutter closed, taking away the vision of those green eyes I love, so I moan, "Eyes open. Watch me."

She obeys me and opens her eyes as I begin to pick up the pace with my fucking her mouth. I'm impressed that she doesn't gag the first time I thrust hard, sending the head of my cock to the back of her throat.

"That's a good girl. Take it all," I say in a low voice as I barely control my urge to let loose and ram my cock down her throat.

Her hold on the base tightens, a sign she might not be handling everything as well as I've been thinking. I gently pry her fingers from around me and thread my fingers through hers so she has something to hold on to.

"It's okay. Just don't let go of me."

Tears begin to roll out the sides of her eyes, making her black mascara streak across the tops of her cheeks when I start fucking her mouth in earnest, but I'm too far gone to stop. She doesn't make a noise, though. I know she's uncomfortable by how she squeezes my fingers at my hip, and as much as I know I should slow down, I can't.

I'm so close, and all I want to do is fill that beautiful mouth. Every stroke of my cock across her lips gets me nearer to the moment when that will happen, but until then, I can't stop myself.

Tears stream out of Aria's gorgeous green eyes, and as much as that should make me slow down, it doesn't. All it does is turn me on even more. My legs hurt I'm pushing my hips so hard, and my fingers ache from how tightly I'm pulling her hair. I'm so close… just a few seconds more and I'll be there.

When it happens, I feel like the top of my head is going to blast off. I thrust into her mouth one final time and fall still as my cock shoots ropes of cum down her throat. My hand still gripping her hair keeps her mouth right where I need it to be, but she begins to shake her head after a few seconds, so I let her go.

Aria runs into the bathroom as I collapse onto the bed, exhausted and utterly satisfied. I hear her running the water in the sink as I wait for her to come out, and when she returns, all the tears and mascara staining her cheeks are gone.

"You should have told me I looked like that," she says with a pout as she stands naked in front of me.

"Like what? I thought you looked great. Totally turned me on," I say with a smile.

She crawls onto the bed beside me and curls up against my side. "You have a thing for strung out crack whores? Because that's how bad I looked."

I turn to look at her and shake my head. "Not that I know of. I thought you looked sexy."

With laser-like focus, she stares into my eyes and asks, "Why? Because I had your cock in my mouth? You men are so easy to figure out."

That makes me smile. She hasn't figured me out at all, but I like the bravado she's showing right now.

"There's nothing wrong with admiring a woman who's going down on you. And I'm not like any other man you've ever met."

She slides her hand over my abdomen and snuggles up next to my shoulder. "Maybe, but you're like every other man in that way."

I wrap my arm around her and pull her close so her head is resting on my chest. I like the feeling of her on me like this. For nearly a month, she's laid next to me in this bed, and I can't count how many nights I wanted to be with her exactly like this. I fought it all that time, but these last few days have shown me I don't want to fight against what I feel anymore.

We lie there silently with just the sound of our breathing between us until she says, "Tell me about her."

I close my eyes as the instant urge to pull away washes over me. I don't want to be that way with Aria, though, so I stop myself and let the memory of Gia fill my head.

"She was kind and gentle, and the person who was supposed to love her most took her life because she loved someone else," I say, the words feeling like knives stabbing me with each syllable that leaves my lips.

Aria doesn't say anything for a long time as the memory of that day I learned Gia was gone from this world makes my chest hurt. She died because I didn't do enough to protect her. I swore I'd never make that mistake again.

"Didn't you love her more than him, though?"

I turn my head and see Aria waiting for my answer. I won't lie to her. She asked, and I want to answer.

"Yes, but I didn't make sure she was safe, so maybe I didn't love her enough."

"Is that why you paid Franco? To get me away from him? I know you said you didn't that first night I was here, but did you?" Aria asks in a soft voice, her warm breath drifting over my chest.

There's no point in lying to her. Her protection was more important than any of the other reasons why I paid that shithead ex-boyfriend of hers to take her for my own.

As I stare up at the ceiling, I answer, "Yes. I couldn't let what happened before happen again."

She falls silent again, so after a minute or so, I look over to see her watching me. I know what she's thinking, but she's wrong. She needs to know that.

"You aren't a replacement for her, Aria. I don't care that you resemble her or what my brother said to you. You aren't, so don't think that."

With a nod, she tries to smile, but it never reaches her eyes. Taking a deep breath in, she lets it out in a rush before pulling away from my body. "Please don't make me a substitute for another woman, Gideon. If that's all this is, then let me go. I can get away from Franco on my own and find happiness for being me."

I roll over onto my side next to her, shaking my head as I try to find the words to make her understand that's not what this is. Cradling her face, I look deep into those eyes that never fail to enchant me and see she truly believes I've brought her here because she reminds me of another woman.

"You're here because of you, no one else. I fell in love with you in the past few weeks. I'm not reliving some memory through you, Aria. I've spent years alone because I didn't want to take a chance on feeling what I felt for her, but you changed that. Gia is my past. You're the only woman I think of now."

"I want to believe that, Gideon. I just can't stop thinking about what your brother said."

Fucking Alex. All he had to do was not be a dick. Too bad he couldn't even do that for me just this once.

"Don't listen to him," I say before kissing her softly. Against her lips, I whisper, "Listen to me. I want you here for you."

"Promise?"

The way she says that makes my heart feel like she's got it in a vice. At this moment, I'd promise her anything to see her happy.

"I promise."

I'm rewarded by a genuine smile that reaches her eyes and makes them light up. So beautiful and mine.

"Gideon, can I tell you something?"

Nodding, I hope it's not that she hated what we just did because I enjoyed it more than she knows. "Yes."

"I think Sasha likes me more than just someone who wants to be nice to her boss's girlfriend."

As the urge to laugh at how innocent she sounds right now comes over me, I pull her to my chest and hold her tightly. "I think you're right."

Aria leans back and looks at me with worry in her eyes. "How do you feel about that?"

"I've told her to stop. She has a mind of her own when it comes to things like that, but if you want me to, I'll make her stop."

A blush makes her cheeks turn pink, and she averts her gaze from mine. "No, it's okay. I guess it's better than thinking she wants you all the time."

I softly press a kiss to her forehead and sigh. "Don't worry about Sasha. All that matters is you and me. Remember that."

CHAPTER SEVENTEEN

ideon

Marcello Angeloni agreed to a meeting with me this morning, so I reluctantly leave Aria in bed and get ready to deal with him. After hearing what Cesare had to tell me about the youngest Angeloni, I'm finally in a position to fix this problem he has with the Rule family.

Sasha meets me in my office earlier than usual since it's a special occasion, and she doesn't hesitate to ask about how things are going with Aria. "So you look happy this morning. Is that because you're about to lay waste to the house of Angeloni, or does it have more to do with that beautiful creature you're keeping all to yourself in your penthouse?"

I smile but don't answer her question directly. "Speaking of that, Aria is no longer required to stay in the penthouse when she's not with me, so if you see her somewhere in the hotel, you don't have to worry."

My assistant's eyes open wide in shock. "Really? You aren't allowing her out of the hotel on her own, though, are you? What about that ex of hers?"

"Relax," I say as I take my seat behind my desk. "She knows she has to be accompanied by one of my security guards if she wants to leave the hotel. We've come to an agreement."

"That's great. How did that happen?"

Sasha takes a seat across from me as she expects an explanation. When I don't immediately offer one, she pushes me. "Well? Don't leave me hanging here, Gideon. You looked like you were going to tear off someone's head yesterday, and now you're telling me you two have come to an agreement. What happened?"

"I hate to admit it, but my brother brought everything to a head. If he hadn't pulled his usual bullshit with Aria, we wouldn't have had our discussion last night. I guess I have to thank Alex this time."

That makes her roll her eyes in disgust. "Don't say that. He shouldn't get any credit for anything after what he did with her. I swear he's worse than that private investigator of yours."

Her irritation with my brother for me makes me chuckle. "Feel free to call him what you want. No need to hold back. I hold no brotherly love for him."

"I would call him a pig, but I think he's worse than that. Why does he take every opportunity to make your life miserable? What did you ever do to him?"

With a shrug, I answer her truthfully. "I have no idea. I can't remember a time when my older brother didn't hate me. He's no better with my sister either, although I don't think he bothers much with Autumn anymore now that she's at school. You'd think being the favorite child of my father would make him happy."

Sasha levels her gaze on me and corrects my comment about Alex being my father's favorite before I can. "I've seen your father around Autumn, Gideon. Trust me. She has him wrapped around her finger. Alex might be his favorite son, but his favorite child is definitely your sister."

She's right. My father adores my younger sister.

"Where does that leave me? I'm like some bastard stepchild, it seems."

With a chuckle, she says, "Well, you always have your place as your mother's favorite. And don't bother arguing with me on that. Whenever your mother sees you, it's like she's seeing the sun rise for the first time. Take comfort in that, I guess."

"I guess."

I've had enough talking about my family. There's a good reason I like living here with them all living far enough away so I don't have to see them much.

"My guest is going to be here soon. I don't want to be interrupted while he and I are talking. I don't care who it is. No one is to bother us."

She nods and hands me a sheet of paper. "Got it. Interrupters will be shot on sight. After you're finished dealing with him, that's the list of events going on at the hotel today. We've got a wedding this afternoon, an engagement party tonight, and all of that is after the two groups that are using the grand ballroom and the secondary ballroom for their lunch meetings."

For a moment, I glance at the words, barely noting them before I set the paper on my desk in front of me. "You have all of this under control?"

Her face twists into a look of utter shock. "Really? How many years have I been handling all the events here at the hotel? I think I might be insulted, Gideon."

I know Sasha well enough to be sure she's not insulted, but I play her game anyway. "I'm sorry. What can I do to make it up to you? Would you like an extra day off this week? Tamsin wasn't so bad the last time you had a vacation day. I think I could muddle through without you for a single day."

A wicked smile brightens her face. "No. That's not what I want, and you know it."

Again with the Aria business. The two of them are nothing short of relentless.

"No, and I've told you to stop asking. You've even got her thinking you like her."

That makes her even happier. "Good! What did she say?"

"She said she doesn't want to have my assistant constantly hitting on her. That's what she said."

Twisting her face into a scowl, Sasha stands up to leave. "She didn't say that, and you know it. Just because you're jealous and don't want to let anyone even see her doesn't mean she feels the same. We could have a good time, you know. We have before."

I shake my head, wishing she'd stop. "No. Aria is different. She's not a plaything of mine. I care about her, so I want you to respect that."

Sasha's eyes open wide at my confession that I truly care for Aria. Other than with Gia, my assistant has never seen me care about anyone.

"Do you mean that? Are you in love with her?" she asks, nearly collapsing into the chair beside her.

There's no point in denying what she'll see with her own eyes in due course anyway. "Yes. I'm in love with her."

"And she said she's in love with you?"

I wish I could say yes, but I'm not going to lie to Sasha. "No, but now that I've given her some freedom and let her see I care about her, she'll come around. So no more hitting on her."

Quietly, my assistant says, "Okay. I won't do it anymore." She stops for a moment before adding, "I don't know what to feel about you being in love, Gideon. I've gotten used to you being the man you've been for all this time since Gia. Does this mean I'll have to find another job?"

Jesus, where the hell did that come from?

"No," I emphatically say, shaking my head. "Why would you ask that? What does you working as my assistant have to do with my being with Aria?"

She slowly stands up and sighs. "You may be in love, but you don't know a thing about women, Gideon. Aria isn't going to want me around. You and I are practically joined at the hip twenty-four seven. No woman will tolerate that. You and I weren't that close when you were with Gia. We're different now, but Aria's not going to want that in her life."

I wave away her concern for the ridiculous nonsense it is. "No, that's not going to happen. I can't run this hotel without you, so that settles that."

"You can, and you know it. You've just grown used to having me as your right hand," she says in a voice tinged with sadness.

I need to lighten the mood in here right now. "Of course I can, but then everyone would have to deal with me, and you and I both know that's never a good thing. I work best as a figurehead for this place. You're the face everyone wants to deal with."

As she walks toward the door, I hear her say, "That's not how love works. You're going to realize that soon."

Sasha seems particularly off today. She's crazy if she thinks anything has to change now that I'm with Aria. What's gotten into her?

I can't think about that right now. I need my head in the game for this meeting with Marcello Angeloni. There can be no chance he gets the upper hand on me today. If so, then I may have to admit to my father that my way of dealing with things didn't work this time.

For five minutes, I prepare myself for a meeting I can't be sure will be as cordial as our last encounter at the masquerade ball. This is no different than any other time I've had to handle things in my tenure here at the hotel.

Well, except for one big distinction. I've never met one-on-one alone with anyone who's sworn to kill anyone with my family name.

When Sasha opens my office door, I look up to see her escorting Marcello in. "Gideon, Mr. Angeloni is here for your meeting. Would you like me to bring in coffee for you two?"

The expression on my assistant's face tells me she's worried about what's about to happen, but I simply smile at her suggestion as I wave it away as unnecessary. "No, thank you. Close the door on your way out."

She gives me one last look to warn me about how uncomfortable she is about this meeting before turning to leave as Marcello walks toward the chairs in front of my desk. I extend my hand to shake his, choosing to make this as businesslike as possible.

At least to begin with. How it ends will depend on how he takes what I have to tell him.

"Thank you for agreeing to meet with me today, Marcello. Please sit down. Make yourself comfortable."

He gives me a smile that's little more than forcing the corners of his mouth up for a split second before unbuttoning his black suit jacket. Sitting down in the chair to the left, he shifts in his seat for a moment and then looks across my desk at me like he finally remembers he's supposed to be some kind of badass who plans to kill all my family, including me.

"Thank you, Gideon. I hope we can keep this meeting as cordial as we are now," he says, practically gritting his teeth.

I'm surprised at how little control he has over his emotions this morning. I expected him to act like he did at the ball the other night. Smooth. Poised. Masterful in handling the situation.

This man seems nothing like that one.

"I hope so too," I say with a lilt to my voice that should give him a clue I doubt the possibility of that actually happening.

He looks around my office and nods as if he

approves of what he sees. "I believe you and I have similar tastes. Your office reminds me of mine, or at least one I used to have before I came back here. Minimalist but opulent. I would love to know the name of your decorator. I have the chore of redoing my brother's office to my liking. As it is now, I can barely think in that room."

So we both have brothers who are unlike us. Good to know.

With a chuckle, I say, "I know I couldn't work in the place my brother calls an office. He's the king of chaos. Papers and nonsense everywhere. There's no order in that room."

Marcello smiles and nods in agreement. "Exactly. A place for everything and everything in its place. It's the way a man keeps his thinking clear and straight."

I silently admit that if this person hadn't threatened my life and the life of everyone with the last name Rule, I could see myself admiring him. He's not that different from me in many ways. I can appreciate that.

Unfortunately, that's not possible.

"Well, we might as well get down to business. As the representative of my family on this coast, I'm hoping you've changed your mind about wanting all of us dead. As I told you before, no Rule is responsible for the death of your brother. You have no fight with us concerning that. However, I'm here to tell you if you can't change your mind, the Rule family will not sit idly by waiting for you to follow through on your threat."

He takes a deep breath in and lets it out slowly through his nose before responding. I sense he's working hard to keep his calm. I plan to use that to my advantage.

Steepling his fingers in front of his face, he takes another deep breath and exhales before saying, "You see, Gideon, I have proof your family was behind my brother's murder. Your cousin was there at the villa the night of his killing. Lucius was planning on marrying your cousin's girlfriend, so you see, I simply cannot change my mind on what's going to have to happen to avenge my brother's death."

As I suspected, he didn't come here to actually talk about anything. Fine. If that's the way he wants to play this game, the time for being a gentleman is over.

"I know all of that, but I can tell you Alaric had nothing to do with what happened. Not that he didn't benefit from your brother's death, but he didn't kill Lucius. However, I see we're not going to be able to reconcile our differences on that point, so let's move on to something else."

Marcello shakes his head, clearly confused about what I mean. "Something else? What else is there to talk about? If you give up your cousin, I'm happy to let the rest of you Rules live in peace. That's my only offer."

It takes everything in me to not laugh in his face. Give up Alaric so this fuck can kill him? No, that's not going to happen. Not even if he was responsible for killing an Angeloni. Hell, not even if he was responsible for killing every fucking Angeloni but the one sitting in front of me.

I slide the manila envelope in front of me as I smile. "That's not going to happen. Alaric, like every other Rule, will not be paying the price for your brother's death. However, I have some things you might be interested in here today, so let's move on to those."

His gaze travels to the envelope in front of me, and as I slowly slide the pictures out, I see his eyes widen. Perhaps Cesare was wrong. Maybe he does know about his girlfriend's nocturnal visits to her older lover. Having to face that truth in front of a man he's vowed to kill isn't exactly something anyone wants to deal with.

I push the pictures across my desk toward him. "I believe you know this woman. You may even know what she does when you're not around. Now I'm happy to keep these pictures between us, assuming you come off your position regarding your threat against my family."

As he lifts them up and begins looking through them, I add, "But if you can't see your way to moving on and leaving my family alone, you should assume these will become public. I'd like you to consider how that's going to affect your ability to head your family's business on this coast."

His hands shake as he moves from picture to picture, but he doesn't say a word. When he finally gets through them all, he tosses them back onto my desk in clear disgust. This man has no ability to conceal his true feelings.

"That means nothing to me. If that's all you have, I'm afraid you underestimated me, Gideon Rule."

With a smile, I take out the smaller envelope from my coat pocket and set it down on the desk in front of me. So he doesn't mind being cuckolded and having the entire world know about it. Let's see how he feels about the other bit of dirt I possess on him.

"I would never underestimate you, Marcello. I make it a point to know everything there is to know about my enemies. The cheating girlfriend, while embarrassing for you, might not make it impossible for you to continue as the head of the Angeloni family. What I have in this envelope will, however. So this is your last chance. Forget about that threat of yours and agree with me that our two families can live in peace, or what I have here will be public by day's end and your time as the new head of your family and its business has an expiration date on it."

His face twists into an ugly grimace as he shakes his head far too fast to pretend like he has any control now. "What the fuck does that mean? I'm the head of my family because I'm the only Angeloni son left, thanks to your fucking cousin. Be careful, Rule. You're playing with fire here."

I take the papers out of the envelope and smooth the creases out before turning them toward him. As he begins to read the words, I say, "It's interesting the way our father's generation saw paternity, don't you think? I mean, I say I have only one brother and one sister, but the truth is my father has children scattered all around the world. That generation certainly liked to sow their wild oats. And then there's the idea of exactly what makes us who we are. Is it blood? Or is it simply calling two people our parents?"

I watch as Marcello's right hand closes into a fist so tight his knuckles turn white. I can only imagine how unsettling it is to find out your position in the world isn't what you've always believed it was.

He remains silent as he reads through what Cesare found out about his parentage and his illegitimate brother's that gives that man, not Marcello, the right to head the Angeloni family. When he finally lifts his gaze from the paper, his eyes are filled with rage enough that if I didn't know my security had already confiscated his gun on the way in, I'd be reaching for my own at this moment.

"This is bullshit. I don't know what you think this does, but it doesn't change anything. I will kill every Rule I can find to avenge my brother's death," he says through gritted teeth.

"I'm telling you right now, Marcello, walk away

from this fight. Not only will I make sure your father's bastard ruins your plans and possibly does what he has to in order to get you out of the picture, but the other members of my family are chomping at the bit to get their hands on you. A promise to live and let live on this coast is all you need give me, and I keep your secret forever and I make sure they find someone else to bother with. If not, then you're about to enter a world you won't survive. Trust me."

He stands up abruptly, throwing the papers across the desk at me. "Fuck you! The next time you see me, Rule, expect me to carry out my threat. The same goes for the rest of your fucking family. Marcello Angeloni will not be forced to take your deal out of fear."

I watch him storm out of my office and smile at how well that went. I hadn't expected to be able to unnerve him that easily. Reaching for my phone, I dial Cesare's number to set my plan in motion.

"Hey, boss. I just saw Angeloni walk out of your hotel, and he looks like someone just ruined his fucking day."

"Try his entire life. He doesn't want to play ball, so I don't have any choice. Make the photos of the girlfriend public, and find me the illegitimate brother."

"Got it!" my P.I. says with far more enthusiasm than usual. "Some people insist on looking a gift horse in the mouth, don't they?"

I sit back in my chair and smile. "That they do. I gave him a choice. He just made the wrong one. Now he's going to feel the pain that comes with it. Let me know when you find the brother."

"Will do."

This calls for a celebration. And I've got just the place for it.

CHAPTER EIGHTEEN

ideon

ARIA LOOKS AROUND MY VILLA LIKE SHE'S impressed, something that makes me happy. Her eyes wide, she studies every inch of the space as I take her on a tour of the place I've just finished having redesigned. From top to bottom, it's been changed from old and outdated to exactly the kind of home I want. Sleek and modern now, this villa is everything the penthouse is and more, and even better, it's far more private and lets me escape the hotel for a while whenever I come here.

"This is beautiful, Gideon," she says as she swivels

her head to look around one more time. "Is this place yours?"

"Yes," I say with pride.

She turns to face me looking so serious. "Then why don't you live here? It's not like the commute to work would be that long. It's not even five minutes away from the hotel."

"It had to be gutted and redesigned. I can live here now."

"Are you going to?"

The difference between can and will is vast in this case. I've gotten used to being at the hotel in case there are any problems I need to handle, but the truth is Sasha can take care of most things. There's no reason I shouldn't move to this villa.

"I don't know. Do you like it?" I ask, searching her eyes for the answer before she gives it.

Confusion settles into her beautiful face, and she scrunches up her expression. "I don't understand."

"I have to consider what you want now, Aria. You live with me. So do you like it, or do you like the penthouse more?"

Aria steps back as her mouth drops open. "I don't know. I don't think I want to be the one who takes you away from your hotel. You love it there."

Sliding my arm around her waist, I pull her to me. "I love being with you. The hotel can do with less of me being there. If you like this place, we'll stay here. If not, we'll stay at the penthouse."

She stares into my eyes and smiles. "Okay, I think I know the only question to ask. Why did you have this villa remodeled?"

I answer her truthfully. "Because it was out of date and needed it. I bought it knowing that and when the opportunity came to have the designer work on it earlier this summer, I took advantage of it."

With a sigh, she shakes her head. "Not the answer I was expecting. Okay, how about this? Did you intend on fixing it exactly as you like and then selling it or living here?"

Now I see where she's going with this. She doesn't want to be the reason I leave my home to live here. What she doesn't understand is I don't care where I live if I'm with her. Penthouse or villa, it doesn't mean a thing to me.

"I planned on living here, although I didn't have a definite date for when I'd move in. To be honest, I didn't think about it much at all."

She loosens my tie and slides it from around my neck as she thinks about all I've said. "Well, it is brand new inside and out, right?"

Smiling, I nod. "Yes."

"And if you don't live here, it's just going to sit empty until you sell it, right?"

"Yes."

"Then I guess you should live here." She suddenly opens her eyes wide and adds, "Who's going to live in the penthouse if you aren't there?"

I hadn't thought about that. With a shrug, I say, "I don't know. I can rent it out to someone who wants to live at the hotel or use it like another suite, just better."

Again, she appears to consider this like all the other information she's gotten in the past few minutes, almost as if it's an important decision. Finally, she says, "I say you should live here."

"We should live here," I correct her.

"Okay. We should live here. But only if our deal from before stands. I don't want to be stuck here all alone while you're at the hotel and not be able to leave the house. If that's the case, I vote to stay at the penthouse."

As I cradle her face in my hands, I kiss her lips and smile. "Our deal stands if we live here. I'll just have to make sure one of my guards is available at all times so you can leave whenever you want to."

That brings a big smile to her face. "Thank you, Gideon."

"Let's go into the dining room. It's time for dinner," I say as I guide her back through the house to where two waiters will serve our meal cooked especially for us by the hotel's chef.

When she sees the two men dressed in their black uniforms just like at the hotel, she spins around to face me, her eyes wide in amazement. "You had waiters come here to serve us?"

"And the chef made our meal just like back at the

penthouse," I answer with a smile, loving how happy she looks that I made such a small effort.

She deserves so much more than she ever expects. I need to make her see that.

I pull out her chair for her, eager to begin giving her all she should have in life. "My lady."

When she looks at me and bites her lip like she loves this, I can't help but feel like we're finally making progress. Tonight we'll have a wonderful dinner and drinks, and she'll see what having a man like me loving her means.

AFTER THE WAITERS TAKE AWAY THE LAST OF THE dishes from dessert, I give them something extra they appreciate and send them on their way so Aria and I can be alone. She looks beautiful tonight, but more than sex, I want us to talk. So much of our time together has been focused on our physical attraction, so tonight's a chance to share an emotional connection.

"What do you want to do now?" Aria asks with a sparkle in her eye.

"I thought we'd talk. Let's go out onto the terrace and sit down," I say as I take her hand to lead her outside. "It's all brand new out there. The original villa only had a tiny little balcony, but I had them build a terrace for me."

As we step out through the French doors, I hear Aria gasp. "It's gorgeous, Gideon! I think it's even more beautiful here than at the penthouse. I like looking out over the water, but this gives you a view of the entire area. Look at all the lights up and down the coast."

She points toward them, and I can't help but love how excited she is. "It's an incredible view. I'm happy you like it."

Aria throws her arms around my neck. "I love it!"

I pull her close to me and hold her in my arms as we look out over the Amalfi Coast. It's never appeared as beautiful to me as it does at this very moment with the sun setting and night falling so the lights reflect off the water.

After a little while, she says, "What did you want to talk about?"

I sense the worry under her words, so I quickly move to show her it's nothing bad. I just want us to share something other than our bodies.

"Don't worry. It's nothing to be concerned about. I just wanted to talk so we can find out more about one another."

She slowly turns in my hold and stares into my eyes. "What do you want to know about me?"

My gaze drifts over her beautiful face before I answer, "Everything. I want to know what you love. What you hate. What makes you happy. What makes you sad. Everything."

Aria doesn't say a word but continues looking into my eyes as if she isn't sure she should believe me when

I say I want to know about her. Maybe the men she's been with before me didn't give a damn about who she was when she wasn't naked, but I do.

"You do love me, don't you?" she asks, her voice full of disbelief.

"I do, and I want to know everything about the woman I love."

That finally seems to convince her that I truly want to hear about who she really is, so she takes a deep breath and lets it out in a rush before she begins. "Well, my favorite color is blue. I love the water, but I hate boats. They scare me."

I can't help but smile at how sweet she sounds. "Why?"

With a shake of her head, she says, "I don't know. Maybe in a past life I was thrown off a boat and drowned. I don't know. I've only been on a few in my lifetime, and I've never been in danger. All I know is every second I was on them, I hated it."

"Okay. No boats for Aria."

"I love cake, especially lemon and blueberry cake. I wanted to be a vegetarian a few years ago, but I found out I liked steak too much, so that went out the window. I've always been tall. All the boys at school made fun of me until high school because I was taller than them."

Although I have a sense I know the answer to my question, I ask it anyway. "What happened in high school to change things around?"

She smiles, but this time it's a wicked grin. "They caught up to me so I wasn't taller than them anymore."

"How tall are you?" I ask, guessing she's got to be nearly six foot.

"Six-one. And before you ask, no, I never played basketball."

The defensiveness in her voice tells me she still feels insecure about being that tall in a world full of women who are usually half a foot shorter than her. She doesn't have to be uncomfortable around me, though. At six-four, I still have three inches on her.

"I wasn't going to ask that. I like how tall you are. I tower over most women, but not you. Three inches is nothing. I don't have to slump when I'm with you. I like that."

Her expression lights up. Her ex, that toady of Marcello's, stands about five ten, I bet. It was nothing for me to look down on him, so I guess he doesn't even reach six foot. She probably intimidated him because of her height.

"Most men don't like really tall women like me. Or the ones who do have some kind of weird fetish. I met this guy once who—"

She stops talking and looks away. "You probably don't want to hear about that. Sorry."

But I gently take her chin between my fingers and pull her face back toward me. "Nonsense. I want to hear everything. What did he do?"

"He asked me out, and I thought we were going to

go out on a date, but instead, all he wanted me to do was pose for his sculptures. No dinner. Nothing. Just me standing still for hours while he chiseled away. Let's say that didn't go on for more than one night."

I kiss her on the forehead and smile against her warm skin. "At least he didn't just want you for sex. That's something, right?"

Aria sighs. "There's something called a happy medium, Gideon. A woman doesn't want to be just an object to a man. Not a sex object or an art project."

Something in the way she says that tells me she's including me in the group of men she's met who don't seem to have a happy medium. She wouldn't be wrong. I went from not touching her for weeks to professing my love for her, but it wasn't as fast as it seemed. I just didn't tell her all the times I was feeling something in those weeks.

"So now it's your turn. Tell me about you. Like why you're not happily married with children?"

With a chuckle, I say, "I guess we're jumping in the deep end to start. I'm not married because I've been committed to my job more than I wanted to be to a woman. As for kids, I'd like them someday. I just don't think now is the time, but someday."

Aria scans my face for a long moment, practically glaring at me, before she says, "I'm guessing you're just assuming I want kids."

It hadn't occurred to me she would want them or not. I hadn't gotten that far with my fantasy about our future life together, but since she said that like kids are the last thing she could ever want, I'm curious.

"No. Do you, though? I'm not talking about double digit numbers. But do you like children?"

As if someone turned a light on inside her, she smiles broadly and nods. "I love children! I don't know if I want double digit numbers, but I think a few would be wonderful. At least a boy and a girl to have one of each."

"I think that's what my parents said until they had my brother and me. Then I think they decided they needed to try until they had a girl. Thankfully, it happened on the first try and my sister Autumn came along. I can't imagine having a long line of brothers behind me until they finally got a daughter."

"I hope that's not what my parents did, or they were sadly disappointed because all they got were my four sisters and me. Not a boy to be found in the bunch. My father was definitely outnumbered by females in my house growing up."

It takes me a second, but I realize I know nothing about Aria's family. "Four sisters? Where are they? Do your parents live here on the coast?"

She smiles like my assumption is the silliest thing she's ever heard. "No. You don't think I'm Italian, do you?"

I had wondered about the lack of any accent, but I never put much thought into why that was. "Yeah, I thought so. You do live here. You look like many

Italian women do. I guess I just naturally assumed you were originally from here."

Shaking her head, she says, "No, I'm from upstate New York. My father runs an antique business, so he comes to Italy often. My parents bought a house here, and I came over after I graduated from high school. It was only supposed to be a gap year, but it turned into six. My sisters all live back in the States. All of them are married with kids. I'm the only one who my mother says doesn't seem to want to settle down."

Now that she's told me where she's from, I can't help but ask how she ended up with that asshole Franco. I don't know if I actually want to know the details, but I sense there's a story there.

"So did you meet your ex when you came over here right after high school?" I ask, refusing to use his name.

"Franco? No. I met him last year. Let's just say that my time here in Italy hasn't been all positive. I got into some tight situations, and I found myself with him one night. That turned into eight months, until you came along."

I want to know what that means—tight situations —but I don't ask. That can be for another time. I'm just happy to hear she wasn't with him for long.

We fall silent because all I can think of is taking her from him, but finally Aria pulls me out of my thoughts. "Gideon, I'm worried he's going to retaliate. I mean, I don't think he loved me, and I didn't love him, but he's a possessive man. I don't think he's going to just let you take me away without trying to do something in return."

She acts as if I didn't pay him handsomely for taking her off his hands. There's no reason for him to retaliate. I didn't steal her away. I offered him money for her, and he took it. The transaction is complete. He got what he wanted, and I got what I wanted.

I caress her cheek hoping to find a smile for me, but still she remains worried. "Don't worry. Trust me. Whatever he thinks he's going to do isn't going to happen. I won't let it."

Aria relaxes against my body and quietly asks, "Can I trust you, Gideon?"

Tilting her head back, I look deep into her eyes. "Yes. I swear you can trust me, Aria. Don't ever think I'd let anything hurt you."

That's enough to make her smile. She can trust me. Whatever Franco has up his sleeve, he won't hurt her again. That's a promise I can keep.

CHAPTER NINETEEN

ria

AFTER OUR TIME AT HIS VILLA, ALL I CAN THINK IS being back at the penthouse feels like a downgrade. Yes, it's a gorgeous place with stunning views, but the villa has a warmer, more welcoming feeling to it that I like having around me.

It feels like a home.

My mind wanders as the thought of it being our home fills my head. I shouldn't think like that. Yes, Gideon told me he loved me, but I'm still not sure he's not seeing me and thinking of the love he had for Gia. I don't want to let myself fall into the trap of thinking another man truly cares when he doesn't.

For now, I just need to enjoy the fact that I have

somewhere safe to stay far away from Franco and I'm with someone I like. That's a lie, though. I don't just like Gideon. How could I? He's taken care of me and protected me just like he promised, and in return, he rocks my world in bed every time. I couldn't just like him, even if I wanted to.

"Aria? Where are you?" he calls out from the bedroom.

I look back inside and yell back, "I'm out on the terrace."

"Come in here! I want to tell you something."

Ooooh, maybe he has another surprise for me.

I hurry inside to find him only half-dressed, even though it's after eight in the morning already. Still naked from the waist up, he looks so sexy standing there next to the bed.

"What is it?" I ask, even as I can't think of anything but how much I wish he didn't have to get dressed and leave for work.

We could have a good time during the day too. I think today would be a perfect time to prove me right on that.

"I'd like you to do me a favor today," he says with such sweet sincerity that I can't help but smile.

"A favor? Like what?"

"I'd like you to go shopping. I think the villa needs something, a special touch that's missing. Not that my designer didn't do exactly what I wanted, but when we were there, all I could think was it needed something else."

Confused, I ask, "Like what?"

Gideon shrugs as he reaches into the closet for a dress shirt to wear to work today. "A vase? Maybe something like that or something for the kitchen. It did feel a little sterile in there without much in the way of decoration. You decide. I want it to be something you like."

"What would you like me to spend?"

While he slides into his shirt and begins buttoning it, he points toward the bed. I look down to see a credit card sitting there on top of the sheets.

"Use that card and price is no object. If it makes you happy, then it's not too expensive."

I repeat what he said, surprised to hear money doesn't matter. "Price is no object? What if you don't like what I buy? Then I bet price will be an issue."

He grabs a tie and walks toward me as he slides it around his neck. Giving me a tiny kiss on the tip of my nose, he says, "No, it won't be. Whatever you buy, I'll be happy if you're happy."

"Even if I buy one of those long-faced boob pictures like in your gallery?" I tease.

He sweetly smiles and nods at my joke. "Even if you buy one of those, although I know you don't like that artist's style."

"I just don't want you to hate whatever it is I buy. It's your villa. Maybe you should buy it."

Shaking his head, he levels his gaze on me like what he's about to say is important. "Aria, I trust you. I want you to be happy at the villa, and right now, it's all my style. So go buy something that you love."

He kisses me and then begins walking out toward the front door as he fixes his tie. Still unsure what he wants me to buy, I say, "You know, you made it seem like you were a bad man when I first got here. I'm pretty sure bad men don't hand a woman their credit card and tell her to buy something for herself."

Gideon stops right before he reaches the door and looks back at me. With a devilish smile, he says, "I am a bad man. Just not with you. Raphael will be waiting to escort you wherever you need to go today. I can't wait to see what you buy."

As the door closes behind him, I don't know what he means about being a bad man. So far, other than keeping me here under that stoic guard who rarely speaks to me, Gideon has been more thoughtful than most men I've met.

But that only means I need to be on my guard because if experience has told me anything, it's that even good men do bad things that can hurt you.

AFTER AN ENTIRE DAY'S SHOPPING AT EIGHT STORES and approximately ten words spoken between Raphael and me, I return with a sculpture of a woman carrying a vase I found in a little artist's boutique tucked away on a side street. Made of black marble, it cost far more than I would have ever considered paying for any one piece of art, but Gideon did say price was no object, and as soon as I laid eyes on it, I knew it would look great in the villa's main room.

I set it down on the table behind the sofa and instantly wonder if he's going to be disappointed I didn't buy anything for the kitchen. He's right that it's quite sterile. All white with black accents and stainless-steel appliances looks modern, but it creates a cold feeling.

Maybe I should have gotten a red or yellow piece for that room instead.

Today felt so great, though, so I can't let myself worry about not getting something for the kitchen. Even though I had to spend it with Raphael, who always does a bang-up job pretending to be mute around me, I enjoyed being able to walk around freely and visit whatever stores I wanted to.

And yes, I liked having the protection of a bodyguard to make sure Franco or one of his friends didn't jump out from out of nowhere and grab me. Even if Raphael didn't speak two sentences to me.

Behind me, the front door opens, and the look on Gideon's face is one of pure joy. I don't think I've seen him this happy in all the time I've been here.

"I saw you and Raphael walk through the lobby and wanted to come up to see what you bought," he says, looking around the living room to locate my new purchase.

Stepping to the side, I reveal the black marble sculpture and watch as he nods his approval. "Do you like it? I didn't get anything for the kitchen that would brighten it up, but I can go back out tomorrow, if you want. Or I can go now, assuming Raphael doesn't have an issue with that."

Gideon takes me in his arms and kisses me like he hasn't seen me in days. "First of all, Raphael has nothing to do other than protect you. That means if you go somewhere, he goes. More importantly, I love what you bought. Where do you think we should put it in the villa?"

Thrilled he approves of the sculpture, I say, "I thought in the main room right over near the doorway out to the terrace. I think it would look great there."

"Then that's where we'll put it. If you want to go back out tomorrow for something to brighten up the kitchen, that's okay too. Keep the card just in case."

Unsure if what I bought or something else has put him in a great mood, I ask, "Did work go especially well today? You seem very happy about something."

He shakes his head as his excitement dims just a little. "Actually, work was work. Nothing good or bad. Just work. I'm happy because you bought exactly what you wanted. I assume there were no issues with Raphael. I didn't ask him how it went today on my way in, but since he didn't say anything, I'm guessing you two got along fine?"

I can't help but roll my eyes. "He didn't say anything because I think he's just like that woman with the vase sculpture. I think she'd say more if she had the chance. I don't think he spoke ten words to me the entire day. It was like having a statue walk around with me for all those hours."

"Raphael does as he's told. He's not supposed to chit chat with you all day," Gideon says with a grin. "I might get jealous if he did."

Surprised to hear him say anything like that, I glance at the door where I know Raphael is standing on the other side and then back at Gideon. "He's not my type. You know how much I hate the silent treatment, don't you? Anyway, I don't think he likes me, to be honest."

"I don't care what he thinks of you. All I need him to do is keep you safe, which he did, so for that he gets to keep his job. You seem to have had a good time despite not having anyone to talk with. Did you see anything else you want to buy?"

"Are you kidding? I saw dozens of things, but you said to buy one thing, so one was all I got."

Gideon takes my face in his hands and presses his forehead to mine. "The next time you go out shopping, feel free to buy whatever you want. I mean it. If you want it, it's yours."

"Really?"

He leans back and nods. "Yes, really. If it makes you happy, then I want you to have it."

"And price is no object?" I ask, sure this time he'll tell me to keep it to a certain amount. He's wealthy, but I can't imagine he wants me blowing his money all over town.

"No object. The only thing that matters to me is you're happy."

This feels too good to be true, but I don't want to ask if it is and hurt his feelings. He's been so kind these past few days that I might ruin things between us if I let him know I doubt his generosity.

It's just that I've never known anyone to give something for nothing.

"I have another surprise for you tonight. Don't ask because I don't want to give it away yet. Just know that I think you'll like it."

He walks toward the bedroom as he undresses out of his work clothes. Following him, I say, "Another surprise? Is it dinner again? I loved that shrimp dish the chef made yesterday."

Looking back at me, Gideon smiles. "Then I'll have him make it again tomorrow night. But that's not my surprise. Now no more asking."

I pout, hating how he won't let me guess anymore. His surprises have been pretty great, so it's not that I'm worried that he's suddenly going to want to dangle me off the edge of the terrace or parade me through the lobby in just my underwear. It's just that sometimes surprises don't turn out to be what you expect.

DINNER WAS DELICIOUS, AS ALWAYS. THE CHEF AT Villa Aurelia never makes a bad meal, and tonight's was a particularly good osso buco. I hadn't expected the dessert of lemon ricotta cake too, but it seems that Gideon wanted to go all out tonight.

"So are you going to give me my surprise now?" I ask, sure I sound like a seven-year-old child on Christmas morning but not caring.

He shakes his head and opens his mouth to say something, but his phone interrupts us. Looking down at the screen, he frowns. "I have to go downstairs for a few minutes. When I get back, we'll get this night going."

"Will you have my surprise with you when you come back?"

Gideon stands from the table and leans down to kiss me. "No, but don't worry. It will happen. In the meantime, why don't you take a bubble bath and I'll join you when I return?"

I can't say no to a bubble bath, and the addition of Gideon to it makes it sound like the perfect way to start our evening. "Okay. I'll be waiting for you in the bathroom. Don't be long. You wouldn't want all the bubbles to disappear."

That gets me a smile that makes Gideon look even

sexier than usual. Maybe he likes bubble baths. Who knew?

Ten minutes later, I'm relaxing in the tub with bubbles and water up to my shoulders. My bathmate is nowhere in sight, though. Closing my eyes, I slip down into the water until the water comes right up to my chin. I take a deep breath in and let it out slowly, loving how calm I feel.

The bathroom door opens, and I turn to see Gideon standing beside the tub with something in his hand. "Is that my surprise?"

He tilts his head left and right. "Part of it."

Sitting up out of the water, I reach for whatever it is, but he yanks his hand away. "Not until you get out and dry off."

I don't attempt to hide my disappointment he didn't join me in our bubble bath, pouting up at him. "I thought you would come in and we could take a bath together."

"Change of plans. Now come on. Get out and dry off so we can get our night going," he says with more than a hint of impatience to his voice.

Still curious about what he's holding, I crane my neck to get a look at it, but he leaves before I can see much. It's black. That I know. It looked like it had a sheen to it of some kind.

As I step out and grab the towel to dry off, my mind races through the possibilities of what it can be. It's not a jewelry box. It seemed too soft for that. It's not clothing since it sat in the palm of his hand. Maybe lingerie?

My heart races at the thought that he bought me a black silk teddy. Oooh, I like this Gideon.

By the time I get back out to the bedroom, I'm convinced I'll see a new piece of lingerie waiting for me on the bed, but there's nothing there. Not even Gideon is there.

Looking around, I wonder aloud, "Was I supposed to do something that you didn't tell me about? Where are you?"

From the living room, he says, "I'm out here."

"Am I supposed to wear something, or can I be in my yoga pants and a T-shirt?" I ask, growing more confused about this surprise by the second.

"Stay in the towel and come out here to join me," he says, showing that impatience once more.

I walk out to see him sitting on the sofa with two drinks on the coffee table in front of him. "I got a red wine for you and a scotch for me. If you want something else, just let me know."

Still dressed in his suit pants and dress shirt he had to put back on when he got that call, Gideon pats the cushion next to him and smiles. "Come. Sit next to me."

I do as he says, even more confused than before. "So I'm going to be wearing a towel for this surprise, and you're going to be wearing your work clothes? I don't understand."

He doesn't respond to my question, and instead, turns around toward the arm of the sofa. "Close your eyes."

Oooh, now I'm getting my surprise!

With my eyes closed, I feel Gideon move behind me. His hands cup my shoulders as he kisses down the back of my neck and down my spine to just above my ribs. Every brush of his lips against my skin sets me on fire, and it takes everything in me not to disobey and turn around to kiss him.

"Mmmm...Gideon, you're driving me crazy! Can I open my eyes now?" I ask, practically pleading with him to give me some relief.

"No, keep them closed," he scolds. "No looking."

"No fair."

He continues to kiss all across my shoulders and neck until he sits up behind me and wraps his arms around me. A second later, he undoes the knot in the towel so it falls away from my body, leaving me naked and craving more of his touch.

"Are your eyes closed, Aria?"

"Yes."

"Good. Now keep them closed when I put this on you," he whispers in my ear as I feel him begin to tie a blindfold around my head.

So that's what the silky black thing in his hand was. The idea of what may happen next now that my eyes are covered excites and thrills me. I had no idea Gideon liked this kind of thing.

When he finishes, the cushion shifts and I feel him get up from the sofa. I reach out, but he's not close enough for me to touch. I feel vulnerable, like anything could happen right now and I won't know it until it's too late.

"Gideon, where are you?"

"Right here," he answers in a low voice that hits me deep inside. "I wouldn't leave you here alone."

I turn my head toward the sound of his voice, a useless gesture since I can't see through this blindfold. "Where? I can't see you."

His hand touches my cheek, and I lean my head into his palm. "Don't worry. I'm right here."

"What are you doing? Why am I sitting here naked and blindfolded?"

Gideon doesn't answer immediately, making me wonder why he isn't talking. "What's going on? I think you're scaring me."

Without saying a word, he presses his mouth to mine and kisses me, and instantly, all my fears melt away. I'm so needy right now I can barely stand it when he pulls away.

"Gideon, is the blindfold my surprise?" I ask, desperate to know something about what he's doing.

"Part of it. Now sit back and open your legs."

Excitement rushes through me, and I immediately lean back against the sofa cushions and spread my legs. I feel him sit in between them and jump a little when his fingers graze the insides of my thighs.

"Now be a good girl and enjoy yourself," he says just before he kisses the spot on the side of my knee.

"Does that mean I can't talk?" I ask, unsure how he wants me to act during this.

His lips leave my leg for a moment before he answers, "No. Feel free to talk all you want. I want you to feel good, Aria, so you might not have time to talk."

He settles in between my legs and opens me up so every inch of my pussy is visible to him. I feel my face grow hot from a blush, which seems silly after all we've done together, but this is the first time he's ever blindfolded me during sex.

The initial touch of his tongue to my body makes me jump again, but it doesn't take long before I'm in utter heaven as he devours me. He slides a single finger inside me that's immediately joined by another as his mouth sucks gently on my clit. It's almost too much to bear, but at the same time, I don't ever want this feeling to end.

"Oooooh, God...Gideon, I'm going to come," I moan as my hands search for his head.

The first touch of my fingers to his hair grounds me, and I revel in how soft it is as I try to put off the orgasm that's about to rush over me. I want this to last longer, but with every lash of his tongue against my pussy and every thrust of his fingers inside me, that grows more and more impossible.

Finally, I can't hold it off anymore and I cry out as

my release tears through my body. I hold Gideon's head to me, riding his mouth like it's the only thing in the world I want right now. His fingers pump into me, fucking me hard through my orgasm. I tighten my hold on his hair to keep him from moving, but he lifts his head, leaving me with only the aftershocks pulsating through my body.

He doesn't speak but kisses me deeply so I taste myself on his lips. It's erotic and sensual, just like him, and I reach out to feel for his cock.

It's rock hard and warm against my palm. I stroke up and down and hear him moan. Sitting up, I open my lips to take him inside my mouth, but he stops me.

"I have something else in mind," he says, and a moment later I feel the sofa move again as he sits down next to me.

"Oh? Like what?" I ask.

My question is answered quickly when he lifts me up and sets me down on his lap. I'm facing the wrong way, though. I can tell because my hands come to rest on his thighs, not his shoulders.

"Gideon? Why did you turn me this way?"

Behind me, he softly presses kisses up and down my back as his hands knead my breasts and pinch my nipples. "This is the way I want you."

He grabs my hips and lifts me off him, and a second later, he lowers me back down and I feel his cock enter me. Instantly, he thrusts into my body, filling me completely. This is an entirely new experience for me, and the angle of his cock pressing against a spot inside me makes my eyes roll back in my head from how good it feels.

I tilt my hips to get more of that sensation, and Gideon pushes his hips hard, ramming his cock into me. He's far rougher than usual, but it feels so fucking good I don't care.

"Ride that cock, baby," he moans behind me, and that's all I need.

Just as he orders, I roll my hips again and begin riding his cock. His hands on my sides keep the pace, making me go much slower than I want to. I open my mouth to complain that both of us would be happier if he'd just let me go, but then I feel his fingers touching around my ass.

A second later, he slides his thumb into my asshole and my mouth falls open. Never before has anything made me feel so good as I do right now. I want to beg for more, but I can't because it's like I've forgotten how to speak.

"Do you trust me, Aria?" he says in a low voice behind me.

"Mmmm…that seems to be a question you should have asked before you stuck a finger in my ass, no?" I answer as I continue to ride his cock.

"I mean it. Do you trust me?" he asks as the slowly slides his thumb back inside me.

Nodding, I moan, "Yes. Yes, I trust you. Oh, God…"

I feel him slide his finger out of my ass and then sit up close behind me. His lips against my shoulder, he whispers against my skin, "Good. Now enjoy yourself."

His words make sense but seem odd for some reason. I have a feeling there's something different about him, but I don't know what.

Then I feel another pair of hands touch my thighs. I reach for my blindfold so I can see what's happening, but Gideon holds my wrists tightly so I can't remove it.

"Whose hands are those, Gideon?" I ask, suddenly afraid.

Someone other than him answers my question. "You are as perfect as I imagined from the moment I met you."

CHAPTER TWENTY

ria

EVERY INCH OF MY BODY FREEZES WHEN I HEAR that voice. I tug against Gideon's hold on my arms, frantic to have control of my hands.

"It's okay, Aria. You trust me, don't you?" he asks in a voice so sweet and caring that I have a hard time reconciling how scared I feel right now with how much I want to believe I'm safe with him.

"Gideon?"

That's the only word I can get out as the uninvited guest softly touches my face. "Not to worry. I promise you're going to love this, Aria."

I shake my head, unsure of how to feel or what I

want to say. Why did he let Sasha in knowing what we were doing?

"No," I whisper, my voice shaking. "I can't."

"Shhhh…Gideon has you, and he won't let go. I'm not here to do anything you won't love," she says in a sultry voice that drapes over me like silk.

I once more tug against his hold, and this time, he lets my wrists go free. But as much as I want to rip off this blindfold, I can't.

This is too much. Gideon is still inside me, and the feel of Sasha softly running her fingertips over my thighs is overwhelming.

"No…" I whimper when she cradles my face in her soft hands.

"Is that what you really want, Aria?" she asks, and even though I know I should say yes, I can't.

"Enjoy this," she whispers against my lips. "I know I will."

And before I can say a word, she kisses me and it's like all the air leaves my body. I search for Gideon's hands to keep me grounded because if I don't, I worry I might float away on this feeling of ecstasy that's coursing through me right now.

Behind me, Gideon whispers against my neck, "I'm here with you, baby. Hold on and enjoy the ride."

Part of me wants to scream because I'm so untethered right now. I want to tell both of them I can't do this. I don't want to. I've never done anything like this, and it's clear they have, which terrifies me.

Even worse, it's obvious that Sasha knew to come here tonight. Why would Gideon do this and not tell me? Did he think I want her?

But then there's another part of me that can't deny how turned on I am at this moment. As Sasha's hands roam over my breasts and stomach and she coos like she's loving every second of touching me, Gideon slowly fucks me, his thrusts punctuating every brush of her fingertips on my skin.

I open my mouth to tell them to stop when all of a sudden I feel the first hint of what she's going to do to me. Her warmth breath tickles the tender skin between my legs before a second later I feel her tongue flick against my clit. Behind this mask, it's like fireworks explode in front of my eyes. Gideon has his hands on my waist and he's moving me up and down on his cock, and Sasha has her lips pressed against my pussy, sucking gently and sending ribbons of need racing through me.

A tiny mewing moan escapes from my throat when she sucks my clit into her mouth, and I know it won't be long before I come. I can't handle the overload of sensuality. It's too much. Thoughts of what will happen next fill my head, frightening me.

Will Gideon then have sex with Sasha because I came too fast? Have they been together the whole time? Is that why he's invited her here to join us tonight?

I feel for his hands on my waist and press down on

them, needing some reassurance. Swiveling my head to the right, I search for his mouth to kiss. Even without speaking a word, he answers my silent prayer, pressing his lips to mine. Instantly, I'm calm, even as the rest of my body feels like it's going to explode.

He softly kisses the blindfold over my eyes and says, "Don't hold back. Let yourself go, Aria."

A tiny sob comes out of me against his mouth, and then a moment later, my body comes apart because of his cock fucking me and Sasha's mouth eating my pussy. He pounds into me as my orgasm makes me feel like I'm soaring through the air.

Every single sensation feels like it's magnified. His hands on my hips pushing me up and down on his cock. Sasha's exquisitely soft tongue lashing my clit. My pussy pulsating as my release intensifies.

My mouth is parched from breathing heavily, and even though I feel like I'm flying, my limbs feel heavy. I want this to be over, but I never want this experience to end.

Sasha slides her hands down my trembling thighs before pressing a kiss to the inside of my knee. I feel her stand in between my legs, and then her mouth is on mine in a kiss that takes my breath away again.

"Thank you, Aria. You are as sweet as I imagined you were in my fantasies."

When she pulls away, my head lolls backwards onto Gideon's shoulder. His arms tighten around me as he continues to thrust up into my body. In all that happened, I didn't realize he hadn't come yet, but I sense he's close.

"I'll leave you two to it," Sasha says as he begins to fuck me in earnest, as desperate to come as I was a minute ago.

His hand finds my neck and encircles it, arousing me against my will. I want to be angry with him. I want to scream that he shouldn't have let her be with us like that.

But all I can do is ride his cock as a second orgasm rushes through me, taking me by surprise. My entire body shakes, and this time, Gideon's follows almost immediately. He floods me with cum, so much that I feel it trail down toward my ass.

He doesn't say anything but moans low and deep as he grunts through the final push into my body. I'm exhausted, my body overwhelmed by too much sensation at once, and when he stills inside me, I climb off him and rip off the blindfold.

As always, Gideon looks beautiful sitting there all satisfied after coming. I can't focus on that though because I'm so angry.

"Why would you do that to me?" I ask, barely containing the tears that want to escape.

He trains his dark eyes on me, and in them I see hurt. How dare he look at me like I've done something to hurt him? I didn't bring Sasha here without telling him. He did that to me!

"Did you two have fun ganging up on me like

that? I bet you spent all day in your goddamned office planning it. Sasha wanted me, so you gave her what she wanted on a silver platter. Did you ever think to ask me if I wanted a threesome with her? No, because you wanted it. Why do you even fucking bother with me? You have her. What do you need me for?"

Gideon winces like he's in pain at hearing all I'm saying. He doesn't answer a single one of my questions, but of course he doesn't. What else is new?

I throw the black silk blindfold at him and sob, "I hate you, Gideon Rule!"

God, I can't stay here. I feel stupid and used, like a plaything he and his assistant decided they wanted to enjoy together.

Still naked, I run into the bedroom and dress quickly, needing to get the hell away from him right now. When I walk back out to the living room, he's still sitting on the sofa, and I swear that look of hurt still fills his eyes.

As if I've done anything to him.

I walk past him on my way to the door and hear him finally speak. "Where are you going?"

The words sound like someone's choking them out of him. Spinning around, I snap, "I need to get away from this penthouse right now. I can still walk around the hotel without being watched or guarded, can't I?"

Gideon winces again and simply nods. Turning on my heel, I march toward the door. I want to say something clever that will make him understand just how terrible I feel right now, but I have no words. My heart is broken. Everything I've feared about Sasha has come true.

He cares about her. If he didn't, he wouldn't have let her come here tonight. She asked, and he gave her what she wanted. It doesn't matter that it was me. He wanted her to be happy.

And as for me and my happiness? I don't think either ever occurred to him the entire time he was planning to give his precious assistant what she's wanted all along.

I fling the front door open and see Raphael standing there doing his usual interpretation of a statue. God, I hate him too!

"Do not follow me. I don't have to have a guard when I'm in this hotel, so stay right there and do your statue imitation."

He doesn't move, thankfully, since I likely couldn't do a damn thing if he did decide to come with me. The man is a fucking giant wall of muscles. All I'd be able to do is grumble about how much I hate him as we traveled down to the lobby.

When the elevator doors open, I step out and instantly look for Sasha. I have a few words to say to that bitch too. Unfortunately, she's nowhere to be found.

Probably insinuating herself in another happy couple's sex tonight.

I make a beeline to the terrace where dozens of

people sit enjoying themselves on a warm September night on the Amalfi Coast as I chastise myself for even using the word happy to describe Gideon and me. Happy? I need to stop being stupid. We were never happy. I may have been for a short while because I thought he truly cared about me, but Gideon never was.

All he was doing was biding his time before he could have his favorite girl join us and humiliate me. Talk about killing two birds with one stone.

Looking around at the tables of happy people on dates or celebrating special occasions, I see the steps leading down to the main road just outside the hotel. Is it possible no one is guarding them, and I could simply walk away, never to look back at this hotel or the man who runs it ever again?

I take a step toward freedom and then another, expecting someone to appear who will drag me back to the penthouse. But no one tries to stop me. Sure it can't be this easy, I stop when two waiters walk toward a nearby table with a cake blazing with candles on top. People begin to sing Happy Birthday, and I make my move.

The stairs are so close I can practically taste freedom. Taking one last glance around, I see no one even notices I'm walking away or cares, so I hurry across the terrace. When my foot hits the first stair, my entire body tenses as I'm sure someone is going to stop me now.

But no one does.

By the time I reach the street, I'm shaking I'm so scared. I'm free!

Unsure where to go, I look up and down the road at all the restaurants and businesses with their twinkling lights illuminating the entire coast. I can go to any of them. Except I can't because I don't have any money.

Then I remember Gideon's credit card in my purse. I can go anywhere, at least for tonight before he calls tomorrow and cancels it.

In the darkness decorated with those festive lights all around, I celebrate my escape from Gideon and everything about his hotel. I never asked to be taken by him. I never asked for what happened tonight.

But now that I can go anywhere I want, the only place I want never to see again is the Villa Aurelia. And Gideon Rule.

Lost in thought about how much what he did hurt, I don't see the man come out from the shadows. Instantly, I recognize him and turn to run away.

I'm too slow. He catches me, and I know what he's going to do now.

He's going to take me back where he thinks I belong.

CHAPTER TWENTY-ONE

ideon

NEEDING TO DO SOMETHING WHILE I WAIT FOR ARIA to return, I get dressed and head down to my office. If there was ever a time I needed to distract myself with work, tonight's that time.

I pass Sasha in the lobby and say nothing to her. She gives me an odd look like she can't understand why I'm down here instead of up in the penthouse with Aria.

Neither can I.

Before I can get seated behind my desk and get lost in whatever issue the hotel has tonight, she walks into my office and glares at me. Great. Yet another woman unhappy with me.

"Why aren't you upstairs with Aria?" she demands to know like she's my boss and I'm here assistant and not the other way around.

"She left, so I needed something to help me pass the time until she gets back," I answer flatly, not really sure I can say anymore than that because I'm still not understanding what happened.

Sasha, of course, doesn't take that answer as the end of our conversation. Sitting down hard in one of the chairs in front of my desk, she continues to glare at me, except now she's five feet closer.

"What do you mean she left? Left where?"

"Somewhere in the hotel. She was unhappy and stormed out after you left."

Seriously, that's all I can tell her, so if my assistant keeps pressing me for more answers, all she's going to get are more vague statements because I don't know anything more.

"Gideon, why was she unhappy? Did you do something after I walked out?"

Now it's my turn to glare at her. "No. Like what could I do? I have no idea what the problem is. She yelled at me and stormed out. You women aren't exactly easy to understand. One minute you're perfectly fine with everything, and the next you're crying and slamming the door as you snap at the guard outside."

Sasha doesn't say another word but stares at me for so long that I begin to feel uncomfortable. "What?"

"Please tell me you didn't surprise her with what happened between the three of us. Tell me you didn't do that, Gideon."

The way she's looking at me reminds me exactly of how Aria looked right before she started yelling. Clearly, I'm not seeing the problem, but there's definitely a problem.

"I told you I was going to do that. Why are you shocked I actually did?"

She angrily pulls her eyebrows in toward her nose, frowning at me. "I told you not to do that. I stood in this very room and told you that surprising her was a bad idea. I then explicitly said to make sure you don't spring what we were doing on her. What were you thinking?"

"That it was going to be a nice sexy night she wouldn't forget. Isn't that what it was supposed to be?"

The look of disgust facing me at this moment tells me I misread something along the way. Sasha shakes her head and stands from the chair, throwing her arms up in the air.

"I swear to God you're hell bent on losing this woman, Gideon. You actually didn't tell her before having me join you tonight. And now you're surprised she's angry with you? How can you be so obtuse?"

Anger and something that looks like

disappointment flashes in her eyes as she snaps at me. Two women yelling at me in one night is not what I want, but like with Aria, I don't seem to know how to make this one happy either.

"I thought she'd like it. It's not like I left her with you. I was right there the whole time, Sasha."

All she can do is shake her head. "No wonder she acted like she did. I thought she was doing a hard-to-get thing, but she was scared. She already thinks there's something between us that's making you not want to be close to her, so you pull this shit? What is wrong with you, Gideon?"

"I've told her over and over we aren't together. I professed my love for her. What else could she want?" I ask, truly not understanding how things went so wrong tonight.

My assistant looks like she wants to slap me as she begins pacing back and forth across my office. "You tell her you love her, and then you bring in the one woman she's worried is standing in the way of that love? You should have told her beforehand. She should have had a chance to say no."

With a sigh, I confess the real reason why I didn't tell her ahead of time. "I wanted her to enjoy herself, but I didn't think she'd do it if I told her about it first. I never thought she'd be upset. She and I have joked about you wanting her. I thought she'd like it. Every other time we've done that the women I was with loved it."

Sasha's frown deepens. "Those women weren't Aria. You told me that yourself. She's crazy about you, even after everything, and you pull this stupid stunt. You're going to be lucky if she ever utters another word to you. If you thought this was the way to make her love you back, you're either blind or stupid. I can't say which at this moment, to be honest."

I stand from behind my desk as her words sink into my head. "I guess I better go find her and apologize."

"You haven't done that yet? Jesus Christ, Gideon! What the hell is going through your head tonight? You're going to be lucky if she hasn't run away from this hotel already. If she has, it's what you deserve."

Hanging my head, I repeat what Aria said just before she left the penthouse. "She said she hated me. I didn't want to tell her she couldn't walk around the hotel without a guard and go back on my word. That would have just made things worse."

My assistant's eyes open wide in stunned amazement. "You're telling me she's wandering around this hotel without Raphael?"

"I told her she could the other day, and after she got upset, I didn't think it was a good idea to make her even more unhappy. I was trying to be nice."

"Better late than never, I guess. I'll check the security cameras and recordings to see where she might be," Sasha says as she hurries out of my office.

I stand at the edge of my desk hating how this

night has turned out. I didn't realize letting Sasha join us would turn into such a disaster.

A few minutes later, she rushes in, nearly tearing my office door off the hinges. "She's gone! I saw it as clear as day on one of the terrace cameras. She walked right down the steps to the street below. She's out there all on her own, Gideon. That's bad."

My heart races at the thought of what might happen to Aria without a guard accompanying her on the streets around the hotel. It's nighttime and God only knows who's walking around.

Even worse, one of Marcello Angeloni's men might be in the area and pluck her off the street to take back to his boss.

Fuck!

"Get Raphael and have him meet me at the front door. Find two more security to come with us. I want her found!"

My mind whirls with the possibilities of what may be happening to Aria at this very moment. Christ, if someone lays a hand on her...if someone touches a single hair on that beautiful head of hers, I'm going to kill them. No asking questions. No threats. Just fucking kill them.

In the most painful way I can think of.

CHAPTER TWENTY-TWO

ria

THE TANG OF BLOOD OVERWHELMS MY TASTEBUDS, making me feel like I'm going to throw up. I've been hit before by the very man who looms over me at this moment, but never has he been so vicious in his attack.

"You fucking whore. I swear to God, Aria, before this night is over, I'm going to take out every ounce of rage I have on that pretty fucking face of yours. And then I'm going to take it out on that cunt," Franco says, his voice pure cruelty like I've never experienced in my life.

I recoil in terror, but there's little room for me to move since he's got my hands tied behind my back and my ankles tied to the legs of the chair I've been in for the past hour. Closing my eyes to get a few precious moments of relief from staring into his angry face, I silently pray Gideon knows I'm gone and is out looking for me.

Then again, why would he? I told him I hated him and ran away when I wasn't supposed to. He's probably happy to be rid of me.

"Open your fucking eyes!" Franco barks, frightening me so every muscle in my body tenses.

I do as he commands and see his fist right before it smashes into my cheek. Pure pain radiates out from the spot where his knuckles slam into my flesh, up into my eye socket so instantly I have a splitting headache that makes tears well in my eyes.

"Please stop!" I beg, but it's no use.

He mocks me, repeating my exact words before he slams his fist into my face again. This time hurts even more, and I can't stop the tears from streaming out of my eyes. They roll down my swollen cheeks and into my mouth so saltiness mixes with blood on my tongue.

"Please, Franco. Stop. I'm begging you."

That makes him step back away from me, and when I look up at him through blurry eyes, I see for the moment his rage has subsided.

"You know what, Aria. You're right. This just isn't as fun as I thought it would be. Time to move on, I say."

I let myself wish he's about to let me go, but that hope is dashed when he rips my shirt from my body, leaving it hanging in tatters against my skin. Lowering my head, I close my eyes in shame. I can't cover myself, so my breasts are exposed, humiliating me.

"Just let me go. Please? Gideon paid you. Why wasn't that enough?" I ask, unsure where my bravery is coming from to say words like that.

Franco reaches back and slaps me across the face. The sting makes my eyes tear up even more. God, I don't think I can take any more of this.

"Don't say his fucking name in my house again, you bitch!" he bellows in my face.

"I'm sorry," I sob, unable to stop myself from crying. "I'm sorry, Franco. Please stop. That's all I ask. Just stop."

Those are the exact words that have always worked in the past with him whenever he became enraged at something I did. All I can do is pray to God they'll do the same this time.

I close my eyes, but then I feel his palms against my cheeks as he cradles my face. It's a tender gesture so wrong for what's happened here tonight. I so want to believe he's done beating me that I lean into his left hand for some warmth and kindness.

"You always know how to make me want to be nice to you, Aria," he whispers in my ear. "What is that power you have that even now I don't want to hit you anymore?"

Too afraid to answer, I keep my eyes tightly shut as I silently hope this torture is over. I don't know what may happen next, but at least if he stops beating me, I might be able to survive.

"So tell me, Aria. What made you run away from him?" Franco says in a low voice that sends chills racing up and down my spine.

I can't tell him the truth. It's too humiliating to admit my jealousy got me here, bruised and beaten tonight. So I lie and say something I know he'll believe.

"He scared me, so the first chance I got, I escaped."

Franco moves back from me, and I brace myself for another punch. When it doesn't come after a few seconds, I slowly open my right eye and see him staring at me. I can't tell if what I said made him angry or if he doesn't believe my lie.

"I've seen him. I can't imagine him scaring anyone. Not even you," he says with a sneer.

So I take the chance he might believe me if I explained more.

"He has a way of being silent for so long you think he's dead, but then he finally speaks and says the most terrifying things imaginable."

"Oh yeah?" Franco says in a tone full of skepticism. "Like what?"

My mind scrambles to come up with something he won't doubt. In truth, Gideon never frightened me. If I'm being truly honest with myself, he never did anything to harm me. Even tonight with Sasha wasn't hurtful. I don't know why he included her in our time together, but I don't think he meant to harm me.

None of that matters now because if I don't tell Franco something genuinely awful, he's going to hit me again. So I conjure up a lie from my time with Gideon's brother, who I definitely know is capable of hurting people.

"He never raises his voice, but it's the words he chooses that frightened me. One time he came to the penthouse and threatened to take me away so no one would ever find me. I knew he meant it too, but thankfully, someone on his staff interrupted us and he left me alone."

Franco seems to think about that for a few seconds before he folds his arms across his chest. "So that night at the ball, you two weren't happy?"

"No, not at all. I wasn't happy the entire time I was with him. I swear. He terrified me. I never want to see him again."

I try to make my voice sound like even thinking of returning to Gideon frightens me, but I'm not sure I'm a good enough actress to make it convincing. The only wish I have right now other than to be free of Franco and the pain he inflicts is to be back in Gideon's arms, safe and sound in the penthouse or his villa away from everyone in the world but him.

The sound of a door opening sends utter dread racing through me, and I quickly turn to look at who's walked in. Marcello Angeloni slowly walks toward me, his head shaking like he disapproves of the sight of me.

"Such a beautiful face with such terrible bruises. What a shame."

I can't decide if he's unhappy that Franco has been beating me senseless for the past hour or if torn up women just bother him. Whichever it is, Marcello's arrival appears to calm Franco, at least for the moment.

"Let's talk for a little while, Aria. I think you can answer some of my questions," he says in a slick voice that does nothing to calm me. "Give me what I want, and I won't kill you. If you don't, I'll put a bullet through your skull. Understand?"

Nodding, I don't say anything because I can't imagine what I could possibly know that would help him. I just know if he's talking, then Franco isn't hitting.

"Now tell me, where are Gideon Rule's father and brother tonight?"

As I suspected, I don't know the answer to his questions. But if I don't give him something to keep him happy, Franco will begin punching me again.

"I think they went home," I say, intentionally vague since I don't know where home is for Helix or Alex.

"So they aren't in the country anymore?" he asks as he pulls up a chair and sits down in front of me.

I slowly shake my head as I pray to God I'm not

telling him something that will hurt Gideon or anyone in his family. "I don't think so, but I don't know. Nobody told me any of their plans."

Marcello smiles like he's happy with my answer. "You're doing very well, Aria. Now tell me. What kind of security does Gideon have at the Villa Aurelia?"

What kind of security does he have? Do these men actually think anyone, including Gideon, ever included me in on discussions of topics like the security at the hotel? I barely left the penthouse until this week, and even then, I wasn't clued in on the inner workings of the place.

"I don't know. There's a guard stationed outside the penthouse at all times. I know that. And there are guards positioned at all events. That I know. But otherwise, I don't know where they are. I just know they're there at all times."

That's a lie, and if either Marcello and Franco think about how I got away, they'll realize that. I need to keep talking and make them think of something else.

"But I know that his guards are heavily armed. That I know for sure. I saw their weapons on more than one occasion," I say, trying my hardest to be as convincing as possible.

Marcello nods and then leans forward to pat me on the knee. "You sound like their guns scared you. Did you tell Gideon you didn't like seeing weapons around?"

I shake my head as tears well in my eyes at his mention of Gideon. I know what this man is trying to do. He wants me to give him something that will make it easer to attack the Rules. I don't want to hurt Gideon or his family, so I won't tell him anything, even if I knew what he wants to find out.

"Okay, Aria. That's enough for now."

He stands and waves Franco toward him as he begins to walk into the other room. I hope I didn't say anything that inadvertently will help him to hurt Gideon. I'd die if I thought I was the cause of anything bad happening to him.

I love him. God, please save me from these men and let me return to Gideon so I can tell him how I feel. Please don't let me die here before I can tell him I love him.

CHAPTER TWENTY-THREE

ideon

My body sags against the stone façade of one of the boutiques near the hotel after five hours looking for Aria. Raphael and two other security guards stand waiting for me to give them new orders on where to look for her, but there's no point.

Somebody grabbed her. I know it. I can feel it in my gut.

"Mr. Rule, where to next?" Raphael asks.

I shake my head as I run my hand through my hair in frustration. "Nowhere. We've searched up and down this coast for her. If we can't find her, that means someone got her."

What I don't say out loud is I know what I have to do now. I have to call Marcello Angeloni and negotiate for her release. So much for having the upper hand for a few fucking days.

I don't care about that now, though. All I care about is having Aria back safe and sound. God help Marcello or anyone else if she doesn't come back to me as perfect as she left.

Without another word, I turn to walk back to the hotel as I silently play out in my head what to do next. Angeloni is going to take full advantage of my weakness in this situation. I would if I were him.

I just don't know what he's going to want in exchange for her. He's got power. He's got money. What else could he want?

I'm going to find out.

Sasha runs up to me as I walk through the front doors of the hotel and head for my office, her expression full of concern. She peppers me with questions I can't answer on my way there, her voice full of worry for Aria.

"Where could she be, Gideon? Where would she go? You have to have some idea."

I let out a sigh and shake my head. "I don't know. She told me her family isn't from here. She's from upstate New York, and that's where they still live."

As she closes my office door behind her, she whispers, almost as if she can't bring herself to say the words out loud, "You don't think she'd go back to that ex-boyfriend of hers, do you?"

"No," I answer, relatively sure she wouldn't go back to Franco. "At least I don't think so."

"Well, what are you going to do now? You can't just stop looking. She's out there by herself at night. God only knows what could happen to her!"

"I know. You don't have to remind me. Christ, Sasha. I'm worried about her too, but you need to calm down. Getting frantic isn't going to bring her back any sooner."

My assistant hangs her head in an uncharacteristic sign of remorse. "I just feel bad. I think I'm part of the reason she ran away. Gideon, you have to find her. If someone takes her off the street, I don't even want to think about what may happen. She's not tough like me. Aria's gentle, and I'm not sure she could fight back if someone tried to hurt her."

Memories of that night at Lucius Angeloni's house when Franco abused her in front of me and everyone else there flash through my brain, making me clench my hands into tight fists. If he got a hold of her and hurt her, I'm going to relish ripping him limb from limb.

When I pick up the phone, Sasha looks at me strangely. "Who are you calling? I don't think now is really the time to be chatting people up."

"I'm calling Marcello Angeloni. I have no choice. I

need to get her back, and after the other day with him, he's bound to want something. I'm willing to trade anything to have Aria back with me."

Nothing I say alleviates the expression of worry that's settled into Sasha's face. I've never seen her so upset about anything in all the time I've known her. I want to ask if there's something she's not telling me, but I've got too much to deal with right now.

"Gideon Rule, I thought I'd hear from you sooner than later," Marcello says when he answers the phone. "Missing anything important lately?"

He's playing with me. That's a mistake. Normally, I'm fine acting the part of mannerly businessman who doesn't want trouble.

But now is not normal times, and he's not dealing with just a man who runs a hotel. Now he's dealing with a man in love and the woman he adores. If he tries toying with me for too long, I'll fucking kill him too and to hell with what my father has to say about it.

"I want her back. Now."

"Her? Oh, you mean that pretty thing with the legs that go on for miles. Damn, I do like a woman with great legs," he says with a chuckle.

"What do you want for her, Marcello?" I ask through gritted teeth, barely able to contain my rage.

"You know what I want. Give me the fuck who killed my brother. He's one of you, and you know it."

Again with the bullshit about Alaric being the one

who killed Lucius Angeloni. Fuck, if it was him, he would have been happy to own up to it. The asshole was planning on forcing the woman he loves to marry him. Alaric wouldn't be shy about admitting to being his killer if he had done it.

But every time I've asked him, he tells me the same thing. "I would have been happy to, but someone else got to the scumbag before me. All the better. I just wanted Sienna away from him, and that's what I got."

He says he doesn't know who offed Lucius. I think he does, but if he doesn't want to tell me, I'm not going to force the issue. The world's a better place with one less asshole from the Amalfi Coast in it.

"It wasn't my cousin. He didn't do it."

"Then we have nothing to talk about. I'll be sure to tell your girlfriend you said hello when I see her next. Franco is more than happy to have his plaything back. You know how he is. Women just amuse the hell out of him, especially Aria."

When I hear him say her name, it's like every fiber of my being wants to kill him. "When I get her back, she better be perfectly fine because if she isn't, I don't care what it takes, Marcello. I will find a way to kill anyone who touched her. Remember that when you see your man again. Now if you let her go and she's back here with me in the next hour, I won't go through with what I told you the other day. If you don't, then this is war. Your choice."

He's silent for a long moment before he says, "She must be one hell of a piece of ass for you to get this upset, Gideon. To be honest, though, I feel pretty good about my position here. I've got all the men I need to secure power, and from where I stand, you've got yourself and a bunch of hotel staff since daddy and big brother left the other day."

My hand holding the phone begins to shake I'm so angry, but I can't let him see that side of me. He wants a war? Now he's fucking got one.

"Remember what I said. She comes back to me unharmed in the next sixty minutes, or you and every one of your men I find will pay."

I hang the phone up, knowing I need to make a few other calls if this is really going to happen. Angeloni's got one hour before I let my family do what they do best.

As the minutes tick by and Aria doesn't come back, I sit in silence knowing I caused this. I took her from that prick because I wanted to protect her, but bringing Sasha into our sex tonight was a mistake.

Finally, I walk out to watch the front door as the hour ends, but Aria's nowhere in sight. Tamping down my rage, I tell Sasha to keep an eye out for her and tell me the instant she returns.

"Do you really think Marcello Angeloni and that son of a bitch ex of hers are actually going to let her go?" she asks like she doesn't believe it any more than I do.

I shake my head. "No, but I needed to give him an hour to give me what I want before I set events in motion I might not be able to stop. He's had his hour. Now it's time to make some calls."

As I turn to walk back into my office to call my father and Alaric, Raphael walks through the front doors holding something in his arms. After a few seconds, I realize it's Aria he's carrying. She looks limp, and for a moment, my heart stops.

Is she dead?

Sasha races up to him to see how Aria is. "Where did you find her?" she asks as she guides him toward the elevator.

"She was left on the steps. She's in pretty bad shape. Somebody's been beating on her. I don't think she has any broken bones, but she's hurting. Should I take her up to the penthouse? She looks like she needs to get looked at and sleep for a long time," Raphael says, speaking the most words I think I've ever heard from him at one time.

I follow them into the elevator, but I can't look at her. If I do, it's going to feel like someone's ripping my heart out of my chest.

She whimpers halfway up to the penthouse, and I instinctively turn to see what's wrong. She's got a black eye, her cheek is swollen like someone hit her hard, and blood trickles from near her ear. It's everything I can do not to stop the fucking elevator and march right the fuck over to Franco's fucking apartment.

But I have to be smart about retaliating, even if my heart is breaking.

CHAPTER TWENTY-FOUR

ria

Beside me, Sasha buzzes around like a busy bee trying to make sure I'm comfortable in Gideon's bed. I want to tell her to go away, but I can't bring myself to say the words because it feels nice to have someone care that I'm hurting.

Even if it is the person who Gideon cares about the most in the world.

For his part, the man himself seems disinterested in how I feel. He hasn't come over to talk to me since we got back here, and he hasn't moved from his position near the door since Raphael set me down on the bed.

"I've got a warm washcloth," Sasha says with a

smile as she sits down next to me. "I promise I won't press too hard, but I need to clean off the blood near your ear, okay?"

She stares down at me like I'm some broken bird she's decided to nurse back to health. If I could raise my arm, I'd push her away. Since I can't, I shake my head, but even that hurts.

"I don't want your help."

"Well, you need it, so sit still while I clean you up."

I try to roll over unsuccessfully, making me cry out in pain. Sasha quickly pulls away, but Gideon still does nothing to come closer or see if I'm okay.

"We should get her something to ease the pain. I have some pills in my desk downstairs. I'll be right back."

Sasha hurries away, leaving me alone with Gideon. He continues to remain silent, and as much as I want to ask him why he won't even speak to me, I don't have the strength. I just don't understand why he doesn't care enough to at least check if I'm okay.

After a minute alone with him, I cover my face with my hands and say, "I'm sure you have somewhere else you'd rather be. Feel free to go there and leave me alone."

For the first time since Raphael brought me into the lobby, Gideon speaks to me. "There's nowhere else I need to be or want to be."

I move my hands away from my face and look across the room at him still standing near the doorway.

"Then why are you all the way over there? Do you know how that makes me feel? Is it because I'm all beaten up? Is that what's making you stay away?"

He can't even look at me when he answers, "I doubt I'd be of much help. Better to let Sasha clean you up."

When he says that, I can't control my emotions. Always Sasha. Sasha wants something, so Gideon has to give it to her so she's happy. Always her and never me.

"I don't want her to help me, but since you don't care, I guess I have no choice," I say, fighting a sob that forces its way out.

His indifference crushes me. After all I went through with Franco and Marcello today and how I never betrayed Gideon, even when they threatened to kill me, the way he can simply ignore my pain and stand all the way over there hurts more than any fist slamming into my face.

"Just leave me alone," I say as the tears come and I don't try to stop them. "I should have told them what they wanted to know. I hate you, Gideon."

He doesn't leave, and when Sasha returns with a glass of water and whatever she found to help me deal with the pain from the beating I took, Gideon watches intently, almost as if he finds someone helping me a curiosity. His eyes never leave me, even if he can't be bothered to comfort me in the least.

"Take care of her. I have things that need to be

handled," he says without a hint of emotion in his voice before walking away.

Sasha puts the glass of water in front of my face, but I push it away, splashing it all over me and her. "I don't want you. I want him. After all I dealt with, the least he could do is make sure I'm okay."

Her usual iciness comes through loud and clear when she glares at me and says, "Well, I'm as close as you're going to get. Now take these pills and drink this water."

As close as I'm going to get. Isn't that the truth?

I do as she orders, although I resent every second of it, before I ease back onto the pillows she's stacked up behind me. Sasha isn't exactly a kind nursemaid, but she is a caring one. I have to give her that.

Closing my eyes, I let the pillows envelop me while I wait for the pills to take effect. If I'm lucky, they'll knock me out so I can sleep and hopefully forget this entire day.

The mattress moves, and I look to see Sasha getting into bed with me. Lying next to me, she gives me a smile I think she intends to be sweet and says, "I'll be here in case you need anything. Just let yourself rest so you can start healing."

We lie there in silence for a long time as I patiently wait for these pills to do something, and my mind fills with all the questions I've wanted to ask about her and Gideon. When it becomes clear whatever she gave me doesn't seem to be working, I look over at her and finally say what's been on my mind.

"Are you in love with him?" I ask into the silence surrounding us and carefully watch her expression as she considers my question.

"I adore him. There's a difference."

So typical of her to answer but say nothing.

"What does that mean?"

Sasha stares up at the ceiling for a few moments before turning her body to face me. Tucking her hands under her cheek, she smiles and says, "The first week I worked for him, I fell for Gideon. He enchanted me. I wanted him more than I wanted to breathe. I don't know how since I'd never fallen for someone so quickly, but he had me under his spell."

I don't say the words, but that sounds like love to me.

"And that's when you two started sleeping together?" I ask as jealousy fills every nook and cranny of my being.

"By week's end, I was down on my knees with him in my mouth. I utterly adored him and would have done anything to have him. But he didn't feel that way for me."

The sadness in Sasha's words comes through loud and clear. As much as I want to hate her, I can't help but feel badly for her. I know exactly what it's like to care for someone and know they don't return the feelings.

"I think you're wrong. He clearly loves you. I think he adores you too, if you ask me."

She shakes her head but the sadness in her voice now moves to her eyes. "No, he loves you. I knew it the first night he brought you here. You were different. He cares about you like I've never seen him care about anyone before."

"Other than you and Gia. I can't tell you how good it feels to play third to you and a ghost."

Sasha snuggles up against me and softly kisses my cheek. "You're wrong. Gia is in the past, and I was someone he never truly loved. It's you, Aria."

"Me what? Tell me because I need to know. As far as I can tell, he barely notices I'm around, until he decides you need something to make you happy and then I become important."

"He handled tonight badly. I admit that freely. I told him he fucked up as soon as I found out he didn't give you a head's up about what he wanted to do beforehand. In his defense, I think he thought you'd love it. It's stupid that he thought that way, but he's a man. They do stupid things."

My emotions well up inside me until I can't control them anymore and tears stream down my cheeks. "Why would he think choosing you over me would be something I'd love?"

Sasha smiles and wipes away my tears. "Oh, honey. He didn't choose me over you. It's true I wanted you from the moment we met, but tonight wasn't about me. It was about you, or at least he thought it was. As I said, men do stupid things. He didn't mean to hurt you. Neither of us did."

I shake my head, not willing to let her be nice when I'm wanting to hate her. "See, that right there? Neither of us? You're the couple. You and Gideon, not me and Gideon. That's how it's been since I arrived here, and it's never going to change. He cares more about you than he does about me."

"No, you're wrong. He made a mistake, Aria. Don't let that ruin what you two have."

I stare at her in disbelief. "What we have? What is that? We have nothing. He brought me here because he wanted to protect me, and all I've been is some plaything he toys with every so often. What you two have is a true connection. What we have is sex. Nothing more. Just sex."

She cradles my face and smiles like she can't believe I could be so foolish. But there's nothing stupid about what I just said. It's the truth.

"Gideon loves you, Aria. He sometimes doesn't know how to show it, but he loves you."

"How many times have you two done a threesome before with other women?" I ask, my jealousy skyrocketing with every second I think about them together.

"I should let Gideon tell you that, but you should know you were the one I wanted more than any of the others. You're as perfect as he believes you are."

Turning my head, I squeeze my eyes tightly shut. "He doesn't believe that, and if he did, he doesn't believe it anymore. Not after today."

She hugs me to her, making me feel less alone. "Oh, beautiful girl, you're so wrong. He loves you even more now that he has to fight for you."

I look over at her and shake my head. "Fight for me? What do you mean?"

"Where do you think he's gone to? He's going to make whoever did this to you pay. Nobody touches Gideon's woman and gets away with it."

The way she says that, like anyone in the world would refer to me by those words, sounds utterly bizarre. Gideon's woman? Oh, maybe his fuck buddy or someone he likes to play with, but his woman? No, that's her, not me.

"He shouldn't bother. That won't change things between us."

I close my eyes as the effect of the pills begins to overtake me. Whatever Gideon is out there doing, he isn't doing it for me. I mean nothing to him.

CHAPTER TWENTY-FIVE

ideon

PACING BACK AND FORTH ACROSS MY OFFICE, I WAIT for my father and Alaric to arrive. I should have gone to Franco's on my own. The problem with that is I don't know what I'd be walking into, which even in my blinding rage I know would be a stupid move on my part.

So I wait and try to control my emotions as they run rampant inside me.

Just seeing Aria like that, all bruised and bloody from what those assholes did to her, made me want to strangle them with my bare hands. I warned Franco that if he ever came back after I paid him that he'd have to deal with me. I let him slide for a week, but now he's made an even bigger mistake.

One he'll pay for with his life. Now it's just a matter of how it happens and how much he suffers.

As for Marcello Angeloni, I tried being professional. I didn't want to do things the way my brother and father think they should be done. They always shoot first and ask questions later. I don't work like that. I don't need to kill people to get my point across. There are other ways—more civilized ways of doing business—but Marcello chose to go the wrong way.

Now he'll pay too. A Rule may not have killed his brother, but one will kill this Angeloni.

My mind wanders up to the penthouse where I know Aria is hurting. I wanted to comfort her. I just couldn't control my anger, and I knew she didn't need that on top of everything else. Sasha's better at that kind of thing anyway. She'll make sure she feels better.

Behind me, my office door opens, and I turn to see my father and brother march through with Alaric bringing up the rear. What the fuck is Alex doing here? He has no part in any of this. Why the fuck would my father let him tag along?

"Time to break some heads!" he announces before I can even ask why he's here at all.

Ignoring him, I look at my father as he sits in my chair behind my desk. "Why did you bring him? He isn't needed here. In fact, you aren't either. Alaric and I can handle things."

"Yeah, you handled things well enough that your pretty little girlfriend got fucked up by our enemies," Alex says with a laugh.

That's it. I'm not putting up with his shit anymore. I told him to get the fuck out of my hotel when I saw him with his hands on Aria. I don't want him here, helping or not.

I spin around and face my brother, my rage boiling over as I stare at him in complete disgust. "If I hear another fucking word out of you, you're going to be the first person I fucking kill tonight. You aren't welcome here. I told you that when I threw you out of my hotel a few days ago. Nothing's changed, so get the fuck out!"

"He's here because I want him here," my father says sternly, like he plans to reprimand me for speaking to Alex that way.

Not today.

Turning to look at my father sitting at my fucking desk, I say, "I don't need you here either. Unless you're planning to woodchipper someone, you can go and take that asshole with you. Alaric is the only one of you I need tonight."

For a moment, it's like the world stops turning on its axis. I've never spoken to my father that way. Of course, Alex finds all of this funny and chuckles behind my back.

"I love that fucking story. Alaric, isn't that a great story? I wish I was there to see the guy get all chewed up. That would have been the best."

God, I hate him.

"Enough about the fucking woodchipper story!" I yell, surprising everyone. "Not every goddamned situation in life calls for chopping someone up into little pieces. Alaric and I can handle this situation tonight."

As usual, my brother starts running his mouth, but I'm not hearing any more of his bullshit. My father, though, seems bothered by my insistence I don't need him here. Why he would care baffles me. Doesn't he have anything better to do on a Saturday night than flying across the world to kill people?

With a frown, my father hums his unhappiness. "I don't think infighting between you two is going to help things get done tonight. Alex is here because I thought he could be of assistance. You have people who need to be taken care of, so now you have three of us to join you in that."

It's as if he heard nothing I just said.

"I don't want him here."

"Still upset about the other day, little brother? Maybe we could have another go at our fight right now. You won't catch me off guard this time."

Fed up with him and the rest of my fucking family, I pull my gun and aim it at the center of his forehead. "I'm not bothering with fighting you tonight. Either get the fuck out of my office and out of my goddamned hotel, or learn how good a fucking shot I am. Your choice."

Out of the corner of my eye, I see my father stand up from behind my desk. "Whoa, let's everyone calm down here. We're not your enemy, Gideon. Put the gun away. We don't pull our guns on family."

Still aiming for my brother's head, I turn to look at my father in astonishment. "What the fuck do you mean? Alex here has pulled a gun on me so many times I'm surprised he hasn't shot me by mistake by now. Then again considering how shitty a shot he is, I might come away without even a scratch. Every time he gets his shorts in a knot, this bastard threatens to kill me."

My father can't even pretend any of that isn't true. Fuck, he's been not five feet away on more than a few occasions when Alex did it.

Alaric carefully walks up beside me and says in a calm voice, "I know how you feel, Gideon. More than you might think. Dealing with family sucks. You know I couldn't be around my older brother for more than a few minutes before I wanted to kill him. And I know what you're going through with Aria and the bastards who hurt her too. You know that. Keep your anger for them. Alex can get it another day."

I slowly lower my gun and nod a silent thank you to him. He's right. I shouldn't be focusing on how much I hate having my brother involved in this problem. I need to focus on the men who deserve my rage tonight.

"All right. I'm fine. You're right. Tonight, I need to keep my eye on the target."

Alaric gives me a tiny smile and nudges my arm. Out of everyone in my family, he understands what it's like to be the second son to a father who can't seem to see anything but the first son.

"Good. Now that we've cleared that up, who's getting killed tonight?" my father asks as he comes around my desk.

"Marcello Angeloni and his man Franco. They're the ones who got a hold of her."

My brother, still needing to feel like he hasn't lost his ability to enrage me, leans against the wall and asks, "How did they get her anyway? I thought you had her tethered to that penthouse of yours upstairs. Did she sneak off away from her captor, Gideon?"

I turn to bark at my brother to shut the fuck up, but my father surprisingly beats me to it. "Enough, Alex! If you don't fucking stop busting your brother's balls, next time I'm going to let him follow through when he pulls his gun!"

Stunned, I glance over at Alaric to see he's shocked at my father's outburst at his favorite too. When I turn to see how my brother is taking this rare pushback, I see he looks like he swallowed something disgusting.

"Now Gideon, can she tell us anything that can help us know if it's just Angeloni and this Franco person we need to take out? I think it would be a good idea to talk to Aria before we start," my father says as he makes his way toward the door.

I want to say she's resting, but part of me wants to see her and make sure she's okay. By the time the four of us get up to the penthouse, I've decided we aren't all going to walk into my bedroom and loom over her with our questions.

Before I open the front door, I turn to the three other men and say, "I'll go in alone. She doesn't need to feel like she's being interrogated."

"No, I'm going in with you, Gideon," my father says.

Jesus, everything is a battle with him and my brother. Instead of fighting him, I simply nod. Nevermind the fact that he's never actually had a conversation with Aria. I'm sure meeting him for the first time while she's laid up in bed recovering from being beaten up is exactly what she's going to want tonight.

Sasha meets us at the door and gives me a quick run-down on how things have been up here. "She's feeling a little better. I think the pills are helping, but she only slept for a little while."

Pulling me off to the side, she looks around me and then asks, "What the hell are they all doing here? Now doesn't feel like the right time to have Aria meet your father, Gideon."

"As if anyone wants that," I say, rolling my eyes.

"We just need to ask her a few questions. Keep my brother busy out here and don't let him touch anything."

With a devilish smile, she says, "And if he happens to walk out onto the terrace, casually push him off the side?"

The simple thought of that makes me smile. "You wouldn't get an argument from me if that happened. My father might lose his mind, but I'm fine with it."

Aria is sitting up when we walk in, closing the door behind us. I walk over to the side of the bed and sit down next to her, taking her hand in mine as I can barely look at her with all those bruises on her face.

"We need to ask you a few questions, okay?" I say softly, forcing a smile so she isn't frightened.

She looks at me like she doesn't understand, and as much as I want to explain to her why I acted the way I did before, that will have to wait.

"Okay. What about?" she asks me, her eyes big and filled with uncertainty.

"We need to know who did this to you."

Aria immediately turns away from me and stares down at her hands in her lap. When she doesn't say anything, I touch her arm to get her to look at me. But she won't.

"It's okay. We just need to know the names. If you know who they were, I need you to tell us."

My father takes a step toward the bed and sits down on the edge. In a voice I've never heard him use with anyone but my sister, he softly says, "I know. This is hard, and you don't even know me. I'm Gideon's father, Helix. I wish we could have met in better circumstances, but we have to work with what we get. We can't let whoever did this to you get away with this, Aria. Any attack on someone we love is an attack on all Rules, so if you can tell us who hurt you, we'll get them back for what they did."

She lifts her head and looks at him before turning to face me. Her eyes full of tears, she says, "It was Franco and Marcello. They grabbed me off the street. They wanted to know things about you. I didn't tell them anything. I swear, Gideon. I don't know if there was anyone other than them there when they did it, but the two of them are the ones who beat me up."

I lift her hand to my lips and kiss it tenderly to silently thank her. "You did great, Aria. Now rest and I'll be back soon."

My father stands from the bed and smiles at her. "Don't worry. We don't let anyone hurt our women. We'll find those two and take care of them."

When he leaves, Aria holds my hand tightly to keep me there with her. "Gideon, I want to believe I'm yours, but why didn't you say anything before? You made me feel like you didn't care."

Cradling her face in my hands, I stare into those beautiful green eyes and give her my sweetest smile before kissing her. "I'm sorry, Aria. I was so consumed with guilt that I didn't know how to handle it when I saw you like this. I'm going to kill Marcello and Franco for what they did. My father's right. We don't let anyone hurt those we love. Please forgive me."

As tears stream down over her cheeks, she sobs against my chest and my heart breaks for how sad she sounds. "I'm sorry for causing all this trouble. I should have never run away. It's just… I was so jealous."

"I know, and that's my fault. I made a mistake. Forgive me, Aria."

When she lifts her head and nods, happiness fills me. If she can forgive my mistakes, we have a chance to be happy.

"I love you, Aria. I know I haven't been good at showing you as much as telling you, but after tonight, that's all going to change. You rest and I'll be back, and then we can start over, okay?"

"Okay. Please be careful. Franco is vicious. He's following Marcello's orders, but he's terrible all on his own. I don't want you to get hurt because of me."

Pressing a kiss to her forehead, I sigh. "I won't get hurt. Trust me. I've got my family backing me up tonight. The only ones who need to worry are the two men we're hunting. I'll be back soon."

I stand to leave, but still she won't let go of my hand. "Gideon, wait. I wanted to tell you something."

"What?"

Aria gives me a hint of a smile and sighs. "I just wanted to tell you I love you and I'd be heartbroken if you don't come back to me."

"Then I better come back because the last thing I want to do is break your heart," I say with a smile. "Don't worry. I know you don't know this, but I'm with three of the deadliest people I've ever met. They won't let anyone hurt me."

She lets out a heavy sigh and releases my hand. "Okay. I'll be waiting."

I glance back at her just before I reach the door and smile. She loves me.

CHAPTER TWENTY-SIX

ideon

ALEX AND MY FATHER STAND OFF TO THE SIDE AS I pound my fist into Franco's ugly face. Nearly an hour I've been at this, and I swear I could keep it up for hours more. Every time I imagine him even touching Aria, all I want to do is crush this fucker's skull.

"Does it feel as good when you're getting beat on as it did when you were hitting her?" I ask through gritted teeth and then slam my knuckles into his cheekbone.

I hear a crack and step back as he cries out in agony. "It wasn't just me who did it! It was Marcello too. Why aren't you fucking him up?"

Behind me, Alaric chuckles. "No honor among assholes, I guess."

"Don't worry," my father says, joining in with Alaric to have a good laugh. "We'll get to him. You just had the honor of being first. Be happy that son of mine is handling you. If it was me or my other son, you would have been dead by now. Gideon likes to play with his food for a little while."

I glance over at him and nod. I don't generally enjoy being this violent. In truth, I prefer to fuck people up other ways. Messing with someone's psyche is a much better time for me than physically beating someone to a pulp, but mind games take time, and that I do not have tonight.

This is going to end just the way my family members would do themselves. Franco isn't long for this world, and I suspect he knows it. But before he goes off to wherever the fuck he's destined for, I want him to feel what Aria felt every time he laid a hand on her.

My fist connects with Franco's face again, and this time his nose gets it. Blood spurts everywhere, and he cries out again, but this time he's begging for mercy.

Should have thought of that when you were hurting the woman I love, asshole.

With his hands tied behind his back, he can't reach up to try and stop the bleeding, so it covers his face and chest in seconds. Stepping back from him so I don't end up wearing any, I shake my head at the mess he is.

"I say you just kill him already," Alex grumbles. "I get that you're enjoying this, Gideon, but Christ, this is starting to look like torture."

My head snaps in the direction of where he's standing. "And you have a problem with that? I thought you loved torturing people."

He shrugs and reluctantly nods, as if he isn't proud of who he is. "I do, but it's not usually this ugly. There's fucking blood everywhere. That two-thousand-dollar suit of yours is going to get ruined if you keep this up."

As I pull my arm back for one more shot to Franco's face, I say to my brother, "Don't worry. I have more at home."

My fist lands hard against his jaw, but I have to admit the fun has gone out of this for me. Time to finish him off so we can go find Marcello Angeloni.

"One question before I put you out of your misery," I say, leaning in close to Franco's blood-soaked face.

Through swollen, black and blue eyes, he looks up at me and waits for me to ask him what I need to know. I've put this off until now because I'm dreading what he may say.

"Did you do anything but hit her?" I ask as calmly as I can.

I doubt this asshole can hear the slight tremble in

my voice as the thought of him violating Aria between beatings tears me up inside. He should have taken my money I gave him for her and stayed away like I told him to.

Franco shakes his head as he sobs out his answer. "No."

I take a few steps back and survey the damage I've done to this motherfucker. I would have been happy to have let him live as Aria's ex as long as he stayed away and left her alone. This didn't have to happen, but once he touched her tonight, his fate was set in stone.

"Good." Pulling my gun out from behind me, I aim it at his head just as I did with Alex earlier tonight. The difference is I have no problem actually killing Franco. The time for threats is over. "Maybe the fact that you didn't rape her will help you wherever you're going."

He sobs something, but I don't hear him. I'm focused on how good it feels to give him what he deserves.

The gun goes off, and a second later, the bullet tears through his skull. Franco's head falls forward, and my fun with him is over.

"I had no idea you could be so vicious, Gideon," my father says with a wicked grin. "And here I thought you were the civilized one out of all of us."

As I stuff my gun back in my waistband, I roll my eyes. "I am. There's just a point where every man knows he has to give up his civilized ways to avenge a wrong. He wronged Aria, so he got what he deserved. Now onto that fuck Marcello."

"Are you going to want to do him too?" Alaric asks, probably wondering what the fuck he's doing here if he doesn't get to kill anyone tonight.

I shake my head. "Not the whole thing. You need to do something, right? Don't want to make it a wasted trip for you. I'll get him started since now I know he laid his hands on Aria too. You can finish him off."

As I turn to leave Franco's apartment, Alex complains behind me, "Why do you and Alaric get to have all the fun? What the fuck are Dad and I supposed to do? Just stand around with our goddamned hands in our pockets?"

I look back to see my father glaring at my older brother. With a laugh, I answer, "I told you Alaric and I could handle things. Just because I don't go around threatening every fucking person I see doesn't mean I can't take care of business."

While he grumbles, Alaric slaps me on the back, and we walk out together. "I'm with your father. I had no idea you had it in you to fuck up someone like that. I guess those expensive suits hide who you really are."

With a smile, I say, "I'm a Rule, just like you. I just tend to be a different kind of villain than you, Alex, and my father. The end result is the same. Franco got what he had coming to him, and now that Angeloni fuck will too."

Alaric leans in and says low in my ear, "I'm thinking your father is going to want to handle him. Anyone have a woodchipper nearby here on the Amalfi Coast?"

"That's fucked up," I say, shaking my head. "I need to live here after all of you leave. Killing Franco the way I did is one thing. Fucking ripping someone up into tiny pieces will make people think the man in charge of the Villa Aurelia is a fucking psycho."

We hit the warm night air and begin walking out toward the street as he says, "It would make handling your enemies easier. Word gets out that the Rule are woodchippering motherfuckers who cross us, I might not have to kill anyone ever again."

I raise my eyebrows in surprise at how happy he sounds when he says that. I'm guessing he and Sienna have plans to get married and have a family, so continuing as a hitman probably isn't high on Alaric's list of things he wants to do in the future.

"For tonight, we'll just have to do things the old-fashioned way. Two to the head should be enough."

My father walks up beside us and pulls me away from my conversation with Alaric. "We'll catch up with you and Alex in a minute."

Surprised my father wants to talk to me alone, I watch my brother and cousin walk away, as curious as I am as to what Helix Rule wants to say. It's rare that my father ever wants to have a conversation with me.

"Go back to the hotel and take care of Aria. We'll handle Angeloni."

His tone tells me he's decided this already, so there's no point in arguing with him. To be honest, I have little interest in beating another man up tonight before Alaric kills him. As much as I'm a Rule, I am civilized, and after fucking up Franco, I'm not really into a repeat performance with Marcello.

But he did join his man in hurting her, so I have a right to get revenge for Aria.

"He fucked with her too, Dad. I should be the one who takes care of him."

My father shakes his head. "He fucked with someone a Rule cares about. That means we all have a stake in seeing him pay. Go back to the hotel and take care of her. I doubt she ever wanted you to be a killer any more than I did. We'll take things from here."

Unlike usual, I don't get the feeling my father's disappointed I'm not like Alex this time. Still, years of being compared to my older brother make me wonder why.

"I thought you'd be happy to see me following in your footsteps like Alex."

A smile lights up his dark eyes. "I thought so too, but it turns out your mother was right all those years ago when she told me you were never going to be like me. I guess you have a heart like her. Tonight, though, I saw some of me in you, and that's enough."

"Okay. Thanks, Dad. Who's going to take care of Angeloni?"

He begins to walk away to join my brother and Alaric. "I don't know yet. It depends on how I'm feeling when we find him. I brought Alaric, so by rights, I should have him do it, but I think this Marcello Angeloni person has pissed me off. First he threatens to kill every Rule he can find, and then he beats up on your girlfriend? Seems like he needs more than just to pay with his life. I think he needs to be an example for the people around here."

Maybe Alaric is right. Maybe there will be a repeat of the woodchipper.

BY THE TIME I GET BACK TO THE HOTEL, IT'S WELL past two. Sasha left me a note to say she had to run an errand, although I can't imagine what she needs to do at this time of night. Stuffing the letter into my pocket, I quietly walk into the bedroom, hoping not to wake Aria if she's finally sleeping.

I stop at the side of the bed and stare down at her. She looks so small lying there, the evidence of what Franco and Marcello did to her vividly black and blue along her cheek and under her right eye. I reach out to gently touch her, even though I shouldn't in case I disturb her.

"What happened?" she asks as soon as she opens her eyes.

"I just got back," I say, sidestepping the details of my time away as I shrug out of my suit coat. "Go back to sleep. You need to rest. We can talk tomorrow."

She shakes her head as she slowly comes around. "I wasn't asleep. Once Sasha left, I couldn't get back to sleep."

Aria reaches for my hand, and I wrap my fingers around her forefinger to give it a tender squeeze. "I'm here now, so you can fall asleep. You're safe."

Her green eyes stare up at me and she asks, "Why won't you tell me what happened?"

I let out a heavy sigh. "Franco's dead."

She winces for a moment before taking a deep breath. "I figured. You didn't do it, though, right?"

My answer is a simple nod, which makes her eyes open wide in surprise. "You killed him? Because of what he did?"

"Yes."

"Was it quick? I think it must have been. You aren't a violent man," she says softly as she pushes herself up against the pillows behind her.

"It was what it was. He won't be beating up anyone from now on. I suspect the same can be said about Marcello by now."

"Your father is the one taking care of that?" she asks innocently.

"Someone in my family. Not me, though. I wanted

319

to come back here to be with you. I need to grab a shower. I'll be back in a few minutes," I say, tugging my hand from her hold.

She nods and closes her eyes, as if she can finally rest easy knowing the men who hurt her are gone. I'm glad I could give her that.

Halfway through my shower, Aria steps in behind me. Wrapping her arms around me, she presses her cheek to my back. "You took too long. I missed you."

I cover her hands in the middle of my chest with my own, noticing how delicate hers feel at this moment. She may be nearly my height, but she's much slighter than I am. I imagine that fuck hitting her and her having no chance to defend herself, and I feel my rage begin to build inside me again.

"Aria…" I start to say the words I must, but they get stuck in my throat as the image of her trying to fend off his fists as they slammed into her face plays over and over in my mind.

"What?" she asks in a small voice against my shoulder.

I turn in her hold to look at her and cradle her face in my hands. "I'm sorry. None of this would have happened if I hadn't done what I did with Sasha. You paid the price for my mistake. I never wanted that."

"It's okay, Gideon. I bear at least half the responsibility. I was just so jealous, but Sasha explained things to me. I'm okay now."

Gently, I slide the pads of my thumbs across the

tops of her cheeks and over the bruised parts of her beautiful face. "I made him pay for what he did, Aria."

She slowly closes her eyes and leans her cheek against my right hand. "Thank you."

I don't need thanks. I did it because I love her.

My father was right. I'm not naturally a killer. For the woman I love more than life itself, though, I can be.

Aria is mine, and her ex made the mistake of not understanding that.

And he paid the price for it.

CHAPTER TWENTY-SEVEN

ideon

Seated behind my desk, I try to shake off the drowsiness from not getting enough sleep last night. Aria and I lay in bed and talked for hours, but this morning I feel like I never got any rest.

My office door opens, and I expect to see Sasha walk in, but it's my father instead. I sit up, eager to hear what happened with Marcello Angeloni. The talk up and down the coast this morning is he's missing and his righthand man was found shot to death after someone beat him to a bloody pulp.

"Good morning," he says as he strolls over to the front of my desk, tapping on the edge before he sits down. "You look like a bus hit you. Rough night? I usually sleep like a baby after killing someone."

Even I know that's not something normal people say to one another. Being a Rule means the regular, run-of-the-mill conversations don't happen, though.

"Yeah, I didn't get much sleep. How about you? I'm assuming you slept well since I hear Marcello Angeloni isn't anywhere to be found."

My father cracks his neck and smiles. "I did, in fact. It's been a long time since I took out my anger on someone like that. As for anyone finding him, I highly doubt it."

I could ask what he means, but I don't. The thought of hearing about the youngest Angeloni spread out in tiny pieces along the local landscape isn't something I can stomach this early in the day.

"Good. So I guess you, Alex, and Alaric will be flying out soon?"

My father stares at me oddly before asking, "Why do I get the feeling you don't like when we come to visit?"

Fighting with him this morning isn't on my list of things to do, so I shake my head and smile to hide the truth of how I feel about him or my brother dropping in on me. "It's your hotel. You can visit whenever you want."

He leans forward and taps on the edge of my desk for a second time. "About that. I think it's time I transfer ownership of this place to you. It's grown and flourished because of the work you've done, so it seems only right."

I stare at him in complete shock. Never in a million years did I ever expect my father to give me the Villa Aurelia. My brother has owned the club he runs for the past two years, but Helix Rule always favors him. I just figured I'd forever be stuck as the manager of the hotel but never the actual owner.

"Thanks, Dad. I have to say this comes as a surprise."

He nods solemnly like he understands what I'm saying. "It's only right. Your mother made me see that after I got back from my last visit here. I never set out to make you feel like you were second to anyone, Gideon. That includes your brother. He's who he is, and you're who you are. I think I just forgot that until your mother reminded me that you're more like her."

"It's okay."

My father stands and gives me another nod. "You've taken care of business here at the hotel and last night. You may not be much like me, but I saw something of myself in you last night when you were punishing that man. That might not make you happy, but there it is."

I smile at his attempt to compliment me for being as vicious as him. "Like I told Alex, I can take care of things when I have to. I simply prefer to do them my way when I can."

"How is Aria this morning? Better?" he asks as he turns to leave.

"She'll be okay. I'm taking care of her, and Sasha watched over her while we were gone."

Once again, he taps on the edge of my desk, but this time he levels a very serious gaze on me. "A word of advice. If you care about her enough to kill for her, Sasha has to go. Let her go work for your brother. He could use an assistant like her."

I struggle not to cringe at the idea of doing that to Sasha. No one like her should be anywhere near Alex. Fuck, no woman in her right mind would want to be around him.

My father walks toward the door just as Sasha walks into my office. "Perfect timing. He wants to talk to you anyway. Gideon, I'll have the lawyers draw up the papers and send them along. Call your mother."

Nodding, I don't answer him but silently remind myself to do just that as Sasha hurries over toward my desk. "What papers?" she asks nearly breathless with excitement.

"He gave me the hotel. It's officially mine now."

Her eyes light up with pure joy for me before she throws her arms around my neck to hug me tightly. "Oh, Gideon! That's wonderful! I'm so happy for you."

"For us," I correct her. "Now we can do all of those things we've talked about for the past few years."

She steps back away from me and slowly shakes

her head. "Not us. You. I'm officially giving my notice. It's time for me to go, Gideon."

Her words hit me like a freight train. Sasha leave? To go where? I've been so used to having her as my right hand that I can't imagine running this place without her.

"No. I won't accept your resignation, so forget it."

Taking my hand in hers, she holds it tightly as she explains, "You don't need me around ruining your life, and that's what will happen if I stay. You and Aria have a real chance at happiness, the kind I've always wished for you. That won't happen if I'm always around."

I can't believe what I'm hearing. Why does she think she'd ruin my life? She's my closest friend in the world.

"Aria and I will be fine if you're around. She likes you. She told me that last night," I say, shaking my head in disbelief.

"And I like her, but it will never work with me here. I know that. So I'm going to work for Alex."

I step back in utter shock. "Work for Alex? My brother? No. You don't deserve that after how wonderful you've been here."

Sasha smiles and shakes her head. "I adore you, Gideon Rule. I have from the moment I met you. But it's time to say goodbye now. The least you can do is wish me luck in my new job. I hear my new boss is a real pain in the ass."

The thought of her being around my brother having to do as he orders her to makes my chest hurt. "No. You can't do this. I won't let you."

She opens her arms and pulls me in for another hug. "This is the part where you say you know I can do this and you'll always be here for me to talk to after a long day working at my new job."

I hear the tears in her voice as I hold her tightly to me. "You don't have to do this, Sasha."

In my ear, she answers, "Yes, I do."

When she steps back, she dries under her eyes and forces a smile. "Now tell me you believe I can handle this because if you don't, I'm going to think you really believe I can't rein in Alex, and I don't need that kind of confidence crusher."

"Of course you can. He's an asshole, but you're tough. You'll be fine."

"And you'll be fine too. You have Aria and this hotel that's finally all yours, as it should be."

I sit down, my mind spinning at what's happened in the past few minutes. "How am I going to run this place without you, Sasha?"

It's not an empty question. She's been with me for so long that I can't imagine not having her to rely on when things go to hell.

"I've trained Tamsin well. She'll be as good as I was, Gideon."

"No, she won't. She's cold and she hates me. Remember?"

With a smile, she says, "No, she isn't, and I think she might actually like you if you act like you did with me. Promise me you'll at least give her a chance. She's very efficient and cares about this place more than you realize."

"I'll give her a chance, but it won't be the same," I say quietly, still trying to wrap my head around the idea of my life here at the hotel without Sasha.

Crouching in front of me, she looks up at me and in a serious voice, she says, "Be good to that beautiful creature or I'll come back and steal her away from you."

In return, I say, "Don't take any of my brother's shit."

She pats my knee before standing to kiss me on the cheek. "You know I won't."

"So how long do I have before you leave?" I ask as she steps back away from me.

Tears fill her eyes even as she tries to smile. "I'm leaving with him this morning. We talked it all out last night, so when he flies out, I'll be going with him, your father, and Alaric."

"Jesus. Are you in that much of a hurry to get away from me?"

Sasha leans forward and kisses me again. "I need to go. You know that. It's not anything about you. It's just time. I love you, Gideon. That's why I'm doing this. Now be happy so I don't feel like I've just made the biggest mistake of my life."

Taking her face in my hands, I press a kiss to her forehead as the reality that she's leaving settles into me. "Thank you. Not just for this but for everything. I wouldn't have been able to do what I did with this hotel without you."

That makes her smile. "I know. Now keep it up and make it even better so whenever Alex complains about you, I'll know it's because he's jealous of how great you're doing here."

"I'm going to miss you."

She steps back away from me and takes a deep breath in, letting it out in a rush. "I know. Goodbye, Gideon."

CHAPTER TWENTY-EIGHT

ria

My body hurts a tiny bit less this morning, but I still won't be running any marathons anytime soon. I sit up slowly and swing my legs off the bed before gingerly standing up. When I don't collapse, I count that as a win. Maybe I'll be able to make it out to the living room.

I assume Gideon will send Sasha up sometime soon to check on me. After our talk last night, I'm feeling better about things with her. Yes, she loves the man I love, but that's not an entirely bad thing. He cares about her, so I'm going to need to deal with that.

At least now I don't think she wants me out of the picture.

A tray with a few muffins sits on the coffee table, along with a piece of paper. I make my way over to the sofa and sit down, happy it wasn't a few feet more because I don't know if I would have made it.

It takes a little effort to stretch and get the note, but I grab it and sit back to read what it says. Opening it, I see it's in Gideon's handwriting.

Eat these for breakfast and I'll be up later this morning. I hope you feel better.

Love,

Gideon

I smile at the words Love, Gideon as reread his note once and then twice. Even today after all that's happened he's a man of few words. I can live with that as long as the words he says are full of love.

Leaning forward, I take what looks like a blueberry muffin off the silver tray and sit back to enjoy my breakfast. Delicious, like everything else the chefs make here at the hotel, it practically melts in my mouth, the blueberries exploding their sweet flavor on my tongue.

As I revel in the taste of my muffin, the front door opens behind me. I'm too achy to turn around to see who it is, so I simply say between bites of my breakfast, "I had a feeling Gideon would send you up this morning. If you haven't eaten yet, definitely try one of these muffins. They're incredible."

A second later, I see not Sasha but Gideon walk around the sofa and stop next to me. Surprised, I look up at him and say, "I figured you would have sent Sasha up to babysit me."

I mean it as a joke, but his expression is almost stony as he shakes his head. "No, all you get is me today."

Reaching for his hand, I take it in mine as I wonder what's wrong. "You look upset. What's going on?"

Gideon sits down, still holding my hand as I wait to hear what's happened. He doesn't answer me immediately, but after a few moments, he sighs and says, "Sasha left this morning. She's going to work for my brother at his club."

My emotions unspool inside me at the news that Gideon's assistant and the one person I know he's had with him for years is gone. Was it because of me? Did she quit or did he have to let her go?

"Why? She didn't leave because of me, did she? I didn't want that, Gideon. You know that, right?"

Finally, his expression lightens, and he turns toward me to give me a smile. "I know that. She resigned because she felt it was best. I know she's right, but I'm just a little surprised. I've had her by my side here for so long I don't know what it will be like without her."

I lean over and rest my head on his shoulder. "I'm sorry, Gideon. I know how much she means to you."

"Sasha was my right hand, but I have to accept she's gone. From now on, it's just you and me."

He says that like it's some consolation prize nobody would want. I kiss his neck and whisper against his skin, "I like that. Don't you?"

Turning to face me, at long last he gives me a smile I know is genuine. "I love that. It's why I accepted her resignation so easily."

"You chose me over her? She's your best friend, Gideon. I'm nobody, or worse, I'm the woman who's caused you nothing but grief. Why would you do that?"

Staring into my eyes, he gives me the most wonderful answer I could dream of hearing. "Because I love you, Aria. Friends come and go, but someone like you doesn't come along every day."

He loves me. And I love him.

Whatever the future holds, it's just the two of us.

CHAPTER TWENTY-NINE

asha

MY NEW BOSS STANDS IN WHAT'S ABOUT TO BE THE doorway to my former home looking around my apartment like he's hoping to find a clue about me. Sorry, bossman. You won't find those answers here. My place is merely somewhere I've slept for the past few years. My life—my everything—was the hotel I just said goodbye to.

"I can meet you at the airplane, Alex. You don't have to wait for me. Feel free to go."

He levels his gaze on me and stares without saying a word for a few moments. I sense he's used this trick before with people to make them bend to his will.

Well, he has no idea who I am. I'm not a woman who withers under a harsh look.

"That brother of mine let you get away with a lot, I think."

Whatever that is beneath his words—jealousy, dislike, I'm not sure—it's not for me. I instinctively open my mouth to defend Gideon, as I have from the day I started working for him, but I stay silent this time.

"So what exactly was your relationship with my baby brother anyway?" Alex asks before taking a step into my apartment as he still looks around like he's searching for something.

I stop packing my bag and sigh as a million thoughts fill my head. Answering his question won't be easy. Gideon and I were friends, lovers, co-workers, the fiercest defenders of one another, and so many other things that changed from day to day.

"Your brother's assistant. That's what I was," I say, distilling all the years I worked beside Gideon to their simplest form.

My answer doesn't seem to make him happy. His expression twists into a deep grimace as he shakes his head.

"No, no. I'm not buying that. You weren't just his assistant. He acted like you were his wife half the time. Having him choose that pretty thing with the big green eyes must have hurt."

He finishes speaking, and I see a grin lift the

corners of his mouth, like he enjoys the thought of my being upset over Gideon's newfound happiness with Aria. I'm not sure what the bad blood is between these brothers is, but I'm not going to spend my days listening to him bash the man I devoted the last few years to.

"That's not the way Gideon and I were with each other."

Taking a step toward him, I stop and stare into his dark eyes that hold none of the hint of softness his brother's possess. "If you intend on talking about Gideon like this while we're working together, you should know something. It makes you look jealous. If that's the way you're trying to come off, then fine. If not, you might want to rethink this petty bullshit you're carrying around for your brother."

Alex's face remains placid, but I sense in his eyes a storm behind that façade of calmness. He swallows hard, making his Adam's apple drop and then rise again before he replies, "You have a problem with a little sibling rivalry?"

"I have a problem with the favorite son punching down for no reason. I'm surprised no one has ever mentioned this to you before."

He smiles and walks up to me so there's barely an inch of space between us. Staring into my eyes, he says, "My guess is no one ever had the balls to."

"Well, I do, and I thought you should know."

"Did you talk like this with my brother?"

I nod as the memories of all the times I set Gideon straight run through my mind. "Yes, and I don't plan on changing, so if that's what you're thinking is going to happen, we might as well dissolve our agreement right now. My job as an assistant is to assist my boss, and part of that is making sure he knows when he's not coming across in the best light. Whatever your issue is with your brother, I suggest you get rid of it and fast."

We fix our gazes on one another, and I wonder if he's about to tell me he doesn't need this kind of shit in his new employees. He'd have every right to. Not every male boss wants a strong female at his side. That's fine. But I won't be some shrinking violet simply because Alex Rule needs a weak woman around.

Finally, he sighs and says, "Well, since I'm now the head of the Rule family in this country, maybe you're right."

Shaking my head in confusion, I ask, "What do you mean the head of your family in Italy?"

"You're looking at the person in charge of the Rule family business here. My father isn't interested in the job, and my brother would never be cruel enough to do what's necessary, so it's me. The Rossettis and Angelonis aren't powerful enough to handle things here, so we Rules get control now."

I step back from him in shock. "So you're not

going to be running the club in Rome anymore? I thought that's where I'd be working."

Now his smile spreads, lighting up his face. "Nope. You and I are going to be running the most powerful crime organization this fucking country has ever seen. So you see, I want you strong. I want you as strong as you can be because you're going to see shit like you've never experienced with that brother of mine. Gone are the trappings of life at that hotel you've gotten used to. You think you're tough? You better be."

Running the Rule family crime organization here in Italy? I didn't sign up for that.

"I'm not sure, Alex. I've known what your family does the entire time I worked for Gideon, but I'm an assistant. That's what I do. Maybe you should find someone else."

Alex nods as I say the weakest words that have ever come out of my mouth. I'm not afraid of cruelty. That's not it.

I'm afraid of this man with that much power.

He runs his fingertip along my jaw in a way that could only be described as a mixture of tender and predatory and levels his gaze on me. For a moment, I feel like I need to turn away, but I won't be intimidated by him or any man.

I don't care who the fuck he is.

"What if I don't want anyone else?" he asks in a low voice tinged with anger.

Unsure what to say, I shake my head. Why does he want me to be at his side in this new job of his? I'm not the kind of person he needs helping him. He should have a righthand man. Isn't that what violent men looking to force others to do what they want usually have?

"Shouldn't you have a consigliere instead of me? I'm just a woman who knows how to manage problems."

He shrugs off that suggestion, shaking his head. "I'll have men around me to make sure the Rule family keeps control here, but I want you by my side, Sasha."

"Why? Is this something you're doing to get back at your brother? If so, you're barking up the wrong tree. He's not unhappy that I'm working for you. As long as I want to do it, he's fine with that."

Alex leans in close to me so I can feel his warm breath against my face. "While I do admit I like to ruffle my brother's feathers whenever I can, my wanting you doesn't have anything to do with that."

As I stare into his dark eyes, I feel myself begin to get lost in them. In him. But how is that possible? I've hated Alex Rule from the moment I met him that first time right after I started working at the hotel all those years ago.

Barely able to speak, I choke out, "Then what does it have to do with?"

"It has to do with you," he whispers against my lips.

My mind whirls in confusion from emotions I

shouldn't feel right now. This man isn't someone I could ever care for or even be with. This job was supposed to be just that. A job. I wanted something I could do without any attachment at all after what I'd had with Gideon. I never believed working for Alex would be anything close to what I felt for my position at the Villa Aurelia, and that was the way I wanted it to be.

But now as he stands in front of me, his lips practically touching mine as he says he wants me because I'm me, I don't know what to do. Alex Rule is cruel and mean. That's all he's ever been in all the time I've known him.

"Why?" I whisper, hoping he'll answer with something crude like he usually does to make me snap out of this daze he has me under.

He doesn't answer before he presses his lips to mine in a kiss that takes my breath away. Pressing his hand to the back of my head, he holds me so I can't move as his tongue slips into my mouth to glide over mine. I should pull away. I want to remember I hate him and I only took this job because it meant I didn't have to search for another one after finally accepting the fact that Gideon and Aria would never be truly happy with me in the picture. I want to remember that, but all I can think of now is how much I want to feel Alex's mouth between my legs.

When he pulls away, he smiles as he runs his fingertips across his lower lip. "Very nice. My brother refused to kiss and tell, and now I know why. A word of warning, though. Gideon likes to play mind games. I'm more physical. My games sometimes hurt, though, I'm guessing you'd be the kind of woman who likes that."

"And if I say that I won't be with you if I work for you and expect you to keep it strictly professional, will you fire me before I even begin?" I ask, my voice trembling at the thought of what Alex and his games would be like.

He runs his tongue across his lips and grins wickedly. "Something tells me you won't be singing that tune for long, but no, I won't fire you. The truth is you're part of the Rule family, so there's nowhere you can go where I can't get to you, Sasha. You're mine now. What that ends up meaning for the two of us we'll see. I know what I want."

Before I can say a word in response to what sounds like a thinly veiled threat, Alex takes a step back from me and begins walking toward my front door. "The first thing we need to do together is find a villa where we can work and live. I assume you know everything there is to know about this coast, so I'll trust you to get a list together so we can begin touring places."

"What do you mean where we can work and live? Won't I be living somewhere else?" I ask, knowing full well I have no other place to stay after mistakenly giving my landlord notice that I was moving since I thought I was going to work in Rome.

Alex turns his head to look at me and grins again. "No. I want my right hand with me at all times. Don't worry. I'll keep it interesting. I hear you like women too. Good. I think we're going to have a good time, you and me."

When he walks out, I shake my head in amazement that I haven't already tried to run far away from this man. Alex Rule is not a man I should be playing with. He's violent and vicious, and I doubt he cares one iota about how anyone else in the world feels when he exacts his cruelty on them.

But I'm not some delicate thing who can't handle herself. I like a challenge, and Alex is definitely that.

I've handled myself with bad men before. This one will be no different.

I'll just have to watch to make sure he never has the one thing his brother had from the moment I met him.

My heart.

LOOK FOR ALEX AND SASHA'S STORY, VICIOUS RULE, COMING SOON. SIGN UP FOR MY NEWSLETTER TO BE ALERTED ABOUT THE RELEASE!

ABOUT THE AUTHOR

Abbi Cook grew up wondering if she was different because she always wanted to know more about the villain than the hero in the stories she read. When she got older, she found there were others in the world like her and devoured their writing, loving every dark word. She's written her own tales for years, but in 2019 she decided it was time to take the next step and publish them. She's never looked back since that day.

Readers can find her at her website at abbicook.com, on FB and IG, and through email at abbicookauthor@gmail.com

BOOKS BY ABBI

Captive Heart (standalone prequel to the Captive Hearts series)

Behind The Mask (Captive Hearts #1)

Beneath The Surface (Captive Hearts #2)

Beyond The Lies (Captive Hearts #3)

Captive Hearts: A Dark Romance Mafia Collection

Covet (Sins Duet #1)

Corrupt (Sins Duet #2)

The Sins Duet

Rule (Villains Club #1)

Take (Villains Club #2)

Burn (Villains Club #3)

Play (Villains Club #4)

Bang (Villains Club #5)

The Villains Club Collection

Savage Mine (Free Born Villains Prequel)

Savage Heart (Born Villains #1)

Ruthless Touch (Born Villains #2)

And be sure to sign up for Abbi's newsletter if you haven't already! You don't want to miss a delicious word and all the great things with each release, and subscribers receive a FREE book just for signing up!